7/28/16 - 11/31/16

ANNIE HAYNES
THE ABBEY COURT MURDER

Annie Haynes was born in 1865, the daughter of an ironmonger.

By the first decade of the twentieth century she lived in London and moved in literary and early feminist circles. Her first crime novel, *The Bungalow Mystery*, appeared in 1923, and another nine mysteries were published before her untimely death in 1929.

Who Killed Charmian Karslake? appeared posthumously, and a further partially-finished work, *The Crystal Beads Murder*, was completed with the assistance of an unknown fellow writer, and published in 1930.

D0366098

Also by Annie Haynes

ANNIE HAYNES

THE
ABBEY COURT
MURDER

With an introduction
by Curtis Evans

DEAN STREET PRESS

Published by Dean Street Press 2015

All Rights Reserved

First published in 1923 by The Bodley Head

Cover by DSP

Introduction © Curtis Evans 2015

ISBN 978 1 911095 01 9

www.deanstreetpress.co.uk

TO DEAR
MRS. W.K. CLIFFORD

IN DEEP AFFECTION
AND PROFOUND ADMIRATION FOR
HER WORK

The Mystery of the Missing Author

Annie Haynes and Her Golden Age Detective Fiction

The psychological enigma of Agatha Christie's notorious 1926 vanishing has continued to intrigue Golden Age mystery fans to the present day. The Queen of Crime's eleven-day disappearing act is nothing, however, compared to the decades-long disappearance, in terms of public awareness, of between-the-wars mystery writer Annie Haynes (1865-1929), author of a series of detective novels published between 1923 and 1930 by Agatha Christie's original English publisher, The Bodley Head. Haynes's books went out of print in the early Thirties, not long after her death in 1929, and her reputation among classic detective fiction readers, high in her lifetime, did not so much decline as dematerialize. When, in 2013, I first wrote a piece about Annie Haynes' work, I knew of only two other living persons besides myself who had read any of her books. Happily, Dean Street Press once again has come to the rescue of classic mystery fans seeking genre gems from the Golden Age, and is republishing all Haynes' mystery novels. Now that her crime fiction is coming back into print, the question naturally arises: Who Was Annie Haynes? Solving the mystery of this forgotten author's lost life has taken leg work by literary sleuths on two continents (my thanks for their assistance to Carl Woodings and Peter Harris).

Until recent research uncovered new information about Annie Haynes, almost nothing about her was publicly known besides the fact of her authorship of twelve mysteries during the Golden Age of detective fiction. Now we know that she led an altogether intriguing life, too soon cut short by disability and death, which took her from the isolation of the rural

English Midlands in the nineteenth century to the cultural high life of Edwardian London. Haynes was born in 1865 in the Leicestershire town of Ashby-de-la-Zouch, the first child of ironmonger Edwin Haynes and Jane (Henderson) Haynes, daughter of Montgomery Henderson, longtime superintendent of the gardens at nearby Coleorton Hall, seat of the Beaumont baronets. After her father left his family, young Annie resided with her grandparents at the gardener's cottage at Coleorton Hall, along with her mother and younger brother. Here Annie doubtlessly obtained an acquaintance with the ways of the country gentry that would serve her well in her career as a genre fiction writer.

We currently know nothing else of Annie Haynes' life in Leicestershire, where she still resided (with her mother) in 1901, but by 1908, when Haynes was in her early forties, she was living in London with Ada Heather-Bigg (1855-1944) at the Heather-Bigg family home, located halfway between Paddington Station and Hyde Park at 14 Radnor Place, London. One of three daughters of Henry Heather-Bigg, a noted pioneer in the development of orthopedics and artificial limbs, Ada Heather-Bigg was a prominent Victorian and Edwardian era feminist and social reformer. In the 1911 British census entry for 14 Radnor Place, Heather-Bigg, a "philanthropist and journalist," is listed as the head of the household and Annie Haynes, a "novelist," as a "visitor," but in fact Haynes would remain there with Ada Heather-Bigg until Haynes' death in 1929.

Haynes' relationship with Ada Heather-Bigg introduced the aspiring author to important social sets in England's great metropolis. Though not a novelist herself, Heather-Bigg was an important figure in the city's intellectual milieu, a well-connected feminist activist of great energy and passion who believed strongly in the idea of women attaining economic independence through remunerative employment. With Ada

Heather-Bigg behind her, Annie Haynes's writing career had powerful backing indeed. Although in the 1911 census Heather-Bigg listed Haynes' occupation as "novelist," it appears that Haynes did not publish any novels in book form prior to 1923, the year that saw the appearance of *The Bungalow Mystery*, which Haynes dedicated to Heather-Bigg. However, Haynes was a prolific producer of newspaper serial novels during the second decade of the twentieth century, penning such works as *Lady Carew's Secret*, *Footprints of Fate*, *A Pawn of Chance*, *The Manor Tragedy* and many others.

Haynes' twelve Golden Age mystery novels, which appeared in a tremendous burst of creative endeavor between 1923 and 1930, like the author's serial novels retain, in stripped-down form, the emotionally heady air of the nineteenth-century triple-decker sensation novel, with genteel settings, shocking secrets, stormy passions and eternal love all at the fore, yet they also have the fleetness of Jazz Age detective fiction. Both in their social milieu and narrative pace Annie Haynes' detective novels bear considerable resemblance to contemporary works by Agatha Christie; and it is interesting to note in this regard that Annie Haynes and Agatha Christie were the only female mystery writers published by The Bodley Head, one of the more notable English mystery imprints in the early Golden Age. "A very remarkable feature of recent detective fiction," observed the *Illustrated London News* in 1923, "is the skill displayed by women in this branch of story-telling. Isabel Ostrander, Carolyn Wells, Annie Haynes and last, but very far from least, Agatha Christie, are contesting the laurels of Sherlock Holmes' creator with a great spirit, ingenuity and success." Since Ostrander and Wells were American authors, this left Annie Haynes, in the estimation of the *Illustrated London News*, as the main British female competitor to Agatha Christie. (Dorothy L. Sayers, who, like Haynes, published her debut mystery novel in 1923, goes unmentioned.) Similarly, in 1925 *The Sketch* wryly noted that "[t]ired men, trotting home at the end of an imperfect day, have been known to pop into the library and ask for an Annie Haynes. They have not made a mistake in the street number. It is not a cocktail they are asking for...."

Twenties critical opinion adjudged that Annie Haynes' criminous concoctions held appeal not only for puzzle fiends impressed with the "considerable craftsmanship" of their plots (quoting from the *Sunday Times* review of *The Bungalow Mystery*), but also for more general readers attracted to their purely literary qualities. "Not only a crime story of merit, but also a novel which will interest readers to whom mystery for its own sake has little appeal," avowed *The Nation* of Haynes' *The Secret of Greylands*, while the *New Statesman* declared of *The Witness on the Roof* that "Miss Haynes has a sense of character; her people are vivid and not the usual puppets of detective fiction." Similarly, the *Bookman* deemed the characters in Haynes' *The Abbey Court Murder* "much truer to life than is the case in many sensational stories" and *The Spectator* concluded of *The Crime at Tattenham Corner*, "Excellent as a detective tale, the book also is a charming novel."

Sadly, Haynes' triumph as a detective novelist proved short lived. Around 1914, about the time of the outbreak of the Great War, Haynes had been stricken with debilitating rheumatoid arthritis that left her in constant pain and hastened her death from heart failure in 1929, when she was only 63. Haynes wrote several of her detective novels on fine days in Kensington Gardens, where she was wheeled from 14 Radnor Place in a bath chair, but in her last years she was able only to travel from her bedroom to her study. All of this was an especially hard blow for a woman who had once been intensely energetic and quite physically active.

In a foreword to *The Crystal Beads Murder*, the second of Haynes' two posthumously published mysteries, Ada Heather-Bigg noted that Haynes' difficult daily physical struggle "was materially lightened by the warmth of friendships" with other authors and by the "sympathetic and friendly relations between her and her publishers." In this latter instance Haynes' experience rather differed from that of her sister Bodleian, Agatha Christie, who left The Bodley Head on account of what she deemed an iniquitous contract that took unjust advantage of a naive young author. Christie moved, along with her landmark detective novel *The Murder of Roger Ackroyd* (1926), to Collins and never looked back, enjoying ever greater success with the passing years.

At the time Christie crossed over to Collins, Annie Haynes had only a few years of life left. After she died at 14 Radnor Place on 30 March 1929, it was reported in the press that "many people well-known in the literary world" attended the author's funeral at St. Michaels and All Angels Church, Paddington, where her sermon was delivered by the eloquent vicar, Paul Nichols, brother of the writer Beverley Nichols and dedicatee of Haynes' mystery novel *The Master of the Priory*; yet by the time of her companion Ada Heather-Bigg's death in 1944, Haynes and her once highly-praised mysteries were forgotten. (Contrastingly, Ada Heather-Bigg's name survives today in the University College of London's Ada Heather-Bigg Prize in Economics.) Only three of Haynes' novels were ever published in the United States, and she passed away less than a year before the formation of the Detection Club, missing any chance of being invited to join this august body of distinguished British detective novelists. Fortunately, we have today entered, when it comes to classic mystery, a period of rediscovery and revival, giving a reading audience a chance once again, after over eighty years, to savor the detective fiction fare of Annie Haynes. *Bon appétit!*

Curtis Evans

CHAPTER I

St. Peter's was rapidly becoming the church for fashionable weddings; but even St. Peter's had seldom been the centre of a larger or more fashionable crowd than was assembling this warm April afternoon to see Lady Geraldine Summerhouse married to the man of her choice. There was the usual gathering of loiterers round the door and on the steps of the church; while the traffic in the street was impeded by the long line of private carriages and motors setting down guests.

Two men came round the corner of King's Street, walking quickly; the sightseers brought them to a standstill.

"Hullo, what is this?" one of them exclaimed. "Oh, I see, a wedding. Well I suppose we shall get through somehow."

Both men, though they wore the conventional frockcoat and silk hat, had the look of travellers, or colonials, with their thin bronzed faces. The foremost of the two had reached the last line of waiting spectators, and was just about to cross the red carpet that was laid up the steps of the church and under the awning. The policeman put up a warning hand, some guests were alighting, another car took its place before the kerb. A group of maidservants, with baskets of flowers, stood immediately before the two strangers. The man behind turned his head idly as a big dark man sprang from a car and handed out a tall exquisitely dressed woman. Together they came up the steps and passed close to the stranger, but the beautiful eyes did not glance at him, did not note the change that swept over his face.

He, looking after them, caught his breath sharply, incredulously. Then as they passed into the church he leaned forward and touched the arm of one of the maids.

"Can you tell me the name of the lady who has just gone in?"

The maid looked a little surprised at being spoken to, but the tone was unmistakably that of a gentleman; there was an obvious desire for information in his expression; she answered after a moment's hesitation:

"That was Lady Carew and Sir Anthony, sir!"

"Sir Anthony and Lady Carew," he repeated in a musing tone, a curious brooding look in his light eyes. "Not Carew, of Heron's Carew, surely—mad Carew as they used to call him?"

"Yes, sir. He is Sir Anthony Carew, of Heron's Carew."

"And she, who was she before her marriage?"

There was something compelling about his gaze. The girl answered unwillingly:

"She was his sister's—Miss Carew's—governess, sir."

"Ah!" He turned away abruptly.

His companion leaned forward:

"Are you going on, old man? Hang it all, if you stay here much longer we shall be late for our appointment, and then—"

"I am not going on." The first man's tone was decisive. "You can manage by yourself, Jermyn. Perhaps I may join you later."

His friend looked at him and shrugged his shoulders resignedly.

"Well, you always were a queer sort of fellow. We shall meet later at Orlin's, I suppose. So long, old man."

He disappeared in the crowd. The other scarcely seemed to hear him. He kept his place in the forefront of the spectators, his eager eyes seeking amid the shadows and the dimness of the church, for one graceful figure. He did not notice that the other man had turned, and was now waiting behind him. At last the service—elaborately choral—was over, the organ pealed out the Wedding March, bride and bridegroom with their attendants came forth, and still those light eyes kept their watch on the interior of the church.

The guests followed, some of them found their carriages without difficulty; others stood waiting in the porch talking and laughing to one another. Sir Anthony and Lady Carew were among the first to come out. Their footman touched his hat:

"If you please, Sir Anthony, something has gone wrong with the car; it is just round King Street. Jenkins can't get it to move. Shall I call a taxi?"

"Yes, no. Wait a minute." Sir Anthony looked anxious. The big green Daimler was his latest toy. He turned to his wife: "I must see what is wrong myself, I won't be a moment, Judith, or would you rather go on at once?"

"Certainly not. I would much rather wait. I hope it is nothing serious, Anthony."

As Lady Carew smiled, it was noticeable that the whole character of her face altered. In repose it was cold, even a little melancholy, but the smile revealed unexpected possibilities, the big hazel eyes melted and deepened, the mouth softened into new curves. She stood back a little as Sir Anthony hurried off, a tall graceful-looking woman in her exquisite gown of palest grey chiffon velvet, with the magnificent sables that had been her husband's wedding gift thrown carelessly round her. Against the neutral tints of her background, against the deep tone of her furs, her clear delicate skin looked almost transparent. Her face was oval in shape, with small perfectly formed features, the eyes were remarkable, big and haunting, of a curious grey blue in the shadows which yet held yellow specks that shone in the sunlight, that danced when she laughed. Set under broad level brows, they had long black lashes that contrasted oddly with the pale gold of her hair.

One woman paused as she passed.

"How perfectly sweet Peggy looked, Lady Carew! Quite the prettiest bridesmaid of them all."

Lady Carew's smile lighted up her face; she was obviously pleased as she murmured some inaudible reply.

The pale-eyed man was just behind her now. As she turned aside again he stepped out of the crowd and touched her arm.

"Judy!"

An extraordinary change passed over Lady Carew's face as she heard the voice, as she turned and met the man's gaze. Every drop of blood seemed to recede from her cheeks, leaving her white as death; only her eyes looked alive as she stared at him, even her lips were blue.

"You!" she said slowly in a hoarse whisper. "You!"

"Yes, I." The man placed himself a little before her, so that in a measure he screened her. "At last I have found you, Judy!"

"But you—I thought you were dead." Her eyes were strained upon his face in an agony of appeal.

"So I should suppose," the man said roughly with a short, hard laugh, his pale eyes burning with an inward fire as they wandered over the lovely face, the graceful svelte form of the woman before him. "But I am not dead, Judy. On the contrary I am very much alive, and—I have come home for my own, Judy."

"Your own!" Judith Carew repeated, slowly. Her face was like a death-mask now, but the eyes—the big, luring eyes—were living as they focused on the man's bronzed face, as they drew forth some dreadful meaning. She gave a low hoarse sob. "Your own—my God!"

The pale eyes grew suddenly apprehensive, but the harsh tone did not soften.

"You know what I mean well enough. When shall I find my Lady Carew at home to me, Judy?"

"Never." She shot the word out quickly. "You shall never enter my husband's house. I will kill myself first."

Sir Anthony was coming back. They could see his tall figure towering over the heads of others, here and there he was stopped by a cheery word of greeting; they could hear his laugh. The pale-eyed man looked at the trembling woman.

"I must see you again and to-day—where?"

She shook her head. "I don't know," she said with difficulty. "I have told you you shall not come into his house."

Sir Anthony was on the top step now, only a few paces away. A tall woman in an outré costume of vieux rose had stopped him; the two were laughing and talking like old friends.

The echo of his light laugh, the sound of a careless word made Judith, waiting in her misery, catch her breath sharply.

"Go!" she cried. "Go! He must not hear. I forbid you to tell him now."

The sullen fire in the pale eyes of the man watching her leapt to sudden life, then died down swiftly.

"If I go now, you must see me—later. Look." He drew out his pocket-book and scribbled an address upon the first page: "42 Abbey Court, Leinster Avenue, 9.30 to-night. There!" He tore out the leaf and thrust it into her hands. "If you fail me, Judy, you know the consequences."

She pushed the scrap of paper mechanically into her glove; he turned and disappeared in the crowd.

Sir Anthony caught a momentary glimpse of him as he came up, and looked after him curiously.

"Who was that, Judith? He looks rather an odd customer, as if he had seen life in some queer places. But what is it, child?"—his tone turning to one of apprehension—"You are ill—faint?"

Lady Carew forced a smile to her stiff lips. "It is nothing. It was so hot in the church," hesitatingly, "and the scent of the flowers is overpowering," she added as a passing waft of sweetness from the great sheaves of Madonna lilies that stood in the nave reached them. "I shall be all right directly. What was wrong with the car?"

"Nothing much," Sir Anthony said carelessly. "Jenkins soon put it right, but you can't wait here. Monktowers said he would send his brougham back for us. Ah, here it is!"

He helped her in carefully, and to her surprise gave their own address.

"I can't have you knocked up, and the reception is sure to be a crush," he said in answer to her look. "I am going to take you home, and make you rest, or certainly you will not be fit for the Denboroughs' to-night."

The Denboroughs'! Judith shivered in her corner; she was deadly cold beneath her furs. Lady Denborough's dinner parties were among the most select in London; her invitations were eagerly sought after; it had been a tribute to the furore that Lady Carew's beauty had excited that she, who but two years ago had been only Peggy Carew's governess, should have been included.

How far away it all seemed to her now, as she laid her head back on the cushions and tried to think, to realize this awful catastrophe that had befallen her. The dead had come to life! All that past, that she had believed buried beyond resurrection, had risen, was here at her very doors.

Through the shadow of the carriage, she glanced at Anthony, at the dark rugged profile, at the crisp dark hair with its faint powdering of grey near the temples, at all that only an hour ago had been so intimately dear, that was now, as it were, set on the other side of a great gulf. Her heart sank, she felt sick as she thought of the other face with its bold good looks. It was impossible, she tried to tell herself despairingly, that this thing should really have befallen her, that there should be no way of escape. Sir Anthony watched her anxiously.

As the carriage neared their house in Grosvenor Square, she sat up, and drew her furs around her with a pitiful attempt to pull herself together.

Sir Anthony helped her out solicitously. As she paused for a moment on the step, a man passed, gazing up at the front of the house.

Lady Carew caught a momentary glimpse of the big familiar figure, a mist rose before her eyes, her fingers closed more tightly over that piece of paper in her glove as she swayed and reached out a trembling hand to her husband's arm.

With a quick exclamation of alarm, Sir Anthony caught her, carried her over the threshold of their home.

"Judith, Judith, what is it, my darling?" he said, bending over her.

CHAPTER II

"You must go to the Denboroughs' alone, Anthony." Judith was looking frail and wan as she came into the study in her white tea-gown, her hair gathered together loosely in a great knot behind.

Sir Anthony was sitting at his writing-table, a pile of unopened letters lay beside him; he was apparently oblivious of them as he studied the card in his hand. He sprang up now.

"Judith, is this wise? I hoped you were asleep."

"I couldn't sleep," Judith said truthfully, as she steadied herself by the table, "and I went up to the boy. Anthony, you must not give up the Denboroughs. I shall go to bed at once. Célestine is going to give me a sleeping draught, so you see you will be no use here"—with a pitiful attempt at a smile.—"And we shall put the Denboroughs' table out altogether if neither of us goes. It won't matter so much about me, people can always get another woman, but you, you must not disappoint them."

Sir Anthony hesitated, some quality in her insistence impressed him disagreeably. Why was she so anxious to get rid of him? The next moment he was chiding himself for his folly. Judith was evidently unwell, she was overwrought, feverish.

"Yes, yes," he answered soothingly. "Of course I will go. That will be all right, Judith."

She drew a little soft breath as she laid her head against his arm.

"And now that is settled I am going to take you back to your room," he went on. "You ought not to have come down, you ought to have sent for me."

But Judith's hands clung to his arm. "No, no. There is an hour yet before you need dress. I want to sit here like this. Don't send me away, Anthony!"

Sir Anthony felt a quick throb of anxiety as he looked down at her ruffled golden head; this attack of nerves was something outside his experience of Judith; he began to ask himself whether it was not possibly the forerunner of some serious illness?

"My darling, do I ever want to send you away?" he questioned, a reproachful reflection in his pleasant voice. "It is because I know that you ought to be in bed. For myself could I ask anything better than that you should be here with me?"

Judith sank down in one of the big saddleback chairs near the fire-place, and drew Sir Anthony on to the arm with weak, insistent fingers. As his arm closed round her she nestled up to him with a deep sigh of content, but she did not speak.

To herself she was saying that this might be the last time that she would see the love-light in Anthony's eyes, feel the warmth of his tenderness.

For this one hour she would forget everything outside. She remember only that she was with the man she loved, the man who loved her. Then everything would be over, she would be no longer Anthony Carew's honoured wife. Her life at Heron's Carew would be as if it had never been. There would be nothing for Anthony to do but forget her. But first there was this one hour—this golden hour that she would have to remember afterwards!

Sir Anthony held her closely for a time in silence, once or twice his lips touched a loosened strand of golden hair that lay across his shoulder. But at last he laid her back very gently in her chair, and straightening himself turned to his writing-table.

Judith clung to his arm. They were running out so fast, the minutes that were the souls of her one golden hour.

"You—you are not going to leave me?" she gasped.

"Leave you, my sweetheart, no!" Sir Anthony said drawing his blotting-book towards him. "But I must just finish this letter that I was writing when you came in, I shall not be a minute. It is to poor Sybil Palmer. Her husband met with a bad accident yesterday. He always will act his own chauffeur, and he is reckless at hills. It seems there was a terrible smash-up, and there isn't much hope for Palmer, I fancy."

Judith stirred quickly, she drew a little away.

"Do you mean that he is not going to get better—that he will die?"

Sir Anthony nodded gravely. "I am afraid so."

With all her power Judith thrust away from her that hideous thought that would obtrude itself. Lord Palmer was going to die and Sybil—Lady Palmer—the beautiful cousin who had been engaged to Anthony in his youth, and whose loss had embittered all his young manhood, would be free.

But then—then Judith's golden hour would be over—nothing would matter to her, she told herself, nothing would hurt her then.

She looked at Sir Anthony as he sat at the table; she could catch a glimpse of his profile; she could hear his pen moving quickly over his paper; evidently it was a long letter he was writing. At last, however, it was finished, and he came back to her.

"Now I am at your service, sweetheart."

Judith's lips trembled.

"When next month comes, we shall have been married two years, Anthony."

"Shall we?" Sir Anthony's deep-set eyes smiled down at her. "You have become so absolutely a part of my life, that I don't like to think of the time when you didn't belong to me, Judith."

Judith lay back among her cool, chintz cushions, and looked at him.

"Don't you," she said, and then, "It—it has been a happy time since we were married?" she questioned wistfully.

"A happy—a blessed time," he said with sudden passion, as he knelt down beside her and gathered her into his arms. "It was my good angel that brought you to Heron's Carew, Judith."

"Thank God for two perfect years," she whispered. "Two happy years together; whatever happens we have had that. You wouldn't quite forget those two years—if—if I died to-night; if you married some one else, Anthony?"

"Don't!" the word broke from the man almost like a sob of pain. "Don't talk of it even in jest. One can't forget what is graven on one's heart. Dead or alive, you are the one woman in the world for me." His arms tightened round her, held her close to his heart. With a little sobbing sigh Judith crept closer to him.

Carew's eyes were passionately tender as he glanced at the waves of golden hair resting on his coat. The pale curved lips were touching his sleeve again now; they were murmuring one word over and over again. "Good-bye, good-bye!" At last the golden hour was over.

She got up unsteadily. "You will go to the Denboroughs', Anthony?"

"And you will go to sleep?" He drew her arm through his. "Come, I am going to give Célestine her directions myself. No more going to the boy to-night, mind!"

She let him help her upstairs, it was so sweet, so very sweet to have him wait upon her.

But upstairs she refused utterly to go to bed; she would sleep better on the large roomy couch, she protested. Célestine would bring her some black coffee, and leave the sedative within reach, and then no one must disturb her; she would have a long rest. Sir Anthony bent down and kissed her tenderly.

"I shall not be late. Sleep well, my dearest."

Somewhat to his surprise, as he lifted his head, Judith drew it down again, and kissed him on the lips with sudden passion. "Good-bye, good-bye," she whispered. Then, as her arms fell back from his neck, she closed her eyes and turned her face into the side of the couch.

Sir Anthony stole softly away.

As he closed the door, she looked round again with wide eyes.

"Célestine!"

"Yes, miladi." The French maid came forward, a demure, provocative little figure.

"You can go now. If I want anything I will ring."

"Yes, miladi! But Sir Anthony, he said—" Evidently Célestine was unwilling to depart.

"That will do." Lady Carew interrupted her with a touch of hauteur. "I cannot sleep unless I am alone. And do not come until I ring, Célestine."

"But, certainly, miladi." The maid shrugged her shoulders as she withdrew.

Left alone, Lady Carew raised herself on her elbow, and looked all round the room. On the other side of the room was the door leading into Sir Anthony's apartments. Judith bit her lips despairingly as she looked at it; presently he would be coming up to dress, she would hear him moving about. A long shivering sigh shook her from head to foot as she buried her face in the cushions again.

Meanwhile Sir Anthony went back to his study. There was plenty of time to dress, he had another letter to write that required some thinking over. As he walked over to the writing-table his eye was caught by a piece of paper on the chair where Judith had been sitting. Naturally, a tidy man, he glanced at it as he picked it up, wondering idly whether his wife had dropped it.

"42 Abbey Court, Leinster Avenue, 9.30 to-night," he read, written in a bold unmistakably masculine hand.

"What does it mean?" he asked himself as he twisted it about. There seemed to him something sinister in the curtly worded command. It was not meant for Judith of course, the very notion of that was absurd. But, as he sat down and opened his blotting-book, the look of that piece of paper haunted him; another thought—one he had believed laid for ever—the thought of the long years that lay behind his knowledge of his wife, rose and mocked him.

He would not have been Carew of Heron's Carew if his nature had not held infinite capabilities of self-torture, of fierce burning jealousy that ran like fire through his blood, and maddened him.

It was so little that he knew, that Judith had told him of her past.

It had been the usual uneventful past of an ordinary English girl, she had given him to understand. But the great hazel eyes had held hints of tragedy at times that gave the lie to that placid story.

Sir Anthony groaned aloud as he thrust the letter from him. He sat silent, his eyes fixed on that mysterious paper: "9.30 to-night." For whom had that appointment been meant?

CHAPTER III

Nine o'clock! Judith Carew stood up. The time had come! Once more she looked round the familiar room, her eyes lingering on the big photograph of Anthony, in its oxydized silver frame on the mantelpiece.

She crossed to the pretty inlaid escritoire, and unlocked one of the top drawers. A piece of paper lay inside; she started as she looked at it with a frown. This was not what she wanted— this was merely a pencilled note that Peggy had sent her in the church that afternoon. A note, moreover, that she had thought she had burnt when she came in.

A moment's reflection and her face cleared; she must have tossed the address the man gave her, at the church door, into the fire, while she locked this little innocent note of Peggy's carefully away. It was strange that she should have made such a curious mistake, but it did not matter, the address was written on her brain in letters of fire. She could not forget it if she would.

She went to her wardrobe, and took out a long dark cloak, that would cover her altogether, pinned a toque on her hair, and tied a thick motor veil over it.

Then she opened the door and listened. At this hour the servants should be at their supper; it would be possible for her to get out unobserved. She calculated that she might be back— if she came back—soon after eleven. Célestine would hardly expect her to ring before then, and her absence would pass unnoticed.

No one was about apparently. Her lips moved silently as she came out into the corridor, as she looked wistfully up the short flight of stairs that led to the nursery. Her husband's door stood open; in passing a sudden thought struck her. She went in and opened one of the drawers, inside was a leather case. She looked at it for a moment, then slowly touched the spring, and disclosed a couple of revolvers.

Anthony had been giving her lessons in shooting of late; with that small murderous looking instrument she would at least be able to protect herself. She saw that it was loaded, and held it firmly clutched in her hand under her cloak, as she made her way down the stairs. She had calculated her time well, there was no one in the hall when she let herself out and closed the door behind her softly.

It was a damp night, typical April weather. To Judith, after fevered tossing to and fro on the couch, its very moisture seemed refreshing.

Leinster Avenue was fairly familiar ground to her; in her governess days she had often brought her pupil to see some friends who lived near. Insensibly her feet turned towards the Tube; she had reverted to the mode of conveyance most familiar to her in early days. From Bond Street to Holland Park was but an affair of a few minutes, and from there she knew her way to Leinster Avenue. Abbey Court must be, she felt sure, one of the great blocks of flats standing at the near end of the Avenue. She found that she was right. Abbey Court, Nos. 1—50, faced her as she turned the well-known corner.

Looking up at the big new building she shivered. She thought of the coming interview. Just then some neighbouring clock chimed the half-hour.

She started nervously, she must not keep the man waiting, and she walked up the steps. In the hall the porter touched his cap.

"Lift, ma'am?"

She stepped in and gave the number mechanically.

They stopped at the fifth floor, the man got out and rang the bell for her.

Judith gave him half a crown, and was conscious that he stood and looked at her doubtfully.

The door opened immediately. Instinctively her hand closed more firmly over the revolver.

"Is that you, Judy? Come in!"

She was drawn through the door quickly. She recognized that there was an indefinable change in the voice since the afternoon.

Inside on the other side of a narrow passage was a door opening into a small room, evidently used as a dining-room, velvet curtains hung over the archway beyond; parted they disclosed a room fairly large for a flat. It looked like a man's den—papers and pipes were littered about. In the outer room beneath the electric light she paused and threw back her veil.

"What do you want with me?" she said curtly.

"Want with you?" The man laughed harshly. "I want you—you yourself, Judy, don't you understand? I meant to find you, I was going to put the search for you in the hands of the best detectives in London, when, just by chance, I saw you this afternoon, saw you another man's wife!"

Judith drew her breath in sharply. "I thought you were dead. I saw it in the papers, I never dreamed that there was any mistake."

"Sometimes it is convenient to die," he said sullenly. "And you—and you were always too much inclined to take things on trust, Judy!"

The woman looked at him, her breath quickening, the first dawning of a horrible suspicion turning her white and cold.

"What do you mean?"

He laughed, though a curious indrawing of breath mingled with his laughter.

"I told you a lie when we parted, Judith. You made me mad, and I meant to bring your pride down somehow, but if I had known how you would take it—"

"A lie," Judith repeated. "A lie!" She drew farther from him, back against the wall, her face absolutely colourless save for the dark rings round her eyes, her lips stiff and cold. "What lie did you tell me?"

The man looked at her, his face was flushed, his eyes were bloodshot; with a throb of disgust Judith realized he had been drinking.

"You know," he said hoarsely. "You haven't forgotten, for all your disdainful ways! I told you a lie when I said you were not my wife—that our marriage was not legal!"

"You did not!" The words caught in a strangled sob in Judith's throat. She put up her hands, and wrenched the fastenings of her cloak apart, tore like a wild thing at the chiffon round her neck. "It was *not* a lie!" she panted. "It was the truth you told me—God's truth. I was not your wife—I was never your wife for a single minute, thank Heaven."

"You were!" A very ugly light burned in the man's pale, prominent eyes—a light that might have warned her to be careful. "You are," he amended. "You are my wife, Judy; you are not Mad Carew's, and I mean to have my own. Come," putting out his hand, "you loved me once, you will not find it impossible to love me again."

"Never!" Judith backed near the archway. For the moment she did not heed the danger of rousing the man, of kindling the fire that smouldered in his eyes. "Love you!" she repeated, "I never loved you, never, never—not for a single moment! I"— with a sob—"know that now!"

"Do you really?" The man sprang forward and caught her arm roughly. "And who has made you so wise?" he questioned with a harsh laugh. "Mad Carew? Never mind, Judy, I can afford to laugh! For, do as you will, you are mine, mine only."

Judith stood still in his clasp. She would not struggle with him, she would not try to match her puny strength against his, but her ungloved hand tightened round the shining toy she held. It might be—it might be that only that way would freedom come!

"Judith," the man went on pleading thickly, "I was mad that night—mad with drink, or I wouldn't have laid a hand on you, I wouldn't have lied to you. Our marriage was legal enough; the woman I had married before had been dead for years, but luck was against me. You would be better without me, that was what I thought, Judy, indeed!" his voice growing maudlin.

Still Judith did not speak. She was standing against the velvet *portière* now, silhouetted against the dark background; her delicate features, the ghastly pallor of her face had a cameo-like effect, her big changeful eyes followed his every movement.

His hand dropped from her arm. "But now, Judy, good luck has come to me at last. For every pound of Mad Carew's I will give you ten. I will give you a title too. Ay, you shall be my lady, still, and hold up your head with the best of them. You come back to me, Judy. I tell you I have loved you always—you only!"

"I think not!" Judith laughed scornfully. "You—what do you—what do such as you know of love?" She went on recklessly. "Nothing, less than nothing! I will never come back to you, never. You may be speaking the truth now, as you may have told me a lie before—I may be your wife—your most unhappy miserable wife—I may never have been—his! But at least I will never willingly see you again. Do you dream that I will take one penny of your boasted wealth? Rather than touch it I would starve."

"Would you?" the man said very quietly, his pale eyes watching her every movement. "Would you really?" His look might have told her that the maudlin mood was passing, that he was becoming quarrelsome. With a sudden movement he jerked up her arm. "What is this?" with a contemptuous laugh. "Ah, I see; well, a revolver is a dangerous toy in inexperienced hands. I think we will dispense with it." He twisted her hand, and catching the revolver from her threw it carelessly on the table, knocking over the glass inkstand that stood in the centre.

The table-cloth was red, the ink poured across it in a black stream.

She glanced at the man who stood very near her now, his tanned face flushed, his light eyes reddened and angry. A shiver of terror shook her; she mentally measured the distance to the door, if only she could get away!

He caught her look and laughed mockingly. "Oh, no! You are not going, Judy! I haven't done with you yet. Think of all we have to discuss after our long parting."

There was a slight sound that might have come from the passage behind—she started with the faint hope that rescue might be at hand. The man heard the noise too; he turned his head and listened.

Judy saw her momentary advantage; she sprang forward. Before he had realized her intention she had reached the other room, caught at the door that must lead into the passage, and was tugging at it with insistent, impotent fingers.

There was a loud laugh behind her. "Ah, I thought of that beforehand! No use crying, Judy; the door is locked and the key is outside. Now—now don't you understand that you are in my power? That you are mine—mine!"

Judith set her teeth as she faced him, standing back against the door. He caught her in his arms.

"Do you know that you haven't given me one kiss yet, Judy? I haven't had the welcome I had looked forward to from my wife."

Judith struggled desperately to get away from him, striking blindly at the handsome face, the broad chest.

In vain, her strength was as nothing against his; she was drawn more closely to him; she could feel his hot breath upon her cheek. With one last mad effort at resistance she threw herself backwards. There was a click, then sudden darkness.

In one instant Judy realized what had happened. She had knocked against the electric switch; and it had given her the opportunity for which she had been longing. The arms that had been holding her so tightly momentarily relaxed; with a quickness born of her terrible plight she slipped out of them into the darkness.

There was the sound of an oath as the man felt blindly for the switch—failed to find it. Then as Judith tried to grope her way to the door by which she had entered, she heard that he was coming after her, swearing, knocking over the furniture. She gained the wall; surely—surely it was the outer room! Where was the door? There was not the smallest glint of light to show its whereabouts, and she had thought so certainly that it had been partly opened. It was horrible, horrible, feeling round the room, trying frantically to find the door, hearing the while the heavy breathing of the man who was pursuing her.

Once they were so near that she actually touched him. At last she felt wood—the door, the blessed door; another second and her fingers caught against a blind. It was the window— great tears came into her eyes. But the door was opposite; surely she could make her way across. Putting out her hands before her, she tried to walk softly. Yes: here was the centre table, where the revolver had been thrown, the ink upset. She felt about, there was the ink certainly, her hands were wet, but where was the revolver?

There came a cry.

"Ah! I have you now!" It seemed a long way away in the other room. "No use struggling now, Judy!"

Then across the darkness there rang out the sharp staccato sound of a revolver shot. There was a groan; a heavy fall.

CHAPTER IV

Judith stood as one petrified. What had happened? What was happening? She became conscious of a new sound—an odd gurgling sound. The darkness was peopled with horrible images, the gurgling died away into silence. What was it? she asked herself, her limbs trembling under her, a sweat of deadly terror breaking out upon her forehead. What had that ping, ping sounded like? Could it have been a revolver shot? If—if it were, who had fired it? And who had fallen on the floor?

Was it possible that the man who said he was her husband had shot himself by accident? He had not guessed that the revolver was loaded, and he had used it to frighten her.

As she stood there she told herself that she was a coward and a fool. He was hurt, perhaps dying. Summoning up all her courage, she managed to raise her voice.

"What is it? Where are you? Are you hurt, Cyril?" the old name seemed to come naturally to her lips.

There was no answer. But as she waited, her head bent forward to catch the least sound, she became aware that she was not alone in the room, that some one else was breathing softly close to her. It was not the man who had been pursuing her, she knew that instinctively. An agony of terror shook her, what did that veil of darkness cover? Who—what was stealthily passing her? It was very near her now—that thing with the horribly soft breath, very, very near her; putting out her hand, she would surely touch it. If it came one step nearer, assuredly it would knock against her.

Her overstrained nerves would bear no more. With a shriek of horror, she fled across the room, hitting herself against the chairs, finally running with outstretched hands against the locked door. It was locked still, but as she dashed herself helplessly against it, one hand touched the switch-board. With a cry she pulled the button down and glanced fearfully over her shoulder into the room. As she turned slowly further round, she caught sight of something protruding beyond the easy chair.

She moved round stealthily, fearfully. A man lay on the floor in a curious doubled-up heap, a man whose fair head and broad shoulders were very familiar. "Cyril! Cyril!" she said hoarsely, beneath her breath. There was no answer; she tottered across feebly. She felt no fear now of the thing on the carpet—only a great pity as she sank on her knees beside it.

A ghastly dark line had trickled down on the carpet, the florid face was white, the eyes sightless and staring. With a cry Judith tried to raise the heavy inert head, she took the nerveless hands in hers. "Cyril! Cyril!" she sobbed, as she felt the dead weight, as a dense mist gathered before her eyes.

Judith never knew how long she crouched there, on the floor beside the dead man. Strange thoughts buzzed through her brain, memories of the past, trifles that had no bearing on the present. But at last she awoke to a consciousness of her surroundings, of the danger in which she stood. People might come in at any moment. How could she explain her presence in the flat? How tell them of the dead man's insults, of the sudden darkness, and the unknown hand that had fired the fatal shot? They would not believe her. They might say it was she—she who had killed the man who lay there stark on the carpet before her.

The terror of that last thought pierced the thick cloud that had momentarily obscured her brain; she must get away, at all costs she must get away.

She started to her feet, shuddering as she saw the dark crimson stain that disfigured the front of her white bodice; she drew her cloak more closely round her, fastened down her veil. Then she turned and her lips moved silently as she looked down at the corpse; moved by some sudden impulse, she stooped and laid her hand for a moment on the cold forehead.

At the door of the room she paused again. What unseen danger might be lurking in the flat? At last she took her courage in both hands, and stepped out into the passage. All was apparently quiet; she could hear no sound, see no sign of the murderer. She opened the door of the flat with trembling fingers and pulled it to behind her. She was shaking from head to foot as she slowly made her way down the stairs.

As she neared the bottom of the first flight she heard some one coming up, whistling cheerfully. She saw that it was a man, a young man apparently; then she glanced away quickly, one hand holding down her veil. The man stood aside politely, then there was a sudden exclamation.

"Why, it is Judy! Judy, by all that is delightful! The very last person I expected to meet here."

It was a voice she had prayed she might never hear again on earth. The sound of it brought her to a sudden standstill. The man was blocking the way with outstretched hands—a man with a fair bronzed face, with smiling blue eyes and white teeth that gleamed beneath his drooping moustache.

"This is a surprise, Judy—a pleasant surprise!" he went on. "I had no idea that you and Cyril had made it up."

Judith's tortured eyes stared straight at him, her cold hand lay in his for an instant. Oh, why had she waited? she asked herself passionately; why had she not got away before this man,—who stood for so much that was evil in the past—saw and recognized her?

He did not seem to heed her silence; he turned and walked down the stairs.

"Cyril is looking fit, isn't he?" he said easily. "I half thought of going to him to-night, but I don't know whether I shall have time; as a matter of fact I have some business with another man in the next flat."

Judith made some inaudible reply. His bold, overfamiliar manner did not alter.

"You will have a taxi," he said as they reached the vestibule.

But Judith shook her head. "I am going by the Tube. Good-bye."

He laughed. "At any rate you must let me see you safely in for old times' sake."

"Oh, no, no!" Judith put out her hands. "You must not. Don't you see that I can't bear it; I must be alone."

The insolent laughter in the man's blue eyes deepened. "I see that you are not disposed to give your old friends a welcome, Judy," he said, mock reproach in his tone. "And there is so much I want to know. I want to hear all you have been doing since our last meeting. And how Cyril found you. Poor fellow, he has been half distracted to hear nothing of you for so long."

"He met me," Judith answered vaguely. "Goodbye."

"It is not good-bye," he assured her lightly. "I shall only say au revoir, Judy. We shall meet again."

Judith hurried away; some instinct made her look back as she reached the bottom of the steps. He was standing just as she had left him, but was it her fancy or was it some effect of the flickering light? It seemed to her that his face was distorted by a mocking, evil smile. With an inaudible sound of terror she turned and disappeared among the crowd.

As she hurried past the end of the street a man standing in a doorway opposite drew farther back in the shadow, then came out and turned after her. But Judith had not glanced at him. All her mind was intent on getting to the station at the earliest possible moment; the man following had some ado to keep up with her hurrying footsteps.

Sitting in the crowded carriage of the Tube, she clasped her hands together beneath her cloak. Oh, it was hard, terribly hard, she told herself passionately, that these two men should come into her life again. She had thought herself so safe, she had never dreamed that the dead past would rise again.

Then her mind went back shudderingly to that flat at Abbey Court and its ghastly secret. Who was it who had stolen in and shot Cyril Stanmore? Whose breathing was it she heard as she waited there in the darkness?

The dead man had made many enemies, she knew that some of them must have stolen in and taken this terrible revenge.

She let herself into the house in Grosvenor Square with the latch-key that she had taken care to provide herself with, and was conscious of a passing throb of surprise at finding none of the menservants in the hall.

She went into her room, where everything looked as she had left it. Evidently her absence had not been discovered. She took off her toque and threw it aside; she unfastened her cloak and tossed it back. Then, all alone as she was, she uttered a cry of horror, as she saw again the front of her white dress all splashed and stained with blood. Then there came a knock at the door, and Célestine's voice:

"Miladi, Sir Anthony, he tell me to bring you one little bottle of champagne, to make you eat one little piece of chicken."

Judith snatched up the *couvre-pied*, and drew it round her tightly. She shivered as she met the maid's gaze, her hands caught tightly at the cloth.

"Put the tray down," she said. "It—perhaps I may feel better presently—perhaps I will take something."

"I hope so, miladi, or Sir Anthony, he will be much distressed when he comes home," Célestine brought up a small table and put the tray upon it.

Judith, with her terrible guilty knowledge, cowered before the girl's eyes. In vain she told herself that there was nothing to be seen, that the *couvre-pied* hid both her hat and cloak as well as the front of her gown. Célestine's gaze told her that something had surprised her, that she had seen something unexpected.

Célestine was spreading out a dainty little supper, the wing of a chicken, some jelly, a small bottle of champagne; she brought the table a little nearer to her mistress.

Judith's eyes followed hers, then she made a quick involuntary gesture of concealment. Célestine's gaze was riveted on the hand that held the couvre-pied firmly over the tell-tale bodice. The delicate skin, the slender pink-tipped fingers were all blackened with ink.

"Miladi will take her supper." The maid's tone was perfectly respectful, but there was a subtle change in its quality.

Judith did not look up. After that first instinctive gesture she had not moved.

"That will do, Célestine, I will ring when I have finished," she said decidedly.

Left alone, she leaned forward and, taking up the wineglass, drank off the contents feverishly.

Then she stood up, a tall slim figure, with great terror-haunted eyes, burning in a white tragic face. Catching a glimpse of herself in the long pier glass, of the disfiguring stains on the front of her gown, she shuddered violently.

Then, she caught at her dress, she tore at the fastenings with her blackened fingers, and threw it from her on the floor. She gathered it up in a heap in her arms and, crossing the room to a small wardrobe that contained some of her oldest dresses and was seldom used, she thrust her bundle deep down in the well, dropped an old skirt over it, closed the door and locked it, and, after a moment's thought, put the key away in her jewel-case. Then she looked down at her ink-stained hands. Pumice stone removed the worst stains from her fingers themselves, but the ink had got under her delicate nails, and no effort of hers would move it.

She brushed on, mechanically. Her thoughts were back at the flat; what was happening there? she asked herself. Had the dead man been discovered?

What would the other man do—he who had met her on the stairs—when he heard what had happened in the flat that night? Would he denounce her, set the police to search for her?

Long fits of trembling shook her from head to foot. She tried to tell herself that it was impossible that anything should connect her with the dead man—that as Lady Carew she was safe, all links with the past destroyed; she felt that she was standing on a powder-mine, that at any moment the explosion might come, and this late-found happiness, at which she had snatched, be taken from her.

Presently there were sounds in Sir Anthony's dressing-room; she could hear him walking about, opening and shutting drawers. A passing wonder that he should be at home so early struck her—that he had not come in to ask how she was. Then a swift remembrance of the revolver she had taken from his room flashed across her mind. She had left it in the flat. Would he find out its loss? A sudden revelation that it must have been with this weapon the fatal shot was fired came to her! She recollected that it was on the table where it had been thrown when she groped for it. The murderer must have found it there, must have used it.

The horror of the thought drew her to the closed door. She tried it—it was locked.

"Anthony!" she said very softly. "Anthony!"

Apparently he did not hear her; there was no answer. She listened; he was still walking about the room. She heard him go to his wardrobe; she heard him give the little cough that was so familiar, the sound of his breathing. Suddenly she was reminded of the darkness of that room in Cyril Stanmore's flat, of the breathing she had heard as she waited and listened—the thought of it sickened her.

She turned and tottered back to her couch.

CHAPTER V

The blind was up, the morning light was streaming in through the window.

Judith raised herself in bed, leaned forward clasping her arms round her knees, and stared straight before her, in miserable, dazed bewilderment. All night long she had been tossing and turning in bed, going over again that dead and buried past, dreading the present—the future.

But this morning as the bright sunshine streamed into the room, it seemed impossible that yesterday's—that last night's happenings could really have taken place.

It was—it must be—she told herself, some hideous dream.

In her ordered life, of late, that past in which Stanmore played his part had seemed so very far away, she had been trying to teach herself to forget it.

Was it possible, she asked herself shudderingly, that it was she, Anthony Carew's wife, who had gone to Stanmore's flat last night, who had stood there, panting like some caged wild creature, while that terrible deed was done?

Was it, could it, be a dream? She slipped out of bed, and stood for a moment with her bare feet on the Persian rug at the side.

She unlocked her jewel-case, and took out the key of the small wardrobe, then, crossing the room quickly with trembling footsteps she thrust the wardrobe door back and felt inside the well. Yes! Yes! there was the dress she had worn last night—as she had known too well in her heart it would be.

Shutting her eyes, she could recall the very shape of those horrible stains, those dull crimson splashes. There was no mistake; she had known all along there could be none.

She stood still until at last some sound from Anthony's room roused her. She started and listened, the colour flashing into her cheeks. She told herself that she could not speak out about last night's doings, as her better angel had been counselling her. She was tied and bound by the cords of Anthony's love, by Baby Paul's tiny hands.

Then, shivering, she got back into bed again.

She could hear her husband moving about in his room for some time; then she heard his door close, and realized with a curious sense of bewilderment that he had gone down without coming to inquire how she was.

At last Célestine appeared with the tea. The sight of it was very grateful to Judith's parched mouth; she drank it eagerly.

The maid uttered a little shocked exclamation as she saw her mistress's face.

"But Miladi has surely the influenza," she cried. "Miladi must remain in bed and summon the good Dr. Martin, is it not so?"

"Certainly not!" Judith negatived decidedly. The very notion of lying in bed longer was hateful to her. I am quite well. Get my bath ready, Célestine. I shall get up at once."

She felt a little better when she had splashed in and out of her bath, when Célestine had arranged her hair in its usual golden crown, but she turned with loathing from the white morning gown the maid brought her. She would never wear white again, she thought with a shudder. Yet when her blue serge was fastened she wondered whether her white face did not look more colourless by contrast. She rubbed her cheeks rosy before she went downstairs.

Sir Anthony was standing at the table when she entered the breakfast room; he was apparently absorbed in his correspondence, a great pile of letters lying at his right hand— the papers were on the fender. He looked critically at his wife as she came in.

"How are you this morning, Judith?" he asked quietly.

He hardly waited for her answer. There was a new, almost an antagonistic note in his voice. Judith was conscious of it, without in any way realizing its significance. Her brain was obsessed by a fresh thought, the papers on the floor had riveted her attention. What would they say about last night's tragedy?

Sir Anthony looked at her. "Do you want anything over here, Judith?" he asked.

Judith had little thought to spare for anything this morning, or she would have seen that his face was pale beneath his tan, that there were new stern lines round his mouth, that his eyes were cold and strained.

"The paper, please."

Sir Anthony's eyes scrutinized her coldly as he passed her the paper, noted the two red spots that were beginning to burn on her cheeks, to tell of her inward excitement.

She ran her eyes down the different columns. No! There was no mention of the Abbey Court flat—of its terrible secret. Evidently nothing had been discovered.

She pushed her untasted egg from her, with a feeling of sick loathing, as she realized that the dead man must be there now, alone in his flat, his eyes still staring glassily.

Sir Anthony was to all appearances still occupied with his letters, but over the top of the sheet his eyes were furtively scanning her, watching her every movement.

Suddenly there was the sound of voices in the hall. Judith started and flinched visibly, then her face cleared, and she looked round with relief as there was a cry, "Judith! Judith!"

Sir Anthony threw down his paper. "Peggy! What in the world is she doing here at this time in the morning?"

"Why, Peggy has come to ask how Judith is, to be sure," the young lady answered for herself as she appeared in the doorway. "We were so sorry you weren't well enough to come to the reception yesterday afternoon, Judith dear," stooping to kiss her sister-in-law, "but you look as fit as a fiddle this morning, real country roses in your cheeks. I am so glad," with another kiss.

Peggy Carew was not like her half brother, Sir Anthony. She did not in the least resemble her mother, Theresa, Lady Carew, who since Sir Anthony's marriage had removed to the Dower House. A friend of Peggy's had once said there was nothing in the world she was like, unless it were a dewy wild rose picked from an English hedgerow.

This morning her cheeks were flushed by exercise, her great brown eyes were full of laughter, her young red lips were smiling, the fluffy brown hair was curling in pretty disorder round her white forehead.

"Stephen came with me," she went on with a laugh. "He wanted to know how you were too."

The dark clean-shaven man who had followed her into the room, and who was obviously considerably her senior, shook hands with Lady Carew with a smile.

"When you were not at the Denboroughs' Peggy and I made up our minds to pay you an early visit."

"Oh, I am quite well again this morning," Judith answered, forcing a smile to her stiff lips. "Last night I had a headache."

"Oh, last night she was absolutely *hors de combat*," Sir Anthony interposed. "I had to exercise my authority, and tell her she really must stay at home."

As he spoke, Stephen Crasster, catching a glimpse of his face in a distant glass, was surprised to see that an odd mocking smile was twisting his mouth beneath its drooping dark moustache. Anthony Carew and Stephen Crasster had been friends ever since their college days. That their paths in life had since lain far apart had not in any way lessened their affection for one another. Carew of Heron's Carew was a rich man, Stephen Crasster had had until six months ago to work hard, to make a name and a living at his chosen profession, the law. Then an old uncle in Australia, of whom he had known nothing, had died and left him a considerable fortune. So far the bequest had apparently affected his career but little; he worked as hard or harder than ever, but he himself was fully conscious that life now held certain sweet possibilities at which he had never hitherto dared to glance.

Noting his expression as he watched Peggy, remarking how constantly he was in attendance on the girl, Judith had come of late to guess the direction his hopes had taken, and to rejoice that her young sister-in-law had won the love of so true a man.

But Peggy was still unconscious; there could be no doubt of that. To her Stephen Crasster was merely her oldest friend—it was obvious that she regarded him as set—both by age and experience—on a very different plane from herself and the young people who were wont to surround her at her parties and dances.

"Lord Milman was at the Denboroughs' last night," Stephen said, addressing himself to Anthony. "He was disappointed not to meet you."

Judith looked at her husband in surprise.

"But, Anthony—the Denboroughs'—surely you went?"

Sir Anthony looked away. He picked up one of his letters and slipped his paper-knife under the flap absently.

"I thought it better not to go. I sent excuses for us both."

"You did not go," Judith repeated in consternation. "Oh, Anthony, I am sorry. Where did you—" A swift wave of colour flooded her face as she stopped short. She looked at him anxiously, timidly. It was not possible that he had remained at home last night—that he had even seen her go out?

There was no response in his eyes as he met hers. "I am very glad I did," he said dryly. "It enabled me to go over to see Venables. I had been trying to get it in for some time."

Judith breathed more freely. "Still, I am very sorry my stupid headache should have come on that very day. Peggy, is your mother going to—"

She paused. Jenkins, the butler, had appeared in the doorway.

"If you please, Sir Anthony, Inspector Furnival, of Scotland Yard, wishes to speak to Mr. Crasster on the telephone."

"Does he, indeed!" Crasster's keen, dark face lighted up. "You will excuse me, Lady Carew. This may be something of importance; they must have put him through from my place."

The telephone stood immediately opposite the door in the hall.

The three left in the breakfast room could hear him speaking plainly.

"Hello! That you, inspector?... Yes, I remember you promised... Yes, yes, quite right; where is it?... Leinster Avenue... Right. I will be with you as soon as possible."

Leinster Avenue! Judith caught her breath; her face was as white as death when he came back.

But Crasster had no attention to spare for her; he had eyes only for Peggy, who was now teasing her brother to take her to Ranelagh on Saturday.

Sir Anthony looked up. "Nothing wrong, I hope, Crasster?"

"Nothing at all!" Crasster returned heartily. "Only that I must get back as soon as possible. Peggy, are you going to give me the pleasure of driving you home?"

"Oh, I don't know; I think you are very tiresome! I wanted to play with Paul. Why must you go?"

There was a smile in the man's eyes as they looked down at her petulant face. "It is all in the way of business, Peggy. But if you don't want to come, I will leave the car for you and get a taxi."

"I will take Peggy home." Sir Anthony got up, tearing several of his letters up and tossing them into the waste-paper-basket. "I want to consult Mother about something, so you will be free, old man!"

Crasster hesitated a moment; he looked at Peggy, but the girl kept her face averted.

"Well, it is from Furnival," he said apologetically. "Probably he is about the keenest-witted detective they have at Scotland Yard. He makes a point of letting me know if anything interesting turns up, and he has often been good enough to say that I have been of real assistance to him. And since the unravelling of mysteries is part of my profession—"

Peggy hunched up her shoulders. "I didn't know you were a policeman."

Carew laughed outright. "A barrister is next door to one. Come, Peggy, don't be cross; I will take you for a long ride another day."

"Where are you going?" Peggy was only half-appeased.

"To Leinster Avenue," Crasster answered, "Furnival tells me that there has been a"—he hesitated a moment—"a curious occurrence at a flat in Leinster Avenue. He is very anxious I should go, but—"

"Of course you must go," Peggy said with restored good humour; her fits of petulance were never of long duration. "And I—perhaps I will come out with you to-morrow, Stephen, if you are good, and ask me prettily."

"What is the name of the flat?" In Judith's own ears her voice sounded loud.

Stephen looked a little surprised as he turned courteously.

"Abbey Court," he answered.

CHAPTER VI

"Do you think I look nice, Judith?" Peggy executed a pirouette before her sister-in-law.

"Very nice," Judith said absently. Her whole being was absorbed in waiting, listening.

The hours that had passed since Stephen Crasster had been summoned by Inspector Furnival that morning had stretched themselves out into an eternity of suspense and anguish. She had not known what the next moment might bring forth.

"Madame Benoit has a very good cut," Peggy went on, twirling herself about in an attempt to get a good view of the hang of her skirt behind. "I believe Mother would like me to wear nothing but white, but one gets tired of always having the same colour. And blue always suited me. It is Stephen's favourite colour."

"He is late." Judith's attention was caught by the sound of Crasster's name. Her eyes barely glanced at Peggy's pretty, graceful figure; they watched the clock with unconcealed impatience.

Peggy looked a little disappointed at her lack of interest. "Oh, no! I came early because I wanted a nice long talk with you, and I must see Paul. Come, Judith," putting her arm through her sister-in-law's, "he looks such a darling in his cot."

Lady Carew yielded. It was not worth while to resist, and it was better to do anything—anything rather than to sit there watching the clock, and waiting. The sisters-in-law looked a strange contrast as they left the room together, Peggy looked the very personification of youth and spring. Judith, with her white face, drawn under her eyes, and new strange lines of pain furrowing her brow, might have sat as a model for care or guilt.

Sir Anthony liked best to see her in white, and to-night, remembering this, Judith had put aside her own shivering distaste, her shuddering remembrance of the dress huddled away in the well of the wardrobe, and allowed Célestine to array her in a gown that she had carefully chosen, in accordance with her husband's taste, in Paris. It was of oyster-white satin, but satin of so soft and supple a texture that it might have been drawn through the proverbial ring—satin, moreover, that merely formed the background for the most exquisite embroidery of seed pearls and crystals. It was too magnificent a toilette for a *partie carrée*, such as had been arranged for this evening—just Stephen Crasster, Peggy, Anthony and herself—but they were going on to a gala performance at the theatre, given in honour of a foreign royalty who was visiting London.

Paul was awake as it happened; he was sitting up in his cot laughing and chuckling to himself, and obstinately refusing to go to sleep. Peggy adored her small nephew; she ran forward and picked him up, regardless of her finery.

"Kiss Auntie Peggy, Paul."

Paul lifted his rosy mouth pursed up into a round O, but his big grey eyes had seen somebody dearer than Peggy, he held out his arms to his mother.

"Mam, mam, dad, dad," he gurgled.

Judith took him almost mechanically, but the pain that had been pulling at her heart-strings all day seemed lulled a little, as the baby nestled his soft downy head into the curve of her neck.

They made a pretty picture, the tall, lovely mother, her eyes softened, her mouth relaxing into a smile, and the bonny, laughing boy. Peggy admired them in her honest, whole-hearted fashion, as she tried to make the baby look at her.

Somebody else was admiring the group, too. Peggy looked up, her ear caught by a slight sound. Outside in the day nursery, looking at them through the open door, stood her brother, Anthony, and Stephen Crasster. Stephen was smiling openly. The gloom of the morning was gone from Anthony's expression as he watched his wife and child. He came forward. She turned, holding the chuckling baby towards him, then, as she caught sight of Crasster behind, her whole face seemed to wither and alter. Stephen Crasster hesitated.

"I must apologize for this intrusion, Lady Carew, Anthony would bring me to have a look at my godson. He is a fine fellow."

"Yes," Judith said quietly.

She let Peggy take her little son from her whilst she set herself to talk with feverish energy to Crasster. Surely, surely he would tell her why Inspector Furnival had wanted him at Abbey Court that morning.

But nothing apparently was farther from Crasster's intention. He talked lightly and easily on a variety of topics, but the very recollection of Inspector Furnival's summons might have passed from his mind. At last, when Paul, now growing sleepy, had been replaced in his cot, and they were all seated at the round table in the big dining-room, Judith asked:

"Did your friend, the inspector, want you for anything important this morning, Mr. Crasster?"

She had succeeded in arresting his attention.

"It was rather interesting," he said slowly, "unusual, perhaps I ought to say. But I rather fancy it is out of my line."

Peggy smiled at him from her seat opposite.

"Are you talking of your imperative work of this morning, Stephen? Don't tell me it was nothing you were wanted for after all."

"No, it wasn't unnecessary," Crasster said, his dark face rather grave. "Only I don't fancy I'm quite so clever as I thought myself, Peggy, I don't imagine that Furnival found me much good."

Sir Anthony laughed disagreeably. "I should start from the idea that you can't trust anyone—that your dearest friend may be deceiving you."

Crasster looked at him in mild surprise. Carew was behaving rather oddly to-day, he thought, but probably he was not well; he had sent away his soup untasted, he was merely pretending to eat his fish.

"Well, I don't know that one's dearest friend would escape if suspicion pointed his way," Stephen answered slowly. "But what I find so enthralling is the fact that most detective work is of necessity a series of deductions. To reduce this to a science is, of course, our aim, but I must confess that in my case it is beset with difficulties. My deductions have a bad habit of not turning out right," with a whimsical smile. "You may remember at Eton, Anthony—"

Usually Lady Carew would have found it interesting enough. But to-day it seemed that it would be impossible to sit there quietly to the end of the meal, to take her part as the courteous hostess, while all the time her whole being was seething in a perfect whirl of unrest, of torturing anxiety. It was maddening to know that this dark-faced, pleasant-voiced man, was in possession of what she would have given half the remaining years of her life to learn, and yet he would not speak, she could not make him tell her. Only by a supreme effort did she retain her self-control until the meal was over. Then at the earliest possible moment, with a quick look at Peggy, she rose abruptly.

It was hot in the drawing-room; Judith felt feverish and oppressed with the terrible sense of overhanging calamity. The French window on the balcony stood open. Declining Peggy's invitation to go up to the nursery for another look at Paul she stepped out.

It was very quiet in the square, only now and again an occasional motor or a private carriage passed. She waited there; the chill of the night air felt pleasant after the fever that was consuming her. Peggy had stolen softly away intent on another visit to her small nephew. Suddenly the silence was broken by a loud, raucous cry coming down Oxford Street. Judith listened to it mechanically, paying scant heed; it was a man crying papers, that was all. As it grew nearer, more coherent, one word penetrated the mists that had gathered over her brain, startled her absorption.

"Murder! Murder!"

She held her breath, she strained her ears; what was he crying? Murder!

"'Orrible murder in a West End flat! 'Orrible murder—"

One of Judith's hands, went up to her throat, tugged relentlessly at the laces in the front of her gown until the delicate fabric gave way. Steadying herself with the other she leaned over the railings. The man was coming in a direct line with the house now.

"'Orrible murder in a West End flat. Latest details."

Judith stepped back into the house and rang the bell.

"Get me an evening paper, please, James," she said when the man appeared. "As quickly as possible. They are calling them outside."

She constrained herself to take the paper from the salver, she forced herself to wait until the man had left the room before she opened it. Then, she almost tore the pages apart. There was no need to search, for the column she wanted stared her in the face.

MYSTERIOUS MURDER IN A WEST END FLAT

"A crime of a peculiarly mysterious nature was perpetrated some time last night in a block of flats, comparatively newly built, called Abbey Court, in Leinster Avenue. The victim was a man who was known to the agent as Mr. C. Warden. He had taken the flat only a week ago and little or nothing was known of him. He is described by the porter as a quiet, inoffensive gentleman, giving no trouble and having no visitors. He was in the habit of having his breakfast sent up to him, the rest of his meals he took out. This morning the porter went up with his tray as usual, but was unable to make Mr. Warden hear. The porter waited a while and tried again. Then he ascertained that the electric light within the flat was still switched on; this made him fear that possibly Mr. Warden had been taken ill, with the result that he went round to the agents, and had the door broken open.

Mr. Warden was discovered in his sitting-room lying dead upon the floor in a pool of blood. Dr. Wilkinson of St. Mary's Street who was quickly upon the scene, gave it as his opinion that the unfortunate man had been shot from behind, at close range, and that the shot had entered at the back of the left ear, and, travelling in a transverse direction, had severed the carotid artery, thus accounting for the excessive hemorrhage. Dr. Wilkinson stated that death had probably taken place a couple of hours, at least, before midnight, and that it could not possibly have been self-inflicted. The revolver with which presumably the fatal shot was fired was discovered in the little dining-room, which was separated only by curtains from the room in which the deceased was found. It is hoped that the weapon may prove valuable as a means of identifying the assassin.

A curious feature in the affair is the fact that the porter states that, last night, for the first time, he took up a visitor to Mr. Warden's rooms in the lift—a lady wearing a long cloak and thickly veiled. He noticed her particularly, first because she was the only visitor who had asked to be taken up to No. 42; secondly, because she was so muffled up that it struck him she did not wish to be seen. A hand-painted fan was found on the floor, partly underneath the body, which is supposed to have been left by this mysterious visitor, and which may ultimately prove a valuable clue. Every effort is being made to discover the identity of Mr. Warden's visitor. She is described by Jenkins, the porter, as being tall and slender, with fair hair. Her features he could not see plainly as she had a thick veil twisted round her hat and face. She had a low, pleasant voice and he says was distinctly a lady. It was after nine o'clock when he took her up. He had no idea when she came down as she did not use the lift. Inquiries with a view to discovering her identity are being diligently prosecuted, and the police are of opinion that, with the clues at their disposal, this will be a matter of small difficulty."

Judith read it through without moving. Then she looked at it again. The printed type seemed to dance up and down before her eyes. With a gesture of despair she let the paper slip to the ground, walked over to the mantelpiece and leaned against the high shelf.

"My God!" she breathed, "My God!"

It seemed to her that the description cried aloud that it was she, Judith Carew, who had been in Warden's flat. Reading between the lines it was perfectly obvious that it was she who was suspected of having caused his death. They were diligently prosecuting the search for her; they expected with the clues at their disposal to find her quickly.

She quivered from head to foot in one long drawn out sob of agony. What was she to do? Where in heaven or earth was there any help for her? She dared not take the course that it seemed to her any innocent woman ought to take, she dared not go to the police and tell them her story. Her hands were tied and bound. Appearances were too terribly against her. The dead man had been shot with the revolver she herself had taken to his rooms; she had the strongest possible motive for desiring his death. She shivered and cowered against the wall as she asked herself how long it would be before they found her.

The sound of the opening door made her start with a cry of terror. She looked across, half expecting to see the police come to arrest her, but it was only Peggy who stood in the doorway, her eyes laughing as she glanced behind her.

The two men followed. Judith heard Anthony's voice; she tried desperately to recover herself, to regain her shattered self-control. She thrust the paper beneath a pile of books and went forward.

"The carriage will not be here for half an hour, Mr. Crasster. What shall we do to amuse you till then?"

"Peggy shall give us a song," Crasster suggested.

The girl made a little face at him. "Not now, sir, I'm going on the balcony," catching up a fleecy wrap and drawing it over her pretty bare shoulders as she stepped out.

Stephen held back the curtains for Lady Carew.

After a moment's hesitation Judith followed. As Crasster placed a chair for her, her ear caught the sound of a measured footstep below. She touched Peggy's arm. "Who—what is that, Peggy?"

The girl looked a little surprised as she leaned forward.

"Only a policeman."

"Only a policeman!" Judith's heart contracted as she sank into her chair, her fears rushed over her, multiplied a thousandfold. Why, oh why had she been such a fool as to come out, to sit here where it would be so easy for her to be seen—to be identified.

She got up jerkily. "After all, I don't think I will stay here," she said unsteadily. "I want to speak to Anthony—to consult him—"

She stepped back quickly. Sir Anthony stood in the inner drawing-room; she heard a rustle, and with difficulty suppressed an exclamation of alarm as she saw that he had the evening paper in his hand.

His back was towards her, but his face was reflected in the opposite mirror. Judith saw that he was studying something intently, that his dark overhanging brows were drawn together in a heavy frown.

CHAPTER VII

There is no doubt that Lady Carew's nerves are overstrained. The prevailing disease of our twentieth century, Sir Anthony!"

Sir Anthony Carew bowed. His dark face was unsmiling.

Judith, looking wan and fragile in her blue linen gown, was sitting in a big easy chair near the window.

Dr. Martin looked at her again. "The remedy is quite simple. Plenty of fresh air, rest and quiet. No need of drugs, though I will give you a simple prescription for the sleeplessness. If you will not think me too cruel, Lady Carew, I must say that the very best thing for you would be to leave London, to go into the country, and do nothing but rest and laze."

A little wave of colour swept over Judith's pale cheeks. She sat up in her chair and looked at Anthony wistfully.

"Oh, I should love to go into the country, to go back to Heron's Carew with nobody but the boy and you, Anthony. Oh, do let us go to Heron's Carew," with a little sob.

"Of course we will go to Heron's Carew, if Dr. Martin thinks it advisable," Sir Anthony said slowly. "Or would a voyage—sea air...?"

Dr. Martin regarded him benevolently over his pince-nez.

"Ah, that may come later. For the present I think Heron's Carew the very best possible suggestion. And remember, Lady Carew," wagging a fat playful forefinger at her, "no house parties, no bridge. A little tennis if you like when you are stronger, but for the present just absolute quiet—a deck chair on the lawn, and Master Paul for your companion, and in a very short time I shall expect to hear that all your roses have returned, that Sir Anthony is quite satisfied with your progress, I shall indeed."

"Yes, yes. I am sure it will do me good," Judith said feverishly. "I love every stone of Heron's Carew, only,

Anthony," her face clouded, "what of Peggy? Your mother is not strong enough—"

"Oh, Peggy will be all right," Carew said with a certain carelessness. "As a matter of fact I have already written to Alethea about her, she is coming up to town next week and she will be only too pleased to take Peggy about."

"You have written," Judith said with a puzzled look.

"The very best thing, my dear lady," Dr. Martin interrupted briskly. "Lady Leominster will look after Miss Carew and you will go to Heron's Carew in search of health. Now, that is all settled, and Sir Anthony will feel more comfortable about you."

When he left the room, shortly afterwards, Sir Anthony accompanied him and Judith was left alone.

The idea of leaving London, of returning to Heron's Carew, had brought a transient flush to her cheeks, a brightness which faded all too soon from her eyes. For some time she waited expecting her husband's return. The day was warm, the wind was blowing from the south, it fanned her cheeks, it brought in the scent of the flowering plants in the balcony.

More than a fortnight had elapsed since that terrible night in the Abbey Court flat; a fortnight which had held for Judith every species of imaginable dread. Every day the papers had made some mention of the mysterious murder; the inquest, after the first sitting, had been adjourned for a fortnight. To-day there had been hints that to-morrow the police would be in a position to place some important evidence before the coroner and the jury. There had been all sorts of rumours that Stanmore's mysterious visitor had been traced, that she was an actress, a noted singer, a society beauty. In her terror Judith had pleaded illness, she had broken all her engagements, she had refused to go out of doors, everywhere, anywhere, she might be recognized!

One feature of the affair puzzled her considerably; so far, the man she met on the stairs had not been mentioned. Yet surely he must have come forward, he must have told the police what he knew of Cyril Stanmore, told them that the mysterious visitor, whose identity was arousing so much curiosity was Cyril Stanmore's wife.

Nothing had leaked out so far with regard to Stanmore's identity. Why should he have taken the flat in the name of Warden, Judith could not imagine, save that with her knowledge of the man she was assured that his silence hid nothing creditable.

It had been stated in one report Judith had seen that the deceased man had left no papers, no valuables, nothing to prove his identity or to show where his relatives could be found, neither had his relatives been forthcoming.

But the man that Judith had met on the stairs knew as much as, or more than, she did herself of Cyril Stanmore's history. How soon would he speak or had he spoken already?

Down below in the Square people were passing backwards and forwards; a couple of men were lounging against the railings opposite. Judith's gaze fell upon them and with a quick movement of alarm she drew back into the shadow of the curtains. It might be that they were waiting, hoping to see her, to identify her.

A great longing for the quietness and the seclusion of Heron's Carew came upon her; there, in the spacious gardens she would at least be free from prying eyes. She listened eagerly for Anthony's return; she would beg him to make arrangements to go down to Heron's Carew at once—to-morrow, or the next day, surely it would be possible.

As she waited she heard the man below whistling for a taxi. She peered out through the pattern of the lace curtain as it drove off. Sir Anthony was the only occupant; his face was grave, even sombre, as she caught a passing glimpse. Judith looked after him, vaguely puzzled. He had gone out after hearing the doctor's report without coming back to speak to her. Then for a moment she roused herself to a fuller consciousness. What was amiss with Anthony? His manner to her, which had remained as lover-like for the two years of their married life as during the brief intoxicating period of their engagement, had changed in this terrible fortnight to one of cold reserve. Was it possible that he had recognized her description, that he had guessed? The very thought drove every drop of blood from her cheeks, her lips; set her heart beating in great suffocating throbs. She hardly realized how long she had been crouching there behind the curtains, shivering with sickly dread at the bare notion of this new possibility, when another thought struck her. If they were to go down to Heron's Carew at once, there was something she must do. She pulled herself up, holding by the table at her side. It was curious how her physical strength had deserted her.

At last, however, she made her way feebly to the bell, and rang it. Célestine made her appearance with such speed as to suggest that she had been remaining purposely close at hand.

"But miladi is ill," she said, as she saw her mistress's ghastly face. "Miladi is surely faint. If she will let me get a glass of Sir Anthony's good wine—?"

"No! I want nothing." Judith held up her hand. "But I am cold. It is possible I have taken a chill. Will you have the fire made up in my room? I shall be coming up directly. I always fancy I rest on the couch there better than anywhere."

"It is one beautiful couch," Célestine assented, her sharp little black eyes scanning Lady Carew's face attentively. "And of course there is already a fire, miladi. Since miladi has not been so well I have kept one there every day, since it might be that at any time she might need it."

"That is right," Judith laid her head back on her chair. "I will come up in a few minutes then."

"Will miladi let me help her?" Célestine's voice and manner were respectfully sympathetic.

But Judith shook her head. "No! no! I will come presently."

She waited a little while gathering her strength together, then she made her way upstairs slowly.

Célestine was waiting for her. The couch was drawn up as her mistress liked it, but Lady Carew looked disappointedly at the fire. "I told you I wanted a good fire, Célestine, a large fire, I am cold."

"A—h!" Célestine held up her hands. "But the other day when the fire was not so large as this Miladi say that it was huge, that it would give her the fever. But, see, Miladi, it will soon burn up, be as big as Miladi likes."

She deftly applied wood, piled up small coal, and presently the fire showed signs of becoming large enough to satisfy her mistress's requirements. Judith watched her with wide-open, miserable eyes. At last she said wearily:

"That will do, Célestine, I feel warmer already. Now perhaps I shall sleep."

"But I hope so, Miladi." The maid stood up and looked with distaste at her blackened fingers. "And if Miladi want anything she need not exert herself to ring the bell; if she would just speak one little word, I am at my needlework in the dressing-room, I shall hear."

Judith raised herself on her elbow. "No! No! I can't have you in the dressing-room, Célestine; I can't sleep if anyone is moving about."

The maid looked aggrieved. "But I will be as quiet as a mouse, Miladi. And I am putting on the lace of Miladi's heliotrope satin. If miladi should want it."

"I shall not want it," Lady Carew said decisively. "We are going down to Heron's Carew directly, Célestine. Dr. Martin says the quiet will be the best thing—best for me."

Célestine held up her hands. "*Ma foi*, it is a *triste* place, that Heron's Carew," she grumbled discontentedly. "Naturally

Miladi does not require her magnificent toilettes there. Me—I expect always to die of megrim at Heron's Carew."

"That will do!" Judith said wearily. "You understand, Célestine, I am not to be disturbed until I ring."

Left alone she waited a while until the fire had burned up briskly, until there was a glow in the hot coals beneath that scorched her face as she sat there. Then she got up, rallying all her self-control, walked across to her jewel-case, and took out her little key. Holding it she paused a moment undecidedly; then with a gesture of infinite loathing she turned to the small wardrobe and opened the door.

She averted her face shudderingly, as she thrust her arm into the well, and brought out the skirt she had thrown over the tell-tale tea-gown. Laying it on the floor beside her she put her hand in again; then, with a quick, startled exclamation she turned, peered into the well, pushed her hands from side to side—the tea-gown was gone!

She sat back on the floor and stared at the empty well. Where—how had it gone? The wardrobe had been locked, the key of the jewel-case had never been out of her possession; she went back feverishly, tore all the things from the hooks, and scattered them around her on the floor, only to make more certain of what had been obvious from the beginning—the tea-gown was gone!

With a slow movement of despair she got up, her knees shaking under her, cold beads of perspiration breaking out on her forehead. Who could have learnt of its presence in the wardrobe—who could have obtained possession of it?

At last her lips moved mechanically, they framed words.

"They—they spoke of a clue to be produced at tomorrow's inquest," she whispered hoarsely. "Was it this? My God, was it this—was it this?"

CHAPTER VIII

Heron's Carew was a big imposing-looking building, standing on the top of the hill, looking down to the Heron's moat. It had no pretensions to any kind of architectural beauty. In ancient time, rumour had it, the old house had stood lower down and the Heron's moat had surrounded it; some vandal of a Carew had pulled it down to build the newer edifice on the top of the hill. Of the house that had been built originally on the hill, much was destroyed by a fire in the days of the first George, the residue formed the kernel of the present Heron's Carew; but to it had been built by different Carews such additions as took their fancy, a new wing here, a large dining-room thrown out there, bedrooms built over any spare space. Time had mellowed the whole, had thrown over the heterogeneous mass a kindly veil of ivy, *ampelopsis* and other climbing plants. The Carews, every one of them, loved Heron's Carew, but it is to be doubted whether any of them had loved Heron's Carew with a greater love than Judith, the wife of the present owner.

It had meant safety to her, the old house, when she came to it. It was there that she had first dared to dream tremblingly that Anthony cared for her, it was there that the golden days of her early married life had been spent, there that her little son had been born—it was small wonder that she loved every stone of the grey walls.

Already, though they had been back only a week, Heron's Carew was beginning to exert its spell over her. Some of the fret and the worry had smoothed itself out of Judith's face; she was looking stronger and better as she sat in her lounge chair beneath the shade of the big cedar.

Paul, fresh and rosy from his afternoon's sleep, was on the rug at her feet playing with a big woolly lamb, and emitting every now and then a satisfied chuckle.

A couple of footmen came down from the house bringing the tea-things; Sir Anthony followed them, a bundle of papers in his hand. He sat down in one of the wicker chairs and smiled at Paul, who was trying in his own fashion to attract his attention.

"Well, young man, how are you? Judith"—a slight subtle change in his voice as he addressed his wife—"you heard from Peggy this morning, didn't you? What did she say to you? Did you gather that she is enjoying herself with Alethea?"

"Oh, enormously, I think." Judith hesitated a moment, and coloured, bending over the baby to hide her confusion. She was conscious that Peggy's letter had received but scant attention. "Lady Leominster is taking her out everywhere, and Peggy is getting lots of admiration, as she was sure to." Judith finished with a smile; her pretty young sister-in-law was very dear to her.

"Did she say anything about this new Lord Chesterham to you?"

"New Lord Chesterham?" Judith wrinkled up her brows. "I don't remember. No, I feel sure she did not mention Lord Chesterham. Why do you ask?"

Anthony drew a letter from his pocket. "I have just heard from Alethea. She says—oh, here it is. The new Lord Chesterham was at the Westropps' the other night. Peggy made quite an impression upon him, I think. It was easy to see he was attracted and, knowing how near Chesterham Castle is to Heron's Carew, my mind could not help glancing at certain possibilities. But it is early days for such speculations yet, so I will say no more. That is all." Sir Anthony folded the letter up and glanced meditatively at it.

"Lord Chesterham!" Judith repeated. "That is the one who has just come into the title, isn't it?"

Sir Anthony nodded. "He didn't bear the best of reputations before he succeeded either, from what I hear. I am sorry Peggy has met him. I should have thought Alethea was to be trusted to look after her. But she seems quite pleased with this," tapping the sheet with his hand. "However, as Peggy says nothing about the man herself, I expect it is all right. She would have been certain to tell you if there had been anything in it."

Judith did not answer as she busied herself about the tea-urn. With her surer knowledge of a woman's heart, she was inclined to think that Peggy's silence might be a bad sign.

"It is time Chesterham came down here," Sir Anthony presently went on, "the estates are going to rack and ruin, but there never was any Chesterham of the lot that troubled about that as long as there was money to pay for their pleasures." He laid Lady Leominster's letter, together with a pile of others, on an empty chair beside him as he spoke, and caught up his heir: "Well, Master Paul, come and tell me what you have been doing with yourself."

Judith watched them with fascinated eyes. To her, after the ceaseless nervous terrors of the past six weeks, it was something like happiness to be here in their own grounds, safe from intrusion, alone with her husband and child. Sir Anthony, too, had seemed more like himself since their return to Heron's Carew. Nevertheless Judith was conscious that the barrier between them remained, that the perfect confidence that formerly subsisted between them was now a thing of the past. Suddenly at the bottom of the pile of letters she caught sight of the evening edition of a London paper. She drew in her breath sharply. The inquest on Cyril Stanmore had been adjourned until this morning—was it possible that there could be any news of it yet? Public interest in the West End flat murder, as it was called, had flagged a little of late.

The disappearance of her tea-gown had thrown Judith at first into a perfect frenzy of alarm; but as the time wore on and she heard nothing of it, her fears began to subside, though the occurrence remained as mysterious as ever. Questioned, Célestine had obstinately denied all knowledge of it.

Her hand stole towards the paper; Anthony was still absorbed by the baby; he would not see her. She drew it out quickly, and opened it with as little rustle as possible. Yes. There it was on the space reserved for intelligence received on going to press.

WEST END FLAT MURDER—INQUEST AND VERDICT

"The inquest on the man known as C. Warden was resumed this morning before Mr. Gwynne Bargrave. No further evidence was offered by the police, who stated that, so far, the clues in their possession had led to nothing tangible. The jury returned a verdict of 'Wilful murder against some person or persons unknown.'"

That was all.

Judith drew a long breath of thankfulness. She had but little knowledge of the law's procedure in criminal cases; and it seemed to her that the Leinster Avenue case was finished now, that she had nothing more to fear.

She let her clasped hands fall on the paper with the gesture of one who had escaped from an intolerable bondage; then, looking up, her eyes met Sir Anthony's. He had the baby on his knee still, but over its fluffy yellow head his eyes were watching Judith eagerly, with a certain furtiveness. He dropped his heavy lids, but not before Judith had surprised an expression of keen watchfulness. It had the effect of a sudden shock upon her, it was as if he had purposely placed the paper there, as if he had been waiting to see the result upon her.

The next minute he had risen with Paul in his arms; he was tossing the delighted child in the air. Judith told herself that she must have been mistaken, that her nerves were overstrained, that she was foolishly fanciful, but the unpleasant impression remained.

She got up and crossed the lawn hurriedly. As she neared the house, Jenkins, the urbane, appeared, preceding a black-robed figure.

"Lady Palmer has called, my lady. She asked to see both your ladyship and Sir Anthony."

"Lady Palmer!" Judith repeated in a puzzled tone, then her face altered. How could she have forgotten? This was the widowed Lady Palmer, the Sybil Carew of Anthony's youth—free, now, while he was bound.

The slender graceful woman in black came up to her quickly. Both Judith's hands were caught. Two liquid brown eyes gazed into hers.

"You are my cousin Anthony's wife, I am sure. How—how beautiful you are! You must forgive my frankness. Anthony will tell you I am nothing if not unconventional."

Judith felt suddenly tongue-tied. She had heard much of Sybil Palmer, of her, beauty, of Anthony's mad love for her. She had heard that the breaking off of his engagement had embittered all his early manhood; she knew that the meetings between the two had since been few and far between. She knew also that her husband had written to Lady Palmer on hearing of her husband's fatal accident.

"You will give me a welcome, won't you?" the sweet pathetic voice went on wistfully. "Ah, there is Anthony." With a final lingering pressure Judith found her hands dropped, and Lady Palmer turned to Sir Anthony, who was coming across the lawn towards them, Paul perched on his shoulder.

"Sybil!" he uttered in an amazed tone. "How in the world did you come here? We had no idea—"

"I know you had not." Lady Palmer's beautiful eyes grew moist; her sweet tones were reproachful. "But I was staying with the Wiltons, and I told them I must come over. I thought you would give me a welcome, Anthony, for the sake of old times."

The last words were uttered in a low voice, but they reached Judith's ears as she waited.

"Of course we have a welcome for you—of course we are delighted to see you," Sir Anthony answered, a certain breeziness in his voice that contrasted curiously with Lady Palmer's languid tones.

"Ah, things have altered since we last met," she went on with a little catch in her breath. "Then my dear husband was with me, do you remember? And it was before your marriage. Now you have your wife, your child, and I—I have lost everything."

"I was—we were so grieved to hear of your loss," Sir Anthony said with some embarrassment.

Judith, waiting, felt with a vague tinge of wonder, that Sybil Palmer was an absolute surprise to her. She scarcely realized as yet the subtle charm of the deep brown eyes, of the transparent pallor of the skin, of the pathetic curves of the lovely mouth.

"Oh, what a beautiful boy!" Lady Palmer was trying to coax the child to come to her arms.

Judith felt an unreasonable thrill of pleasure when Paul, usually so good with strangers, turned obstinately away and held out his tiny arms to his mother. "Mum, mum!"

"Ah, well! he will make friends with me later. Children always do," Lady Palmer said easily, though Judith saw that she did not look quite pleased as she turned back to Sir Anthony. "Dear old Heron's Carew! How often I have dreamt of it! The love of it is in the Carew blood." She sighed. "DearLady Carew, I know you will let me ask my cousin's advice, you will not grudge it to poor little me, for I am in such trouble now, Palmer made such a complicated will. You will help me, won't you, Anthony?"

"If I can, I shall be delighted," Sir Anthony said courteously, but with a certain reserve in his tone. His gaze had wandered from the eyes raised so appealingly to his, to his wife's graceful figure.

Lady Palmer's eyes followed his. "How lovely she is," she murmured. "An ideal Lady Carew, Anthony. And yet, and yet—" she broke off musingly.

"And yet?" There was a slight touch of hauteur in Sir Anthony's voice.

Lady Palmer bit her lip, and then laughed. "How absurd of me! I was trying to think—I fancied I had seen her before. I remember now, it was at Monte Carlo. We were there, Palmer and I, and there was a terrible scene. A young man was missed, he had shot himself."

"And there was somebody there who reminded you of my wife." Sir Anthony frowned as he looked at her.

Lady Palmer laughed. "Well, yes! I did see a face that reminded me of Lady Carew's. At least I thought so at first, the resemblance is not quite so striking now when I see more of Lady Carew. Do you know Monte Carlo, Lady Carew?"

"No!" But if Lady Palmer could have seen the face bent so closely over Paul's head, she would have noticed that it turned several degrees paler.

The flute-like voice trickled off into laughter. "But of course it could not have been you; I must have been mistaken, though at first I thought it was the same face."

"Of course you were," Judith said hurriedly. "Of course you were mistaken."

CHAPTER IX

"My lady said she expected to be home next week, but perhaps Miss Peggy might stay awhile longer with Lady Leominster. I was to be sure and write back soon and tell her how your ladyship was looking."

Judith smiled. "You must tell her that the air of Heron's Carew has quite set me up."

"I was saying so to Célestine last night," said Gregson.

"Was Célestine down here last night?" Judith enquired with a little air of surprise. "I thought she went down to the village."

"Oh, no, she didn't, my lady." Gregson's pleasant old face, that always reminded Judith of a wholesome winter apple, grew suddenly grave. "Célestine generally goes off to the Spring Copse nowadays; she just looked in on me in passing. I have said myself that I didn't believe your ladyship knew what she was doing."

Something in the old woman's tone arrested Judith's attention. "Why, what is she doing, Gregson? If she likes to walk in the Spring Copse, instead of in the village, I can't see that it matters."

"Not if she walked alone," Gregson said significantly. "I have heard say that Célestine meets a young man there, my lady—not that I have seen it myself."

"A young man!" Judith repeated slowly. "Oh, well, you know, Gregson, there is nothing very surprising in that, is there?"

"Perhaps there isn't, my lady," Gregson returned. Her expression was uncompromising. She had been the Dowager Lady Carew's confidential maid, then she retired to the nursery when Peggy was born, finally she had accompanied Lady Carew to the Dower House. She had known Judith as Peggy's governess before she became the wife of the owner of Heron's Carew, and it was no small tribute to Judith's charm of manner and natural dignity that Old Mrs. Gregson always spoke of her as a real lady and the right wife for Sir Anthony.

"I say nothing against Célestine having a young man," she said now after a pause. "As your ladyships says, that is natural enough, and when it is all open and above board, I should be the last to make any objection, but when it is meeting after dusk, and in woods and such places, why it seems to me that nothing but harm can come of it."

"Oh, well, I don't know," Judith said with a slight smile. "I fancy Célestine can take care of herself. But I will give her a hint. Good-bye, Gregson; I shall write to Miss Peggy and tell her all her pets are going on well."

Gregson curtsied. "Yes, my lady, we take good care of them, but they miss her bright face sorely, as we all do."

Judith was looking much better now. The air of Heron's Carew and its restful atmosphere had done wonders for her, though her beautiful eyes still held the shadow of a terrible dread. She made her way through the Home Wood. Already it was brilliant with the promise of early summer.

Absorbed in her own thoughts, as she reached the gate leading to the park, she did not heed a faint rustle of the undergrowth; she caught no faintest glimpse of the two men who, hidden behind the budding rhododendrons, were peering out after her. She walked quickly up the hill to the house. As she turned across from the avenue, however, and made her way to the rosery, she caught the sound of voices, and paused with a quick throb of disappointment. Anthony was there, and a visitor!

Another moment and she had recognized Lady Palmer's voice. Judith's face clouded over; with a restless sigh she turned back and went in by the front door.

She could not bring herself to like Lady Palmer in spite of that lady's protestations of affection for her cousin's wife.

Lord Palmer had apparently left his affairs in a considerable tangle. Lady Palmer was still staying with her friends, the Wiltons, and almost every day found her at Heron's Carew, intent on getting Sir Anthony's opinion on some knotty point. Sir Anthony, for his part, seemed nothing loath to act as general adviser.

Judith went up to her own room; its windows overlooked the rosery. She could see her husband, his dark head bent down to his companion, pacing up and down the centre walk by Lady Palmer's side. Lady Palmer was talking softly; she was gesticulating with her small white hands.

Judith's eyes were strained and bright as she watched them. It seemed to her that the reason of her husband's coldness to her was perfectly clear now. It dated from the day of Lord Palmer's accident. Lord Palmer's premature death had set Sybil free, still young and beautiful, and Anthony— Anthony, who had well-nigh broken his heart for the loss of her in the days of their youth—Anthony was bound.

Was he?

The question pierced like a sword stab through Judith's heart. It was the first time, in any serious sense, that the threats uttered by Stanmore on the night of his death had recurred to her memory. The manner of his death had been such as to overshadow and absorb all lesser things. Until now Judith had not realized that, if his words were true, even dead he stood between her and Anthony. As she watched Anthony and his cousin, a new terrible pain gripped her heart; she bit her under-lip till two red beads of blood stood out. Then, with a resolute effort, she turned away; she would not look at them again, she would not even think of them, she would put that last horrible suggestion from her.

She turned away, and, moved by some sudden instinct, opened the door of Anthony's dressing-room, and looked in. All was just as usual. Then, as she stood there, her eye was caught by something bright on the floor near the dressing-table. She went over and picked it up with an exclamation of surprise. It was a diamond stud—one that she knew her husband particularly valued. How it had escaped the attention both of the valet and the house-maids was a mystery.

The dressing-case was unlocked, but Judith knew that it held a secure hiding-place—a concealed drawer, the secret of which Anthony had shown her in the early days of their married life. She remembered that he kept the stud there.

She pressed the spring and the drawer sprang open. There was not much in it. Judith took up the stud-case and fitted the diamond in. Then, as she put it back, her eyes were caught by a piece of paper that lay beneath—"42 Abbey Court, Leinster Avenue. 9.30 to-night."

The fatally familiar words stared up at her in the man's big characteristically bold handwriting. She stood still and gazed at them, her breath coming in quick shallow gasps, her eyes dilating—it was Cyril Stanmore's writing, she could not mistake it.

She put out her hand, shaking as if from ague, and picked it up. Yes; there was no possibility of error—it was the identical piece of paper that Cyril Stanmore had given her on the steps of St. Peter's, when he had ordered her to come to his rooms.

How had it come into Anthony's possession? And what could its presence in the secret drawer signify? It was self-evident that she had dropped the paper, that Anthony had picked it up, but when and where? Its presence there in his drawer showed that he attached some importance to it. Was it possible that he had found it before she went to the flat? She remembered that he had not gone to the Denboroughs' on the night of the murder. Where had he been? Where had he gone? She shivered all over as if from ague as she dropped the paper, pushed the stud-case over it, and replaced the secret drawer.

Shaking still with internal cold she tottered back to her room and closed and bolted the communicating door. Then, leaning against the wall, her mind went back to the night of the tragedy at the flat. She recalled every little incident with the precision and the certainty of a photograph.

She retraced every step mentally. She saw that it would have been perfectly easy for anyone to have followed her; the only difficulty was as to how it would have been possible to obtain access to the flat. She could only imagine that Stanmore in his anxiety to hurry her inside, had fastened the door insecurely—some one who had been waiting and watching must have stolen in behind them.

Judith put her hand up to her throat, her mouth suddenly parched and dry; somebody had stolen in and waited in that outer room, had heard Stanmore's threats, and when the light was switched out had taken up Sir Anthony's pistol and used it!

Judith's eyes were full of sickening terror, her mouth twitched down at one side, big drops of moisture stood out upon her forehead. Whose breathing was it she listened to? If she had found the door earlier, if she had turned the light on, whom would she have seen?

CHAPTER X

"Eh! What! What is the meaning of this?" Sir Anthony was reading his letters. He looked up now, and glanced at his wife as though he expected her to explain what was the meaning of their contents.

Judith's mouth gave a little nervous twitch; from her seat behind the tea-pot she glanced out half-fearfully at her husband. She was growing much thinner, the graceful rounded curves of her figure were changing to positive attenuation. The improvement in her health that those first days at Heron's

Carew had wrought had not been maintained, but Judith was resolute in determining to stop there.

"What is it, Anthony?" she asked nervously. There was a curious shrinking now in her manner to her husband; it was obvious at times that she avoided being left alone with him.

"It is Peggy," Sir Anthony returned somewhat illogically. "This letter is from my stepmother and there is another from Alethea. Peggy is engaged to Lord Chesterham."

"Peggy is engaged to Lord Chesterham!" Judith echoed. "Oh, I am sorry. I was afraid she was attracted by him, but I didn't think there would be anything definite settled at present."

"I never heard of such a thing," Sir Anthony went on, frowning and tapping the letter. "Peggy is a mere child; she does not know her own mind, and as for Chesterham—I disapprove of it entirely."

Judith looked troubled; she had dreamt of a very different husband for Peggy. "Is there really anything against Lord Chesterham?" she questioned.

Sir Anthony shrugged his shoulders. "One does not want one's sister to marry a man simply because there is nothing against him. The Chesterhams have never been a particularly reputable family, in my opinion. The last lord had anything but an enviable reputation in his youth, but he lived to a great age, and in his case the sins of the past were forgotten. This man, his successor, as I have understood, was always a *mauvais sujet*."

"Still, he may have reformed," Judith said hesitatingly. "I don't want to put myself into opposition, Anthony, but we are bound to look at this from every point of view, for Peggy's sake."

"I shall do my best to stop it—to put an end to the idea at once, for Peggy's sake," Sir Anthony retorted folding up his papers with a determined air. "Why, the fellow must be three times her age, if there were nothing else."

Judith sighed. "I am afraid that sometimes to a girl like Peggy that is part of the attraction."

"It is an absurd, an unheard-of thing, that they should try to settle the affair," Sir Anthony grumbled, paying scant heed to his wife's remarks. "Peggy can't have known him a month, and here is my stepmother writing that the engagement, as she calls it, has her warmest approval. While as for Alethea she positively seems to imagine that I shall be grateful to her for having brought it about. I shall give them both a piece of my mind. I shall tell them—Why!"—getting up and going over to the window—"who is this, coming through the rosary? It looks like—I declare it is Stephen Crasster. What in the world brings him down here?" He opened the window as he spoke, and stepped out on to the terrace. "Stephen, old man, is that you?" he called out in my heartiest greeting. "You have come in the nick of time, for I have just heard a piece of news that has taken away my appetite for breakfast."

With her quick womanly intuition, Judith knew what the news would mean to the man who was coming towards them across the rosery, his keen kindly face bright with smiles. She went out on the terrace too; touched her husband's arm.

"I would not speak of it yet, Anthony; they—Peggy might not like it, I mean," stammering a little as she met his astonished gaze. "Something might happen to prevent it."

"No such luck," Sir Anthony said ruefully. "They mean it to be announced formally next week unless I can put a spoke in the wheel."

"Bad news! Have you?" Stephen questioned as he stepped on to the terrace. "Nothing very bad, I trust. How do you do, Lady Carew"—a certain formality creeping into his tone—"For my own part I hope, Anthony, old man, that you may consider I am the bearer of good news this morning. I am conceited enough to think you will. You see before you the new owner of Talgarth."

"What!" Anthony exclaimed with a great laugh, and a hearty squeeze of his friend's hand, while Judith caught herself up in an exclamation that betokened anything but pleasure, and bit her lip. "You don't mean to say that it is settled? How quiet about it you have been. Why didn't you tell me you were thinking of it?"

"I had a fancy for surprising you," Stephen smiled. "And you knew I was looking out for something in the neighbourhood. I have had my eye on Talgarth for some time. Do you remember we rode over to see it on our way to Mereham Park?"

Certainly Crasster's news had the effect of diverting Sir Anthony's mind from Peggy's misdeeds. His countenance lighted up. He looked thoroughly pleased.

"I remember. It will want a lot of doing up, but there are endless possibilities about the old place, and if you got it cheap I daresay you will do very well there. I know Judith and Peggy always say it is the prettiest place in the county."

"I know they do," Crasster assented. "I hope they will honour me by coming over some day soon and suggesting improvements."

"Why, of course they will," Sir Anthony began hastily; then his countenance clouded over. "That is to say, they will if anything happens to prevent Peggy from carrying out this wild scheme of hers. That is what is upsetting me. I have only just heard of it."

Stephen Crasster's grey eyes twinkled. "What scheme of Peggy's do you mean? I have heard nothing of it. What has she been doing now?"

"Worse than ever," Sir Anthony grumbled dismally. "She is going to marry Lord Chesterman."

"What!" The exclamation sounded almost like a groan as it broke from Crasster.

Judith, watching, saw that his dark face had paled suddenly beneath its tan.

"Peggy is going to marry this new Lord Chesterham," Sir Anthony repeated, his tone growing more aggrieved. "How in the world she and Alethea can think I am likely to approve of such a match for her I am at a loss to imagine. Had you any idea that such a thing was in contemplation, Crasster?"

"I? Not the slightest," Stephen answered quietly. After that first movement of involuntary self-betrayal he had dropped as it were a mask over his features. "It is rather sudden, isn't it?"

"Sudden? Of course it is sudden," Sir Anthony said impatiently. "She didn't know him when we left town. And now Alethea sends me word she is engaged to a man I never saw and never heard any good of. Do you know anything of him?"

"I have met him, I think," Stephen said slowly, drawing his dark brows together thoughtfully. "Yes, he was at the Derehams'. He is a good-looking man."

"Good-looking!" Sir Anthony repeated scornfully. "What do I care about that? I want to know what sort of a man he is."

"I am afraid I can't help you there," Crasster said, forcing an apparent lightness into his manner. "But, more earnestly, "my knowledge of Peggy tells me that there must be some good in him if Peggy loves him."

"I don't feel so sure about that," Sir Anthony growled. "Peggy wouldn't be the first girl who has been made a fool of. Well, well, I suppose talking won't mend matters. And, anyhow, it is a great thing to know we are going to have you for a neighbour, Stephen, old fellow. How soon do you expect to be down?"

A slight change passed over Stephen's face. "I am down now, that is to say, I am staying in the house and seeing into things generally; there is a lot that wants doing. But I haven't any intention of settling at Talgarth for the present. I am too fond of my profession for that. When I have finished the necessary improvements, I must look about for a suitable tenant, or dispose of it in some way. Perhaps—"—with a little laugh in which only Judith's quick ear detected any bitterness—"I may give it to Peggy for a wedding present."

"Nonsense!" Sir Anthony tore the greater part of his correspondence across and threw it into the wastepaper basket. "Nonsense, my dear fellow. You will have to settle down yourself and receive our wedding presents instead. I used to think—"

He was interrupted. Jenkins opened the door and announced Lady Palmer. That lady fluttered in with outstretched hands, and her pretty uncertain smile.

"You must not blame Jenkins, dear Lady Carew. I insisted on being shown in to you at once. I have just heard this delightful news from Alethea, and I felt I must come over at once and offer my congratulations."

Judith submitted with as good a grace as she could to the little airy touch on her cheek which passed for a kiss. Sir Anthony frowned.

"Alethea has been in a hurry," he said shortly. "I have not given my consent yet, and I am Peggy's guardian conjointly with her mother, a fact Alethea seems to forget."

"Oh, I am sure she doesn't. Only you couldn't but approve of this marriage," Lady Palmer rejoined with a deprecating smile. "Lord Chesterham is a great *parti*. He is the most perfectly charming man, besides being enormously rich, and his title is among the oldest in the country. Our little Peggy will be a very great lady, the envy of all her contemporaries."

"Will she indeed?" Sir Anthony questioned ironically. "I suppose the fact that Lord Chesterham is three times her age, and that he bears a bad reputation will not be taken into consideration."

Lady Palmer opened her great dark eyes to their fullest extent. "Dear Anthony, what does age matter? If Peggy is willing to overlook the little disparity, certainly it does not seem to me that it matters to anyone else. As to Lord Chesterham's reputation, well, you must not rake up old scandals. And now I must confess I had another, a selfish reason, for coming over this morning. I have had a letter to say that some of my jewels—the sapphires poor dear Palmer gave me on my first birthday after our marriage—were heirlooms. Now I know—"

"But, my dear Sybil, I have heard from Spencer, and he says—" Sir, Anthony drew her outside on the terrace.

Judith glanced at Stephen Crasster. In the clear morning light his pleasant dark face looked worn a little weary. He laughed a trifle cynically as he looked after the two on the terrace.

"I fancy the trustees will have some difficulty in persuading Lady Palmer to part with the sapphires," he remarked caustically.

"I dare say they will," Judith assented absently. She was trying to screw up her courage to question Crasster about the flat tragedy; probably she would never have a more favourable opportunity. "Have you been very busy lately?" she asked tentatively. "I saw in the paper that that case you were interested in, when some one was shot in a flat, had come to an end."

There was a pause. Stephen's eyes were still fixed on Sir Anthony and his cousin as they strolled up and down on the terrace. The echo of Anthony's remonstrances, of Lady Palmer's exclamations, could be heard plainly in the breakfast-room.

"Yes," he said slowly at last. "The inquest is finished, anyhow; so one stage is over."

"One, stage!" Judith repeated blankly. "But I thought it said the police had no clue—that they had given up the case. I fancied it was all over."

Stephen smiled. "Furnival is not so easily beaten. It was no use adjourning the inquest again. But nothing would surprise me more than to hear that he had given up the case. I happen to know that it excited his interest enormously; there were so many curious points about it."

"Were there?" Judith said faintly. She had sat down again in her place behind the tea-urn. She was touching the cups aimlessly. "Won't you have some tea or coffee, Mr. Crasster? I fear in our excitement over this morning's news I must have appeared very inhospitable."

"I think I will have a cup of coffee, thanks." Crasster followed and took a seat near her at the table. "I believe Furnival feels sure that the capture of the real criminal in the flat case is only a matter of time," he went on after a minute or two. "With all the clues the police have at their disposal it is hardly possible the criminal should escape."

CHAPTER XI

"I thought Anthony would be pleased," Peggy said wistfully.

She and Stephen Crasster were standing on a wide grassy path that ran down the centre of the rosery at Heron's Carew. All round them was a wealth of roses, great climbing *gloire de Dijons*, crimson ramblers, pink and crimson ramblers, golden glowing William Allan Richardson. Peggy, in her white gown, with her big dewy eyes, her exquisite pink and white skin, her soft red lips, looked the fairest rose of them all, the man thought, gazing at her with a very human longing in his kind eyes.

"Up in London everybody was so kind about it. And now— now I have come home it is all different. Anthony is quite unkind; he says Lorrimer is too old, and that he doesn't like him for other reasons. And Judith—well, Judith doesn't say much, but she looks white and—and disapproving. It is all very miserable."

Crasster took the girl's hand in his. "Anthony is naturally very anxious for his little sister's happiness."

Peggy's soft fingers clung to his; her pretty lips quivered. "Tell me, you are glad, aren't you, Stephen?"

Glad! For one moment the man caught his breath. A red mist rose before his eyes. He thought of what had been, of what he had hoped would be, then with a supreme effort he recovered his self-control.

"Of course I am glad, Peggy," he said softly. "If you are happy, that is all I ask. Are you, Peggy?"

"Very—very happy!" the girl whispered, her cheeks flushing hotly.

"Then I am very, very glad, Peggy." With all his might the man was battling down the mad temptation that bade him take the girl in his arms, tell her that the love that had never failed in all her bright youth was hers now; would be hers for ever.

Peggy looked up at him with grateful, humid eyes. "Oh, you never disappoint me, Stephen. One is always sure of your sympathy."

Crasster smiled a little sadly. "You will not need my sympathy much longer, Peggy. You will have Lord Chesterham's." His voice changing in spite of his efforts, as he spoke his successful rival's name.

"Oh, but I shall—I shall always need every bit of your sympathy." Peggy had dropped his hand now; she tucked her arm within his in the old playful confiding fashion, and drew him on with her. "I don't think that being happy," with a deepening of colour, "ought to make one forgetful of other people."

Stephen could not forbear a grim smile.

"Oh, what a child you are still, Peggy," he said involuntarily.

The girl pouted. "You are not to say that. Please to remember that I was eighteen last month; Lorrimer is always forgetting, and you are almost as bad. But come, they are taking tea out, and I am simply dying for some. What is wrong with"—lowering her voice—"Stephen Anthony and Judith?"

"Wrong with Anthony and Lady Carew!" Stephen brought back his thoughts with a start. "What would be wrong with them? Lady Carew does not look well; probably it is the heat."

"It was much hotter than this last year, and she was quite well," Peggy remarked wisely. "Anthony is altered too. He walks about by himself and broods over things. Heigh-ho! The only one that seems unchanged at Heron's Carew is Paul, and he isn't really unchanged, because he gets sweeter and sweeter every day."

As she spoke she sprang forward and pounced upon her small nephew, who was just then passing the rosery gate in his nurse's arms.

"Come to Auntie Peggy, and we will go and have cakes with Mummy." She carried him off in triumph, seated on her shoulder, clutching at her hair with fat dimpled hands.

Stephen followed, smiling at them both, though his heart felt heavy as lead.

Tea was served under the big beech as usual; Judith came across the lawn as they made their appearance. She was wearing a cool-looking gown of pale blue foulard. Against the blue of the gown her face looked transparently white; there were hollows in the cheeks, shadows under the eyes. Crasster was struck anew by her air of fragility as she shook hands with him.

Peggy subsided on to the rug with Paul, gurgles and shrieks of laughter testifying to his pleasure in Auntie Peggy's society; Stephen, his hat pulled down over his eyes, watched them as he talked to Lady Carew. Suddenly he looked up.

"Why, there is some one coming across the park from Home Wood. Surely, it is not Anthony?"

"No, Anthony was going the other way," Judith said easily. "And I am afraid he will not be back just yet. Who can this be?"

She leaned forward wrinkling her brow.

Peggy sat up, holding the chuckling Paul on his feet. "There, soon you will be able to run races with Auntie Peggy, darling!" Then she caught sight of the tall figure now rapidly advancing towards them. "Who is this?" she paused, her colour rose in a wave, flooding cheeks, neck, temples, as she sprang to her feet. "Lorrimer, oh!" She sped across the grass to meet him.

Judith gave one swift glance at Stephen; she saw that his face was strained and tense. She looked away. Peggy had reached the advancing figure now, they were coming back together. Peggy hanging on the man's arm, as she used to hang on Stephen's. But, as she watched the two advancing figures, it seemed to Judith that there was something oddly, fatally, familiar about the carriage of the tall form that was bent over Peggy in so lover-like a fashion.

A black mist rose before Lady Carew's eyes, blotting out Stephen's tortured face, the advancing lovers; she sat very still, one hand grasping the arm of her chair. Paul, clutching at her skirts, whimpering a little in his astonishment at Peggy's desertion of him, found himself for once unnoticed.

"Judith! Stephen!" It was Peggy's voice, eager, appealing. "It is Lorrimer! He got his business in town over sooner than he expected. He came over from Chesterham to the Dower House this afternoon, expecting to surprise me, and Mother sent him on here."

The mist before Judith's eyes was dispersing: she was pulling herself together, her eyes strained themselves with pitiful intensity on the bronzed face, the tall broad-shouldered figure by Peggy's side. Then a sudden icy cold gripped her, the touch of a deadly fear; so it was true then, Peggy's lover, Lord

Chesterham, was the one man whose coming must spell calamity and ruin to Judith, the man she had hoped and prayed she might never meet again.

Stephen, standing up, moving forward to meet the man who had taken Peggy from him, saw that Lady Carew's face had changed, that an odd sickly pallor had overspread her cheeks. The horror in her eyes, their dumb agonized appeal, reminded him of some wild trapped thing. Moved by some sudden impulse he put himself before her.

But Judith rose. She leant heavily on the back of her wicker-chair; for one moment Stephen thought that she was going to faint, he turned quickly to her. She waved him imperatively back, her strange changeful eyes looked black as they strained themselves on the two who were very near now.

"Judith, Judith, don't you see, don't you understand—this is Lorrimer!" Peggy's excited voice rang out again.

Stephen, standing aside, as the man came forward with his ready smile, his outstretched hand, noted how over Peggy's unconscious head Judith Carew's eyes met those of the new-comer; noted how the beautiful face had assumed a look of mask-like rigidity, in which nothing seemed alive but the great burning eyes. He saw too, in the moment, before the heavy lids drooped, the look of triumph that flashed across from Lord Chesterham.

"I hope that Lady Carew will give me a welcome to Heron's Carew, for Peggy's sake," Lord Chesterham was saying as he bent over Judith's hand.

Lady Carew's lips moved, but there was no audible answer.

"Of course she will!" Peggy said joyously. "Only she hasn't been well lately, and you have rather taken us by storm, you know, Lorrimer. I think we have startled her. Sit down, Judith, dear, you are paler than ever."

But Judith put her aside. "I am quite well, Peggy. You are forgetting Mr. Crasster."

"Oh, no, I wasn't," Peggy said with her light laugh. "I never forget Stephen. This is Stephen, Lorrimer, who is to be your very greatest friend. I have told you all about him, haven't I?"

Lord Chesterham laughed as he held out his hand. "You have indeed! I hope the friendship Miss Carew proposes meets with your approval, Mr. Crasster."

Glancing into his rival's smiling eyes, Stephen knew that his secret was his own no longer. "I hope that Peggy's friends will always be mine," he said slowly.

"Why, of course they will be," Peggy cried.

Judith had not moved, she stood a little behind. What was it that her eyes held—repulsion, entreaty, fear? Stephen, watching her, could not make up his mind.

He looked again at Peggy's lover. Lord Chesterham was apparently at his ease. Many people would have called him handsome, but Stephen's keen gaze, accustomed to read the faccs of all sorts and conditions of men, saw that the light smiling eyes were set a trifle too closely together, that there was a thickening of the lower part of the face, as well as certain lines round the mouth that spoke of an evil temper.

But he was all amiability to-day as he watched his young fiancée playing with Paul, and presently, when Judith had turned back to her tea-table, addressed a few casual remarks to Stephen.

At last Peggy got up. "I am going to take Paul back to the house."

"No! You are not to come with me, sir," with a mischievous glance at Chesterham, who had sprung forward. "I want you, Stephen, because I wish most particularly to know what you think of Lorrimer."

CHAPTER XII

Stephen and Peggy walked slowly across the grass towards the house, Paul nestling in Peggy's arms, the echo of her soft laughter reaching the two who were left behind.

Judith did not look after them, did not move so much as an eyelid; she sat beside the tea-table, absolutely motionless, her hands clasped together in her lap, her eyes staring straight before her.

Lord Chesterham drew up one of the chintz-covered easy chairs and sat down near her; apparently she did not even see him, she remained absolutely immobile.

Presently he leaned forward. "It is a great pleasure to meet you here, Lady Carew," he said in his pleasant well-modulated tones. "Delightful to think that one of one's friends at any rate is safely in harbour, in spite of the world's storm and stress."

Then at last Judith turned her head slowly, and looked at him. Hardened sinner though he was, the man momentarily shrank from the horror, the loathing in her eyes.

"How—how dare you!"

He laughed brazenly. "My dear Lady Carew—"

Judith was still staring at him with big frightened eyes. She shuddered as she heard the sound of his laughter. "You—you are Lord Chesterham!"

"I am Lord Chesterham," he acquiesced, still with that evil smile. "Sometimes I have thought, I have wondered whether you knew, dear Lady Carew, whether you guessed—"

"Guessed—" Judith shrank away from him with unconquerable aversion. "Great heaven! how should I guess, how should I dream that such a thing should be—that heaven should let you come here—to torture me?"

He laughed softly. "I don't know that heaven had much to do with the matter. As for torturing you—if I had had any of the intentions with which you so kindly credit me, I might have said a few words that would have materially altered your son's position. But you see—" spreading out his hands.

"Ah, Paul!" Judith's throat twitched miserably, her staring eyes were dominated, held by the wicked smiling gaze of the man opposite. "You—you devil," she said hoarsely.

He laughed again. "Ah! Now if you talk to me like that I shall forget I am being honoured by a *tête-à-tête* with Lady Carew. I shall fancy I am back again at the Casa Civito with Judy—"

"Hush!" Judith's voice rose almost to a shriek; she threw up her arm with a gesture of despair. "You shall not mention that name here, you shall not. I forbid you, do you hear?"

The man glanced round uneasily. It was no part of his plan that she should be tormented into self-betrayal:

"Hush! Hush!" he said imperatively. "You are foolish! If I had intended to tell your secret should I not have spoken sooner? Come, we must be friends, you and I. We shall soon be related—let me see, what shall we be? Brother and Sister-in-law, I believe that is the precise term, is it not?"

Judith raised herself. "No!" she said jerkily. "No! We shall not be related; you shall never marry Peggy! You shall never be Peggy's husband!"

Chesterham's eyes darkened; he leaned forward and looked her fully in the face.

"How do you propose to prevent me?"

For one moment Judith struggled vainly for speech, her mouth twitched painfully.

"I will go to my husband, I will tell him—"

A sneer contorted the man's sensual lips. "What will you tell him? Where we last met, for instance? I can imagine your story interesting him enormously if you do. Come, Judy, don't be a fool!" as she stared at him helplessly. "Don't you see that you can't hurt me without betraying yourself? Don't you realize that you are hopelessly in my power? That instead of threatening me, you should be begging for my mercy, for my silence? Don't you think that Sir Anthony Carew, as well as the public generally, would be intensely interested to hear the circumstances of that last meeting?"

Judith caught her breath sharply. "Why haven't you told them? Why have you kept silence?"

He did not answer for a moment; his eyes were watching her face keenly.

"Because I was sorry for you," he said slowly at last. "Because I knew, none better, what your life had been like in the past; because I could guess something of what led to that last mad act." He shrugged his shoulders. "No. Let the police blunder on; I felt in no way bound to help them. You may rely on my silence, unless you interfere with my plans. Come, is it a bargain?"

He held out his hand; Judith struck it aside.

"No! No! How can I? How can I let you marry Peggy—you?"

Chesterham's expression was not pleasant to see as he tugged at his moustache.

"I think you are forgetting one thing," he said at last, gazing towards the rosery where a glimpse of the tail of Peggy's white gown was to be caught. "I may not be good enough to be Peggy's husband—Heaven forbid that I should contradict you," a momentary softening in his voice. "But," his eyes hardening to steel again, "I put it to you, should I not be at least as suitable as a husband for her as you for a sister-in-law? Do you think you are precisely in a position to throw stones?"

Judith quivered from head to foot, her throat was parched and burning. She drank feverishly of the tea standing by her side. It was cold now, but it seemed to steady her nerves, to cool the fever in her blood. She found courage to turn, to look fully at that mocking face at her side.

"I—I should like to tell you—to let you know that though you met me coming away from the flat that night that I never harmed him—Cyril," she said, speaking fast and jerkily. "I know that you think I did. It is natural perhaps, that you should, but I had nothing to do with his death—nothing."

"Then who had?" the man asked quietly. His eyes watched every movement of her face, every fluctuation of her colour.

Judith raised her eyes despairingly. "How should I know? I was there in the darkened room, and I heard the revolver shot, that is all I know. I did not see anyone, I—I only heard the breathing."

There was a pause. Judith's voice had ceased, her eyes were downcast. Still leaning forward, his elbows on his knees, Chesterham watched her intently.

Then at last he laughed aloud. The sound of it struck across Judith's flagging spirit like a lash of whipcord. She raised her head, her colour mounting hotly. Chesterham laughed again.

"I am afraid you will have to try another story, Lady Carew," he said lightly. "I will think over the affair myself. Perhaps I might be able to help you to something more probable. As for what you have told me—"

A certain amount of courage had come back to Judith. "I have told you the truth!" she said icily.

"Have you?" Chesterham questioned lightly. "Then I am afraid that it will hardly carry conviction. Let me put it to you. You had the strongest of all motives for getting rid of Stanmore. You are young, beautiful you have attained an assured position; you are happy in the love of your husband and your child. Stanmore's coming to England, his discovery of you spelt ruin for you. He insists on seeing you. Presumably, at any rate you visit him at his flat alone, late at night. The next morning he is found dead—shot. As far as can be ascertained by the strictest inquiry you were the only visitor; you were met and recognized coming away. No, no! I'm afraid your story won't do, Lady Carew."

"Nevertheless, it is true," Judith said wearily.

"Well, then," Chesterham shrugged his shoulders. "I should delay making it public for as long a time as possible, dear Lady Carew. In all probability it will be received with a good deal of scepticism. In the meantime, I assure you, you may rely upon my silence as long as you do not interfere with my plans. Now allow me to suggest that you pull yourself together. Peggy is coming back, and some one is with her; it is not the estimable Crasster. I conclude, therefore, that it must be your—it must be Sir Anthony Carew."

Judith looked up. Yes, it was Anthony who was coming towards them from the rosery at Peggy's side; Anthony, with his dear dark face downbent, looking by no means pleased at the prospect of making his future brother-in-law's acquaintance.

Lord Chesterham got up and went to meet them. Judith heard Peggy's introduction. "This is Lorrimer, Anthony." She saw that Sir Anthony only bowed stiffly; that he paused noticeably before taking Chesterham's outstretched hand. Peggy left the two men together and flew across to her sister-in-law.

"Stephen was obliged to go," she complained. "Wasn't it tiresome? Just when I particularly wanted him to stay and make friends with Lorrimer."

Sir Anthony and Lord Chesterham joined them in a minute or so. Chesterham was evidently laying himself out to make a good impression on Peggy's brother. Under the influence of his genial manner and ready, pleasant smile Sir Anthony's first ill-humour was apparently thawing.

Yet Judith saw that his eyes had a puzzled expression. After a minute or two Chesterham noticed it also.

"I wonder whether you have marked the great likeness that is said to exist between the portrait of my ancestor who fell at Fontenoy and myself, Sir Anthony?" he asked tentatively.

"No," Carew answered slowly, "though I see it now that I hear you speak of it. You are very like him. I suppose it must have been that after all. Or possibly there is a resemblance to the last lord. I believe there is."

He relapsed into silence as Peggy claimed Chesterham's attention.

The lovers strolled away and walked up and down under the trees.

Left alone, husband and wife sat silent, constrained. Judith told herself that she would have told Anthony everything, that she would have thrown herself upon his mercy and trusted to his love to understand and forgive, if she had not found that incriminating paper in the secret drawer of his dressing-case, if she could have rid herself of the horrible doubt its possession implied. She watched Anthony furtively from under the shadow of her long lashes. He for his part was stirring up the contents of his tea cup, and gazing at them in a gloomy abstracted fashion. Suddenly he started and uttered a sharp, inaudible exclamation.

Judith raised her eyes. "What is it?"

Sir Anthony did not answer. He was looking across at Chesterham. At last he turned his eyes back to his wife. Their expression was so curious, such an odd mixture of accusation and yet of horror that Judith involuntarily shrank from him.

"It was nothing," he answered her slowly at last. "Only a stitch in my side. I have had several lately. I was just thinking that undoubtedly Lord Chesterham is very like some of his family portraits. That was why"—with a slight stammer—"his face and figure seemed vaguely familiar to me at first."

CHAPTER XIII

The Wembley Horticultural Show, and the athletic sports, which were held together in the Wembley People's Park, was a very great event to the country folk around Wembley. It would be a particularly brilliant function this year in the estimation of the country people, since not only was Lady Carew to distribute the prizes to the successful competitors, but of course the new Lord Chesterham would be there in attendance on his fiancée, Miss Peggy Carew.

Sir Anthony Carew, in his position as Peggy's guardian, had insisted that there should be no recognized engagement, no talk of a wedding for at least a year. He had declared that Peggy was too young to know her own mind, that the year would give her breathing space, and also allow them an opportunity of knowing something of Lord Chesterham, who was at present practically a stranger to them all. That Peggy, as well as her mother and her lover, thought this absolutely unreasonable, went without saying.

The morning of the Wembley Show dawned fine and clear; as the day wore on, it became almost oppressively sultry; Sir Anthony and Lady Carew motored over, arriving on the scene in good time. Stephen Crasster was with them, and they were soon joined by General Wilton and his family, and Lady Palmer.

In the tent given over to the exhibition of table decorations they encountered the Dowager Lady Carew and Peggy, with Lord Chesterham in attendance. His stepmother attached herself to Sir Anthony now in her gentle wavering fashion. Peggy turned eagerly to Stephen, and Chesterham managed to place himself by Judith.

She was wearing an exquisite gown of painted muslin, her leghorn hat, with its bunch of feathers and big brilliant buckle shaded her face, and a long veil of exquisite Chantilly lace was thrown behind.

"Have you seen to-day's papers?" Chesterham asked with apparent carelessness.

"No!" Judith turned paler. "Why, what do you mean—is there anything about the—?"

Chesterham slowly unfolded a piece of paper. "I thought you would be interested, so I cut this out, in case you had not seen it." He handed it to her, and she read:

THE ABBEY COURT MURDER

"It is understood that within the last few days the police have made an important discovery with regard to this case. They are, naturally reticent, but it is rumoured that further developments are expected hourly, and that an arrest will be made very shortly. Report has it that the suspect is a person of good family, moving in the highest social circles."

"Well," Chesterham was smiling as she looked up.

She put the paper back in his hand, with a gesture of despair.

"The hopes of the police seem to be rising, do they not?" he went on in a conversational tone. "It will be quite a *cause célèbre*. I wonder whether you have noticed one thing, it says 'a person'; now hitherto it has always been assumed that the Abbey Court murderer was a woman. Does this vagueness mean that the police have changed their minds, I wonder?"

Judith gazed at him, a nameless fear gripping her heart. In the days immediately following the murder, and their first return to Heron's Carew, it had seemed to her that she had sounded every depth of misery; but since she had found the paper in her husband's dressing-case she had discovered that there were yet unknown abysses of woe, into which she might be plunged.

"Have you heard something? What do you mean?" she questioned hoarsely.

The smile in the man's mocking eyes deepened. "Well, you know I have been thinking over what you told me the other day," he said slowly. "I was rude enough to doubt it at the time, but when I thought it over later I saw a certain possibility that had not occurred to me before. It was possible that—some one might have overheard your appointment with Cyril, or have discovered it in some way; that this person—if we use the newspapers' judicious phrase—might have followed you, and fired the fatal shot. It is possible that this theory has occurred to the police. In this latter case"—his voice becoming softer, more persuasive—"don't you see how valuable the evidence I could give might become, as proving the person's identity?"

Judith opened her lips, but for a moment she literally could not speak, no sound would come from her dry parched mouth. Chesterham was folding the paper, placing it in his pocket-book; his expression as he turned to her was one of evil triumph.

"Do you think that Sir Anthony is quite in a position, all things considered, to place obstacles in the way of my engagement with Peggy? I think I shall have to ask for an interview, and put matters plainly before him."

"You—you couldn't!" The cry burst from Judith's tortured heart. In truth it did seem to her that the refinement of cruelty suggested by his words would be impossible even to the man before her.

His look at her, as he raised his brows, made her feel that he would stand at nothing to obtain his ends.

"I had hoped that you would spare me the trouble?" he said, in a quite unemotional voice. "But I want you to understand definitely, Lady Carew, that my silence is only conditional."

"Conditional!" Judith repeated. "What is the condition?" she questioned, with the same odd feeling that nothing mattered much; yet, though her voice was perfectly steady, her face, her lips, had faded to an absolute pallor, her eyes had a fixed ghastly stare.

"My condition is Sir Anthony Carew's free consent to my marriage with his sister," Chesterham said in his slow level voice, with its grim undertone of rigid determination.

CHAPTER XIV

Judith got up quickly, the scene around her was growing dimmer, the only thing, it seemed to her, was to get away, to be alone. But Chesterham rose too. He overtook her and walked beside her, his long legs keeping pace with her hurrying footsteps without difficulty.

People were gathering round the cricket ground now; Judith and Lord Chesterham made their way behind them quickly.

An old woman separated herself from the crowd, and came towards them, an old woman with a withered face that still bore traces of past comeliness, with white waving hair and big sunken eyes. She put herself directly in their path, curtsying deeply.

"Sure and your lordship hasn't forgotten old Betty Lee?"

Judith moved aside and went on quickly.

For an instant Chesterham stared at the old woman, then, as their eyes met, he smiled and held out his hand.

"Why, no! of course I have not forgotten my old friend, long as it is since we met. How has the world been using you, Betty?"

The old woman started a little as she heard his voice.

She peered forward and looked up into his face, then she curtsied again with a little cackling laugh.

"I have nothing to complain of, my lord; a little rheumatism now and then, and a cough in the winter."

"And how is my friend Ronald? You see I haven't forgotten him, either."

"No!" Again the old woman gave that cackling laugh. "No, I see you haven't, my lord. But"—her keen eyes watching the relief in the man's face—"he is dead, young Ronald is—years ago; or it is a proud man he would have been to-day, to see his old playmate come back the lord of Chesterham."

"Ronald dead!" Was it sorrow or relief in Chesterham's eyes. "Why, I had not heard. I must come up and have a crack with you over the old times, Betty. Are you living alone?"

"I have got my son Hiram with me, my lord." The old woman bent forward gazing apparently at the man's hands. "You'll remember Hiram maybe, Hiram that used to take you and Ronald out fishing? You'll have the Chesterham star, my lord?"

The sudden question seemed to take Lord Chesterham aback. He stared at her a minute without answering, then his face changed, his eyelids flickered. Without speaking he moved up his right cuff, and showed a blue mark, star-shaped, just above the wrist.

Old Betty's expression altered almost to fear as she stared at it. "Your lordship will forgive me—if I have been too free."

The man smiled with a furtive glance at her withered face, as he pulled his cuff down. "Free! Not a bit of it; I am glad you spoke to me." He gave her a smiling nod as he walked away.

Old Betty stared after him, amazed look on her wrinkled face. Her lips moved slowly. "It seems I were wrong, and yet I could ha' took my oath to it!"

The smile was still lingering in Chesterham's eyes as he strolled back to the tents.

Judith had not lost a moment when old Betty stopped them. She hurried onwards, intent only on getting away, on hiding herself from this mocking fiend of a man. She scarcely recognized Stephen Crasster as he crossed the soft turf to intercept her.

"Lady Carew, Peggy wants you to see the roses from the Dower House. She declares that they have beaten Heron's Carew. But what is the matter. You are ill," as he saw Judith's ghastly face.

Judith put out her hand. Stephen Crasster had never been wholly her friend; she had always felt that Anthony's marriage had disappointed him, that in some way he disapproved of her. But she was thankful to see him now, at any rate he would protect her from Chesterham's insolence.

"It was the heat that was too much for me, I fancy," she said incoherently.

"But Chesterham," Stephen looked bewildered.

"He went to speak to somebody, I think." Judith said vaguely. "Mr. Crasster, I must go home. I am not well enough to stay. Make my excuses for me."

Stephen turned with her. "I am exceedingly sorry. Won't you take one of the seats? And I will bring the motor round."

"No, no," Judith contradicted him feverishly. "I am going there to it, and indeed you must not leave the others. Don't let them know I have gone if you can help it."

"You must at least let me see you to the car," Stephen said gravely.

Towards six o'clock the Wembley Show was at its height. The people from the surrounding villages were pouring in, eager to see the sight, to discuss the quality of the exhibits, and to congratulate the prize-winners. The prizes were to be distributed in front of the grand stand on the sports ground at seven o'clock. It had been decided that, as Lady Carew was unfortunately indisposed, her place should be taken by her young sister-in-law, and, as the time grew near, Peggy made her way to the centre of the stand in a flutter of excitement tempered by nervousness. Her brother and mother were with her, and Stephen Crasster and Chesterham stood behind.

Lady Palmer was there, and glanced at General Wilton with a smile, but he, too, was watching Peggy, and with a little sniff of superiority, Lady Palmer leaned back in her chair.

Two ladies passed. Lady Palmer leaned forward and looked at them earnestly. She saw a pretty fair-haired girl, and with her was a slight graceful woman with silver hair. Her face seemed familiar, but for a moment Lady Palmer could not place her. A moment later, however, her face cleared, and she put out her hand.

"Mrs. May, how stupid of me not to recognize you before!" She drew her skirts aside. "Do come and sit down. Is this one of your girls?"

"No, this is a little niece who is staying with us, Sophie Rankin, Lady Palmer." Mrs. May hesitated a moment. Good vicar's wife as she was, she had thought Lady Palmer haughty, disagreeable; to-day she came to the conclusion that she had sadly misjudged her. She took the chair next to her, and sat down, Miss Rankin remained standing, biting her full underlip, her eyes misty.

Lady Palmer glanced at her. "Won't your niece sit down?" she asked sweetly. "She looks in trouble. Is there anything the matter?"

"She has had a little disappointment, poor child," Mrs. May said with slight reserve. "And she is young and shows it, that is all."

Lady Palmer looked again at the girl standing up beside them.

"What was the disappointment?" she asked lightly.

The girl's lips quivered. "I had been looking forward to seeing Lady Carew. I used to be so fond of her."

"Were you really? Ah, well, you must see her some other time," Lady Palmer responded with seeming indifference. She turned to her host. "I'm sure you remember Mrs. May, general," she said sweetly.

The general turned somewhat unwillingly from his admiration of Peggy.

"Why, bless my soul, of course I do. Is your husband here, Mrs. May? I wonder what he thought of my exhibits? I always like to know his opinion."

Mrs. May smiled with much gratification. "I am sure, general, he would be delighted." This was Lady Palmer's opportunity; she knew the general. She felt certain that Mrs. May would not get away from him very easily, now that he was once launched on the topic of his hothouse and gardens, with a fresh auditor. She turned to the tall, fair girl who was leaning forward, as if trying to catch a glance of Sir Anthony Carew.

"Come and sit here, my dear, we must have a little talk together, I am so sorry you are disappointed." She spoke lightly, and motioned the girl to sit beside her.

Sophie's face brightened as she took the vacant seat.

"I am sure Wembley Show is delightful," she said shyly. "It is only that I have been looking forward to it so tremendously, because I heard that Lady Carew was expected to give the prizes away, and when I knew that she was not coming I was so dreadfully disappointed. I am afraid you will think me a terrible baby," she finished with a sigh.

"Indeed I don't!" Lady Palmer smiled, with well assumed quasi-maternal interest. "Do you know Lady Carew very well?" She could not help the undertone of deep interest that crept into her voice.

But Miss Rankin apparently noticed nothing. "Isn't she a darling?" she cried enthusiastically. "I always adored her. And I believe really I was her favourite, though we were all fond of Miss Latimer."

"Miss Latimer," Lady Palmer repeated, raising her eyebrows. "Then it was before her marriage that you knew my cousin. But of course, I believe I have heard her mention your name"—mendaciously—"of course you are—I mean, you were—"

"Yes! She was our governess," Sophie Rankin said eagerly. "And you have really heard her mention us, Lady Palmer. I wonder what she said?"

Lady Palmer's eyes had narrowed, her mouth was smiling still, but her expression had altered. A touch of subtle triumph mingled now with its sweetness. Fate itself must have sent Sophie Rankin to her at this particular moment, she thought.

"She has not said very much, naturally," she said slowly. "But she has always spoken of you as if she was fond of you."

Sophie clasped her hands, her blue eyes lighted up. "Oh, she was—I know she was. Nobody shall ever make me believe she was not."

Lady Palmer glanced at her quickly. "But of course she was fond of you," she observed with decision. "Who can possibly try to make you think she was not?"

"It is Mother," Sophie said confidentially. "She thinks Lady Carew does not wish to remember us because she has not written to us since her marriage. She wrote me that my aunt was not to take me to Heron's Carew. I was not to seek out Lady Carew in any way. And of course I haven't. But I thought I shouldn't be putting myself in her way," continued Sophie, "if she had been here to-day, just to stand somewhere where she could have seen me; and then perhaps if she would have remembered me—she would have spoken to me!"

Lady Palmer laughed. "Of course Lady Carew would have spoken to you. Now I have been thinking, I will take the responsibility. As Lady Carew is ill, it would be no use going to Heron's Carew to-night, she would not be able to see us, but to-morrow, if Mrs. May will spare you, I will drive over with you. I know the dear general will let me have his carriage."

Sophie's ingenuous countenance turned pink all over. "Oh, how kind you are, and how I should love to come, but it is impossible; I am going home in the morning."

"I am sorry," Lady Palmer's tone showed that she meant what she said. "Couldn't you possibly put off your journey for a day?"

Sophie shook her head. "Mother has already let me stay a week longer than my original invitation. I must go back to-morrow, but thank you very much for thinking of it, Lady Palmer, all the same."

Lady Palmer's active brain was busy. Even to herself she would hardly have acknowledged that her dislike of Judith Carew lay in the fact that the latter was her cousin's wife. That, as Sybil Carew, Lady Palmer had made a big mistake when she threw over her cousin Anthony for Lord Palmer, she had long known; but for the presence of Judith at Heron's Court, she felt certain that her mistake might have been repaired. Lady Palmer had watched her cousin's wife. She had seen the beautiful eyes darken with fear. She had seen her start and glance round at any sudden noise, as though haunted by some never-ceasing dread. More and more was she convinced that Judith's past held some secret; more and more determined did she grow to find it out, to use it to her own advantage.

"How long was Lady Carew with you?" she asked Sophie abruptly. "A long time was it not?"

"Two years," the girl answered simply. "She stayed until I was nearly seventeen."

"Only two years?" Lady Palmer repeated. "I thought it had been longer. Stay; perhaps it was some earlier pupils I was thinking of. Do you remember the name of the people she was with before she came to you?"

"I don't know." Sophie's voice sounded altered. She was trying to catch Mrs. May's eye apparently. "I have forgotten."

Mrs. May was taking leave of the general. "I am sure my husband thinks as you do, general."

"So does every sensible man," the general returned, as he shook hands.

Mrs. May's eyes were a little anxious as she glanced at her young niece. "Come, Sophie, dear, I believe we ought to be going now; we have a long drive before us, you know."

Lady Palmer saw that her opportunity was over. She glanced smilingly at Sophie. "You must give me your address, my dear."

The girl looked red, a little confused. "St. Barnabas' Vicarage, Chelsea," she said hastily. "Father is Canon Rankin."

"Canon Rankin! Why, of course I know—I mean, I have heard of him," Lady Palmer exclaimed, with a sudden memory of a clergyman whose work among the outcasts of London was obtaining a grudging recognition from all classes. "I believe my sister—Mrs. Dawson—knows him quite well. We shall meet again some day, my dear." She nodded and smiled as Mrs. May drew the girl away.

The prize-giving was nearly over now; Peggy turned to exchange a smile with Chesterham. Stephen Crasster's hand went up to his chin and pulled it restlessly. He told himself that he could stand no more, that since Chesterham was there he would not be missed, and he made his way out by the back of the stand.

Outside he nearly collided with an unobtrusive-looking little man with a bushy, sandy beard, and stopped with a sudden exclamation.

"What, Furnival! Is it you?"

The sandy bearded one glanced round apprehensively. "Hush, if you please, sir! My name is Lennox—Walter Lennox. I have come down to see a friend."

"On business?" Stephen drew him away from the crowd, now all gathered round the sports ground. They walked across the bowling-green in the direction of the tents. "I thought you were so busy with that flat case."

Inspector Furnival looked at him with a mildly-interested smile.

"So I am, sir! But I am sure you must recognize that every one must have a holiday sometimes. I have been going a bit too strong lately, and the doctors tell me my heart isn't what it was."

"I see." The two men were as much alone to-day on the quiet little bowling-green as if they had been on a desert island. Stephen glanced at his companion with a whimsical smile.

"And so you call yourself Lennox when you come out for the benefit of your health?"

The inspector's wide, humorous lips relaxed a little beneath his sandy moustache. "I like to be incog. sometimes, sir. And, besides"—he took counsel with himself a moment before he went on—"it isn't altogether health that brought me down, though the doctor did order me into the country, but I took the liberty of choosing a spot where I thought a stay might be profitable."

Stephen laughed outright. "I guessed as much. Well, you must come up and have a pipe and a taste of bachelor fare at Talgarth one of these days, inspector. And, if your business is anything in which I can help you, you know there is nothing I like better than a bit of detective work."

Inspector Furnival was looking at the ground now. "Thank you, you are very kind. I know your advice has often been most valuable."

"What do you say to coming back with me now?" Stephen went on. "My car is round at the Lion. And you can tell me what you think of my port. I know you are a bit of a connoisseur."

The inspector hesitated a moment. Manifestly the offer tempted him.

"You are very good, sir, but another time, if you please. Mixing with a crowd like this one picks up hints that come in useful sometimes. I am hoping I may do so to-night."

"Ah, well, another time, then," Stephen nodded. "I understand. Good-bye and good luck to you, inspector."

He strode off.

The inspector strolled back to the sports ground. The prize-giving was over. Peggy was standing near the table talking to one of the winners. Her mother and Sir Anthony, with Lord Chesterham, stood behind him with a group of county magnates.

The inspector's eyes glanced across reflectively.

CHAPTER XV

"Oh, but Miladi is better, much better, and she desires that I come to the fête," Célestine said virtuously.

"I am glad she did. We could not have afforded to have missed you," her companion declared gallantly.

He was the same, dark moustached, smiling little man whom the gossips of Heron's Carew had averred the French maid was meeting in the Home Wood. However that might be, it was obvious that he was expecting her at the Wembley Show. He had been waiting at the entrance gates for quite a considerable time before she had appeared, and he went forward to meet her, hat in hand, with considerable *empressement*. Célestine looked by no means averse to being escorted into the grounds by so presentable a swain. She herself was looking her vain coquettish best. She smiled up at the man walking by her side.

"So I am glad, Mr. Barker! Your fête makes a little change. Ah, but it is a *triste* place, Heron's Carew!"

"It isn't lively," the man agreed with a laugh. "I want you to do me a favour, mademoiselle."

Célestine looked gracious. "What is that, Mr. Barker? You know—"

"I want you to let me introduce a friend," Mr. Barker proceeded. "He came down from town yesterday, my friend did. He is going to stop a bit for his health, and I think the poor fellow feels lonely. There he is walking about by himself, so if you wouldn't mind him joining us—not that I want to share your society with anyone else," he finished with a complimentary glance.

Célestine bridled. She looked across at the solitary figure that Mr. Barker had indicated. Her quick French eyes noted that, though there was nothing particularly noticeable about the man's face and figure, he was immaculately dressed, with a care that reminded her of London. Her eyes brightened, it seemed that there might be possibilities about Mr. Barker's friend.

"But of course I shall be delighted!" she allowed graciously.

They went across together. "Mlle Célestine Delafours, may I introduce Mr. Lennox?" Mr. Barker said with a flourish.

Mr. Lennox bowed with a deference that pleased Célestine. He had fine eyes she said to herself, and, though she might not admire sandy beards, tastes must differ, and the stranger had at least an air.

"You are down here, at Wembley, for your health, Monsieur?" she questioned in her pretty broken English.

Mr. Lennox bowed. "I am staying at Carew Village, at the Carew Arms."

"Ah!" Célestine gave a melting glance upwards. "As is Monsieur Barker. And you are an artist like him is it not so, monsieur?"

Mr. Lennox shook his head. "I am not so clever, mademoiselle, I am only a collector."

"A collector," Célestine echoed with a pretty little puzzled air. "I do not understand, monsieur. What is a collector?"

Mr. Lennox laughed. "Well, it is more a hobby than a profession, mademoiselle. I am lucky enough to have an income to cover my small wants, and I have a natural taste for collecting objects of art. Why, what is this?"

A boy with a telegram was coming towards them. "For the gentleman as is staying at the Carew Arms, Mr. Barker!" he said looking from one to the other.

With a quick exclamation Barker took it from him, tore it open and ran his eyes over it.

"Nothing wrong, I hope," said Mr. Lennox sympathetically.

"Well, yes!" Mr. Barker seemed to have difficulty in finding his words. "My mother has been taken suddenly ill. I shall have to be off at once. I shall just have time to catch the express. Mademoiselle"—turning to Célestine—"how can I apologize to you? You will think me absolutely unmannerly, but my mother—"

"Mademoiselle will understand that your departure is unavoidable," said Mr. Lennox, cutting the other's halting words short. "And, if you are to catch the express, my dear fellow, you haven't a moment to lose. I will take your place as far as it is possible with Mademoiselle, if she will allow me the pleasure of escorting her."

"But Monsieur is too good!" And Célestine made play with her eyes.

Mr. Barker hurried off, with many incoherent apologies. When he had finally departed, Mr. Lennox looked at Célestine with a smile.

"Which way will you go, mademoiselle?"

"I would like to walk among the people, if you please, monsieur; not right in the crowd, but about here, where you can see people—and feel that there is life."

"You find it dull at Heron's Carew!" Lennox observed sympathetically.

Célestine held up her hands. "But of all things. And to me, who understood that miladi was to spend the season in town, it is all that there is of the most horrible. I would never have engaged to come to Heron's Carew all the time, like this— never!"

He glanced at her comprehendingly. "It is hard on you, mademoiselle. But I suppose Lady Carew is not strong enough for the gaieties of the season."

Célestine shrugged her shoulders. "Miladi has a constitution of the most *magnifique*. But one day she has a migraine, and your English doctors are fools. She is sent down to this *triste* Heron's Carew, where there is never any person to speak to but Sir Anthony and Miss Peggy, and what can you expect?"

"She is not getting better?" Lennox questioned.

"But no," Célestine answered energetically. "How should she be here in this dullness? And it is impossible for her to be gay when Sir Anthony—he mopes always, and is sulky."

Mr. Lennox looked interested. "Perhaps they don't get on. I saw him just now when they were giving the prizes away. He looks as if he had a temper of his own."

Célestine raised her eyebrows. "Was there ever a Carew of them all that had not?" she demanded. "The mad Carews, the people round here call them. I think it is a good name—me. But, as for getting on, Sir Anthony and miladi used to be like lovers always. It was wearisome to see them together, until the night of Lady Denborough's dinner-party. Since then all has been changed."

"They quarrelled perhaps," her companion suggested, as she paused and looked mysterious.

"Perhaps," she said slowly, lifting her shoulders. "I do not know. At any rate, miladi and Sir Anthony went to a wedding, Lady Geraldine Summerhouse's, in the afternoon. Then miladi had her migraine and did not go to Lady Denborough's. It may have been that Sir Anthony was sulky because he did not want to go alone. Most men are like that—thoughtless, what you call, selfish!" with a swift upraising of her dark lashes.

Mr. Lennox rose to the occasion gallantly. "I should not be thoughtless or selfish if I had a sweet little wife like—" His eyes pointed the unfinished sentence.

Célestine smiled, did her best to blush.

"But men are all alike—before," with a coquettish glance.

"Not all—any more than you ladies," Mr. Lennox contradicted playfully. "Now you, mademoiselle, if you had a headache, you would make a struggle to go out with your husband, I know; you would not leave him to go alone."

The maid pursed up her lips. "If it suited my purpose I might or I might not, monsieur. Sometimes—sometimes it may be that a migraine is—shall we say—convenient?"

Mr. Lennox looked at her, his face a study of good-humoured surprise. "I don't understand, mademoiselle. You say that Lady Carew's headaches are convenient."

"Not all of miladi's migraines are," Célestine contradicted. "But that first one, on the night of Lady Denborough's dinner, was a convenient one, all the same. But there, monsieur, sometimes it happens that my tongue runs away with me; we will talk of something else."

Lennox looked at her a moment, and then he threw back his head and laughed.

"Do you think I should gossip, mademoiselle? Bless my life it isn't as if I were a married man with a wife to whisper my secrets to," casting a sentimental glance at the girl.

Célestine's eyelids flickered coyly.

Mr. Lennox drew a little nearer. "Sometimes one does get led away, mademoiselle; one meets somebody suddenly, the very sight of whom seems to alter one's life. It is hard to realize that the feeling is not mutual, that one is suspected, doubted;

but I suppose, if one weren't a fool, one would be prepared for it."

"But suspected, monsieur, doubted?" Célestine glanced up quickly into the mild blue eyes that were watching her with such evident interest. In her shrewd little heart she was calculating the possibilities; it was apparent that the new-comer was greatly attracted to her. There was an air of prosperity about him which impressed Célestine. Decidedly, she thought, it appeared as though he would be a better match than Barker. Altogether she thought it might be as well to temporize. "It was only that though miladi had strange ways I do not speak of them usually; but to you, monsieur, who seem not like other men, it is different. Only you must understand that I do not gossip—me."

"Good heavens, no." The man laughed again with every appearance of good faith. "And what does it matter to me whether Lady Carew has her own little game to play, if she breaks engagements in order to get out of doors to—perhaps better say no more."

"But, monsieur," Célestine was staring at him with wide open eyes, "what do you mean, what do you know?"

The tragic intensity of her tone seemed to amuse Mr. Lennox, his smile broadened. "Only the ordinary gossip of the town about a lady so well known as Lady Carew," he replied lightly. "You know she is a society beauty, a famous person whose every movement is chronicled. There have been whispers of Lady Carew of late, that there is a lover in the background, but I should not speak of them to anybody but you, mademoiselle."

"And I never knew, I never dreamed that anyone had guessed." Célestine clasped her small exquisitely covered hands tightly together and spoke with dramatic intensity. "All I know is that Miladi says she has a bad headache, that she can not go to Lady Denborough's dinner, and that she sends me

away, and afterwards when the house is quiet she comes
stealing down the stairs and lets herself out like a mouse."

"Oh, you ladies—you ladies!" apostrophized Mr. Lennox. "It
would take a clever man to be even with some of you,
mademoiselle. So I suppose Lady Carew spent a pleasant
evening with her lover, while poor Sir Anthony went to Lady
Denborough's dinner alone, and made himself miserable all
the evening, thinking that his wife was ill."

Célestine did not answer for a minute; her carefully arched
eyebrows were drawn together consideringly.

"No! Sir Anthony—he did not go to Lady Denborough's
either!" she said slowly. "Though Miladi thought he would. He
went out, somewhere, I do not know where. And he did not
come back till after Miladi had come back, and then he came in
and shut his door with a bang—so." And Célestine brought her
two hands together smartly. "But when you speak of Miladi's
lover, you make a mistake. Miladi may have secrets, but a
lover, no, I do not think it. She loves Sir Anthony."

Mr. Lennox's interest in the story was evidently only second
to that he felt in Célestine herself. "But if she is meeting a
man—outside," he said. "And all London says she is."

Célestine shook her head. "It is not a lover she meets,
monsieur. And I do not speak without reason."

"Reason," Mr. Lennox repeated thoughtfully. "But,
mademoiselle, how can you know?"

Célestine's black eyes looked important. "Ah, now,
monsieur, you are asking more than I can tell. That is my
little—what you call—secret."

CHAPTER XVI

The Dowager Lady Carew was giving a dinner-party at the
Dower House. She had had her way now. Peggy's engagement
to Lord Chesterham, was formally announced, and Sir Anthony

had withdrawn all open opposition, though his private opinion of his future brother-in-law remained much the same. Stephen Crasster's representations had turned the scale, for Crasster, putting his own feelings on one side, had pleaded for Peggy's sake. But, although as Peggy's guardian he had given his formal consent, Sir Anthony was looking distinctly sulky to-night. To his mind this dinner savoured of triumph on his stepmother's part.

From his seat at the bottom of the table, he glanced down at Chesterham, seated between Peggy and her mother. Peggy was looking radiant to-night. There could be no question that she was perfectly happy in her engagement, or believed herself to be so. She was wearing a gown of palest pink chiffon that harmonized perfectly with her delicate colouring; with the light in her soft brown eyes, the glint of the gold in her curly hair. Chesterham was bending over her in the most lover-like fashion. As he watched him, Sir Anthony's brow contracted afresh.

From the lovers, Sir Anthony's eyes strayed involuntarily to his own wife, who was sitting almost immediately opposite. Judith was wearing a wonderful gown, one of Renard's masterpieces. Stephen Crasster was lower down on the same side. Old General Wilson was opposite. The long dinner was drawing to an end and the general was getting talkative, for the wine was unusually good, having been sent down from Heron's Carew cellars. The general's voice grew louder. "He came over to sketch my bit of place, but I refused him permission—told him I didn't want any of his sort round me; I could hardly get rid of the beggar. He had been to Talgarth, he told me, and Heron's Carew."

"Talgarth," Stephen Crasster repeated. "Who are you speaking of, general?"

"That fellow that has been staying at the Carew Arms," the general repeated. There was a lull in the conversation round, his voice sounded unusually loud. "Barker, he called himself, and gave out that he was an artist. Been round everywhere; wanting to make sketches. But he did not take me in; the fellow is no more an artist than I am."

"Not an artist?" Sir Anthony leaned forward. "I think you must be mistaken, general. He took several sketches round Heron's Carew."

"Did he really?" The general laughed until his mirth threatened to become apoplectic. "Don't know whether you will be so flattered by his attentions, Carew, when you hear what he is; he is a private detective."

"A detective!" Stephen Crasster looked up quickly. A momentary sight of Lady Carew's face caught his attention. It was not only that it had turned absolutely white, but that it had a look of unmistakable fear. Forgetful, he stared at her in surprise.

Chesterham leaned over the table; for one instant Crasster fancied he intercepted a glance of warning, the next he told himself that he must be mistaken. Chesterham was speaking lightly.

"You remember the aquamarines you were speaking of the other day, Lady Carew; I have been fortunate enough to pick up some wonderful specimens. Peggy must show them to you after dinner."

"I must ask her."

Judith's eyes met his for a moment. Then she pulled herself together and turned to her right-hand neighbour with an easy question. Stephen told himself that of course he was mistaken.

For Judith, smiling and talking as she compelled herself to do, it was veritably a time of torture, a nightmare from which she rose with relief at her mother-in-law's signal. But in the drawing-room she endured a perfect torment of anxiety. What had the general meant about the detective who was staying at the Carew Arms? If a detective was staying in Carew Village, what was his business in the neighbourhood? Was it—could it possibly be connected with the flat murder? Judith's cheeks blanched anew as she asked herself the question.

Her mother-in-law drew her on to a great roomy couch. "The child is so happy now that Anthony has given way," her eyes growing wistful as she looked at her pretty, tall girl. "And it is nice to think she will be settled near me."

"Yes!" Judith said slowly. She shuddered to think of Peggy as Chesterham's wife, in Chesterham's power, yet with a terrible cowardice she shrank from the only course that could save Peggy.

Lady Palmer crossed the room to them with her graceful, undulating step. "May I make a third on your delightful couch, Aunt Geraldine?" she asked the dowager with her melancholy smile.

The Dowager Lady Carew did not look quite pleased as she made room for her. She had never altogether understood Sybil, or forgiven her share in the past wrecking of Anthony's life.

Little as Judith cared for Lady Palmer, she was inclined to welcome the interruption. It seemed to her that anything was better than sitting there *tête-à-tête* with her mother-in-law, discussing Peggy's engagement, Peggy's prospects of happiness.

Lady Palmer began by offering profuse congratulations; then, gliding gracefully from the subject of the engagement, she turned to Judith. It is such a pleasure to see you so fully recovered tonight, dear Judith; we were all so anxious about you on the day of the show."

"You are very kind." There was a faint touch of amusement in Judith's eyes as she glanced at the speaker.

"One poor little girl was frightfully disappointed," Lady Palmer went on sweetly. "She had been looking forward to seeing you so much, an old friend of yours. I consoled her as well as I could, but I am afraid she found me a very inefficient substitute for you."

Judith drew her level brows together in a puzzled fashion. "An old friend of mine? How unfortunate I should have missed her. But you are a little vague, aren't you, Sybil? You haven't told me her name."

"Her name was Miss Sophie Rankin!"

A soft little breath escaped from Judith. "Sophie Rankin. Ah! You mean my old pupil. How extraordinary that she should be at Wembley Show. And how sorry I am that I missed her. I used to be very fond of Sophie."

In spite of the fact that her tone was one of ordinary polite interest, that she met Lady Palmer's gaze smilingly, the latter had an instinct that in some way she was nearing that secret of the past that she had set herself to discover.

As she paused before speaking again she could see that, as Judith waited, an expression of being on guard settled on her face, that her smile was purely mechanical.

"Poor little girl! She seemed to have quite a romantic attachment to you," Lady Palmer proceeded in soft purring tones. "And I fancy you have ill requited it, Judith dear. She complained that you had never written to her since your marriage."

"Since my marriage. Oh, surely Sophie exaggerates," Judith said quietly, her eyes turning to the door as the voices of the men became audible outside.

With the entrance of the men Lady Palmer's opportunity of questioning Judith had for the moment departed.

She turned to her cousin with a smile as he sat down near her. Nor did she manage to get near Judith again that evening. Sir Anthony was determined to leave early, making his wife's recent indisposition the excuse, nor was Judith by any means loath.

In the earlier happier days of their married life, it had been the Carew's custom to walk up to Heron's Carew from the Dower House, but of late both had dreaded the lengthy *tête-à-tête* it would have involved. To-night, by some mistake, the carriage instead of the motor came for them. Sir Anthony frowned as he saw it; he objected to his horses being brought out at night. Yet as he took his seat beside his wife, as he felt her nearness in every pulse of his being, as the faint undefinable scent from the flowers she wore was wafted to him, he could have found it in his heart to bless the mistake that had prolonged their drive together.

He glanced sideways at Judith; in the bright summer moonlight it was possible to watch her face almost as closely as in the daytime. He could see the pure pale profile, the droop of her eyelids, the exquisite curved lips that were quivering ever so slightly.

Some subtle sense told Judith that he was moved. She turned her face towards him, her breath quickened, she swayed nearer, her ungloved hand touched his. Her husband's arms closed round her like a vice. "Judith!" he murmured, "Judith, my wife!"

Judith did not speak; she rested motionless, silent in his clasp. By-and-bye two big tears forced their way through her closed lids, and trickled slowly down her cheeks. It was rapture to her, after their long sad estrangement, to be once more in her husband's arms, to know that for the time being, at all events, all that had divided them was forgotten and forgiven.

But all too soon, like most of the perfect things of earth, the drive was over, the carriage stopped at the door of Heron's Carew. As Anthony helped his wife out she saw that his face was very pale, that there were dark rings round his eyes. He drew her into the morning-room and closed the door, then standing on the great white bear skin before the fire-place, he took her hands in his. "Judith! Judith!" he questioned, his strong voice breaking in a note of appeal. "You are mine; you care for me."

Judith's soft fingers held him tightly, her strange, beautiful eyes met his. "You—you know, Anthony;" she murmured. "I love you."

Sir Anthony drew her to his breast.

Judith looked up at him, she touched his cheek with her hand. "You are ill, Anthony! You are shivering, and yet your hands and face are burning."

Sir Anthony's clasp loosened a little. "I am all right, child, but I am worried. I wish I knew what to do for the best; this engagement of Peggy's is all wrong like everything else. I feel I ought to have prevented it, and yet what can I do? Peggy and her mother, and even Stephen Crasster, are all against me."

They were standing a little farther apart now; involuntarily when he mentioned Peggy's engagement, Judith shrank from him. Anthony's eyelids twitched as he noticed her movement.

"There was never a Chesterham of them all that was any good," he said bitterly. "The Chesterham star is a sure sign of the rottenness in their blood."

"The Chesterham star!" Judith repeated, her voice curiously lowered. "I don't understand what you mean. What is the Chesterham star, Anthony?"

Anthony's grey eyes were moody now; the change in her expression had not escaped him. "A blue mark something like a star," he answered slowly. "I saw it on this fellow's arm to-night. General Wilton asked him about it."

All the happy light had faded from Judith's eyes, from her face now; she was staring at her husband, a frozen horror dawning in her gaze.

"A blue mark like a star," she repeated. "Where did you say—on the arm?"

Her husband was looking at her curiously. "Of course. All the Chesterhams have it on the right arm just above the wrist."

"Ah!" Judith drew a long fluttering breath. The light in the room was growing very dim. She could see nothing, not even Anthony's face. It could not be true—this monstrous thing that had entered her brain? The darkness was rising nearer, she swayed to one side with a hoarse sob. Sir Anthony sprang forward in time to catch her in his arms before she sank in a dead swoon to the floor.

CHAPTER XVII

"Ah, yes, Miss Peggy, she is a lucky girl!" Célestine said reflectively. "Milord Chesterham is a fine man—a very fine man! And he have taste too! He is not like Sir Anthony, who looks at you as if you were wood—so! Milord Chesterham, he is always polite very."

Mr. Lennox laughed. He was leaning over the stile that gave access from the Heron's Carew footpath to the Home Wood. "But who would not be polite to you, mademoiselle?"

Célestine humped up one shoulder. "But lots of people, I assure you, monsieur. They are not all so agreeable—your compatriots."

"Are they not?" Mr. Lennox questioned. "I am sorry to hear that. But it is you that I want to be agreeable this afternoon, mademoiselle."

"Does Monsieur mean that usually I am disagreeable?" Célestine demanded, glancing at him coquettishly.

Mr. Lennox lifted his hands in protest. "You know that I think you are all that is most charming, mademoiselle. How can you pretend to misunderstand me? But to-day I want to show you—you remember I told you I was a collector?"

"But certainly, monsieur." Célestine's black eyes watched his face.

"Well, latterly I have been getting together a few things that I think would interest you. I want to show them to you, for I know you are an expert, and it strikes me that I have a collection of fans, ancient and modern, that it would be hard to beat."

"Fans, monsieur." Célestine looked eager. "But of course I shall be delighted."

"I have got them down here," Mr. Lennox said, indicating the Carew Arms with a backward jerk of his head. "Some of them are inset with jewels, some of them are made of ivory and rare old lace, one or two are painted. One in particular, said to have belonged to Marie Antoinette, has a pretty little scene by Watteau upon it."

"A—h! How I should like to see them." Célestine's eyes were sparkling. "I love fans. Miladi has some of the most superb. She too, had a Watteau painted one, but it is lost, alas!"

"Lost! That is a pity," Mr. Lennox said quietly, though there was a gleam of interest in his large blue eyes. "Well, mademoiselle, I should like to ask you whether it beats mine, not that I can part with it even to replace Lady Carew's. How did she manage to lose it?"

Célestine held up her hands. "*Ma foi*, but I do not know, monsieur! Truly such carelessness would be impossible to me. Miladi had it put to wear with her magnificent gown for Lady Denborough's; then, she did not go, but she lie on the sofa and fan herself with it, that is the last I know. A day or two afterwards, when I am looking for it she tell me she has lost it."

"Nice piece of carelessness that," Mr. Lennox commented. "Mademoiselle, you will walk up to the Carew Arms with me and look at my collection? I have got a private room."

"Monsieur!" Célestine gave a slight scream. "But that would not be *convenable*—not at all! Even in your England a young lady cannot do that."

Mr. Lennox leaned a little farther over the gate; his tone grew more persuasive.

"You know I would not ask you to do anything I would not like my own sister to do, mademoiselle. Why should you not walk up to the Carew Arms with me? I have got a delightful little sitting-room looking upon the garden, or if you don't like to come into my room"—as Célestine emitted another little shriek—"I dare say they would let us have the bar parlour. You know Mrs. Curtis, don't you?"

"But a little," Mademoiselle answered, a trifle haughtily, shaking some dust from her skirts as she spoke.

"She has been like a mother to me," Mr. Lennox went on obtusely. "And she would get you some tea; no, not tea, coffee—real continental coffee, mademoiselle. I have taught her how to make it myself, I tell you what, mademoiselle, I dare say she would let us have it out in the garden, and I might bring my fans out and show them to you in the summer-house. The most prudish person couldn't see any harm in that, could they?"

Célestine was inclined to think they could not. After a little more coquetting she yielded the point.

The footpath to Carew village was a short cut from the Home Wood. The Carew Arms stood at the near end of the village street, a big old-fashioned hostelry, facing the village green on the one side, with its large well-stocked garden on the other. Mr. Lennox, mindful of the proprieties, did not go in by the open door under the porch, but turned instead to the garden gate. The arbour stood at the bottom of the rough lawn, and thither Lennox and Célestine made their way. Lennox busied himself carrying the chairs and table into the open.

"There now, mademoiselle, now you will be comfortable, while I go and see about the coffee," he said, as he dusted them with his handkerchief.

Célestine seated herself with a simper. She felt that after this there could not be much doubts as to Mr. Lennox's intentions as she watched him walk up the path. It was evident, too, that he was well off; the match would be a good one, and Célestine lost herself in rosy visions of the future.

Presently a smiling country maid appeared with the promised coffee, and Lennox followed, a large wooden box in his arms. "Just the cream of the collection, as it were, mademoiselle," he said, as he deposited it on the grass beside her. "I couldn't think of troubling you with the whole lot."

He did the honours of the coffee, and some small wafer-like biscuits he had imported from town, and Célestine, feeling exceedingly comfortable, sank back in her chair and allowed him to wait upon her.

But at last the alfresco meal was over, and Lennox turned back to his fans. He lifted the box on to the table and opened it carefully.

Célestine uttered a little cry of surprise as she saw the glitter of jewels on the handle of the first one; she bent over it carefully.

"But it is all that there is of the most beautiful, monsieur, it is superb! Miladi herself has nothing finer."

"Hasn't she really?" Lennox questioned as he went on raising the layers of tissue paper.

"But, monsieur"—Célestine leaned forward with a quick motion of surprise—"what is that you have in your hand now—that painted one? It is precisely like Miladi's, the one she lost that I was telling you about."

"It is a beauty anyway." Lennox was holding it in his hand now, he was moving it backwards and forwards. "I like it the best of them all myself."

Célestine stood up and put out her hand. "One moment, monsieur. Yes," turning to the ivory sticks, "it is the very same. It is indeed Miladi's fan that she lose—it is marvellous— *extraordinaire*! How did you come by it, monsieur?"

Lennox looked at her in apparent amazement. "It was brought to me by a dealer, a man who knows I am always on the look-out for such things. But about it being Lady Carew's—I can't believe that, mademoiselle. You must have made a mistake."

"I have not," Célestine affirmed positively. "See you here, monsieur, there are the Queen Marie Antoinette's initials, in diamonds, do you see? And there beneath is a tiny diamond bee, which is of the most recent. Sir Anthony, he had that put there to show it is my lady's."

Mr. Lennox stared at the bee in the most obvious astonishment. "Are you sure, mademoiselle? That bee—but it is a most marvellous coincidence!"

"Most marvellous, monsieur!" Célestine agreed, twisting the fan about. "And yet I suppose it is not so, for if it were stolen the thief would take it to a dealer. I expect Miladi would give a good deal to get her fan back, monsieur."

"She must not get it back," Lennox returned with real alarm. "It is the gem of my collection, I would not part with it for untold gold. See you, mademoiselle, there is no need for you to say a word about it—it is just an accident that you recognized it. Promise me that you will not mention it."

Célestine revolved the situation rapidly in her own mind. After all it was as Mr. Lennox had said—it was pure accident that she had recognized the fan. Lady Carew was already reconciled to its loss. Moreover, the probability was that if she spoke of her discovery she would offend Lennox and destroy those golden *châteaux en Espagne* that she had been so busy building of late.

Her mind was made up; she flashed a captivating glance at Lennox, who was watching her, with more anxiety than seemed quite necessary.

"Very well, monsieur, I cannot say you no, it shall be as you wish. It shall be our little secret—yours and mine."

Lennox's smile and quick look of relief repaid her; he took out one of the fans not yet unfastened and handed it to her.

"If you will honour me by accepting it, mademoiselle."

Célestine gave a gasp of delight as she unfolded it and noted the exquisite carving of the ivory, the beautiful old lace.

"But you are too good, monsieur; it is too exquisite, too lovely for me."

"I don't think so!" Lennox said bluntly, laying the Marie Antoinette fan back in the box.

The church clock chimed the hour. He looked up. "How the time has flown, to be sure!"

Célestine started in dismay. "And I—miladi will be wanting me. You must be a magician, monsieur; you make me forget everything." She rose quickly.

Lennox fastened up his box and took it back to the house, then he caught up the maid before she reached the gate.

They walked back to the wood together, Célestine keeping up a voluble conversation in her broken English, Lennox for the most part listening with a smile that showed him to be well satisfied with his companion.

When they had parted, and he turned back, he found himself confronted by a tall broad-shouldered figure that seemed to rise up suddenly behind. A deep voice said:

"Well, inspector."

"Lennox, if you please, Mr. Crasster, sir." He glanced round. "One never knows who may be within hearing."

"Lady Carew's French maid, for example," Stephen said deliberately. "What do you imagine Mrs.—er—Lennox would say if she could see you now, my good friend?"

Mr. Lennox laughed sheepishly as he drew his beard through his fingers. "She has had to get used to it, sir, in the way of—"

"In the way of business," Crasster finished. "But surely that can't lead to Lady Carew's maid?"

Lennox coughed. "Not directly, sir; I can't say it does. But—well, it is a matter I should like to consult you about if you could spare me a few minutes, say, to-morrow or the next day."

CHAPTER XVIII

"How awfully good of you to come!" Lady Palmer went forward with outstretched hands. "I hardly dared to expect you, and yet there was no one else I could appeal to, and I stood so sorely in need of help. What is a poor little woman like me to do with all the lawyers against one?"

Sir Anthony Carew took her hands in some embarrassment. "Ah, well, you know, Sybil, that anything I can do to help you—"

"You are always more than kind," Lady Palmer said gratefully as she sank into one of the big easy chairs by the window, and motioned him to the other.

She had left the Wiltons rather suddenly in the end, summoned up to town to a conference with her lawyers, and, since interviews seemed inevitable, she had decided to take a suite of rooms at the Imperial Hotel for a week or two until matters were more settled. An urgent appeal from her for personal help had coincided with a growing restlessness on Sir Anthony's part, and he had hurried up to town for a week-end, on the pretext of giving her counsel.

As he sat there, however, his thoughts were not with Lady Palmer, and the thousand and one airs and graces she was assuming for his benefit, they were back at Heron's Carew with Judith.

He could not but be aware that, as far as anything she had yet related, there seemed but scant need for Sybil to have summoned him to London, but she spoke as if an interview with her lawyer were imperative.

He had been there perhaps half an hour when the door of the outer room sprang open, and voices became audible outside. Lady Palmer sprang to her feet.

"I told them that I was not at home, that I could not see anyone. Oh"—after listening a moment—"I had quite forgotten. It is Charlotte. She did speak of coming in, and I did not stop her, for I knew it would be such a pleasure to her to see you again. And, really, she has such a head for business—so unlike poor little me."

Surely never two sisters were more unlike, Mrs. Dawson was tall, sinuous-looking, with a complexion so dark as to suggest a mixture of foreign blood, and curious light eyes that contrasted oddly with her black hair and swarthy skin.

She came into the room now with her graceful languid air, and to Sir Anthony's annoyance he saw that she was followed by another visitor, a middle-aged woman with a pleasant rosy face, which somehow gave him a strange sense of familiarity.

Mrs. Dawson kissed her sister affectionately. "I have only a few minutes to spare, Sybil, for I am on my way to a meeting at the St. Clery Nertells'. Mrs. Rankin is going with me, so I brought her in. You remember her, don't you? But who is this?" gazing at Sir Anthony with wide-open eyes. "Not—surely not—Anthony Carew?"

"Am I so much altered?" Carew asked, smiling in spite of himself. "I should have known you anywhere, Charlotte."

"Well, I don't know," Mrs. Dawson replied, sitting down and looking at him. "You are older of course, we all are," with an affected little laugh. "But you look troubled, worried—your very eyes are altered—anxious."

"An active imagination," Sir Anthony laughed. "What should I have to worry me?"

"Indeed, I don't know," Mrs. Dawson answered with a little sigh, as if giving up the subject. "You have everything a man can have, it seems to me—a beautiful home, a large income, a lovely wife. Oh, how strange that you should be here to-day, and that I should happen to bring Mrs. Rankin in."

"Why strange?" Sir Anthony inquired in his leisurely fashion.

Mrs. Dawson looked a little embarrassed.

"Oh, it is only that Mrs. Rankin is an old friend of your wife's. But perhaps I ought not to have spoken," as Sir Anthony looked surprised, and a decided shade of annoyance crossed Mrs. Rankin's pleasant face.

"A friend of my wife's," Sir Anthony repeated in a puzzled tone, then his face cleared. "Why, that is how it is your face seemed familiar to me directly I saw it. I have seen your photograph in Judith's album. Of course; now I remember, my wife was with you before she came to Heron's Carew, wasn't she?"

Mrs. Rankin's pleasant comely face was still darkened by vexation. She made an obvious effort to respond to Sir Anthony's smile.

"Yes, Lady Carew was with us for two years; we were all exceedingly fond of her," she said, a certain reserve apparent in her tone.

"I am sure you must have been," Lady Palmer chimed in. "I assure you when your daughter found that Lady Carew was ill; and unable to give away the prizes at the Wembley Show, she was so frightfully disappointed that I had hard work to console her."

"What?" Sir Anthony looked across in some surprise. "Is it possible that Miss Rankin was at Wembley Show? Why didn't she come over to Heron's Carew? I am sure my wife would have been delighted to see her."

"Silly child, so I told her," Lady Palmer agreed.

"Oh, Sophie was not in the neighbourhood very long," Mrs. Rankin said hurriedly. "She stayed for a few days at Marchfield Vicarage with the Canon's sister, but I know she had a good many engagements. I dare say she had no time to get over to Heron's Carew, kind of you as it is to think of it, Sir Anthony. Another time perhaps—"

"Another time she must certainly come," Sir Anthony said decidedly. "You must let us know when she is in the neighbourhood, please, Mrs. Rankin."

"Thank you, you are very kind," Mrs. Rankin returned in a distinctly non-committal tone.

"Oh, dear Mrs. Rankin, I don't think it was altogether want of time," Lady Palmer said plaintively. "I gathered from Miss Rankin that you had told her she was not to go to Heron's Carew unless Judith spoke to her first, or something of that sort. That was why the poor child was so disappointed not to see her at the show."

It did not escape Lady Palmer's eyes that as she spoke one of Mrs. Rankin's black-gloved hands suddenly tightened itself upon the arm of her chair, that there was a certain momentary compression of her lips.

She did not answer for a moment then she looked at Sir Anthony, a lurking shadow in her blue eyes, though her lips were smiling. "As you have said so much, Lady Palmer, I think I must explain. To tell the truth, though perhaps I ought not to say it, we have felt a little hurt, both Canon Rankin and myself, that Lady Carew has taken absolutely no notice of us since her marriage. I would not have Sophie thrusting herself upon her, and therefore I told Mrs. May that, much as Sophie might wish it, I would rather she did not go over."

Sir Anthony looked embarrassed. "I am sure there is some mistake, probably a letter has miscarried, or Judith may have called, and your servants may have forgotten to tell you. In any case I am sure Judith would never forget her old friends; it would not be like her. I have always heard her speak of your family in terms of warm affection, and I am sure she will be delighted to hear I have met you, and will look forward to renewing your acquaintance."

"You are very kind. I think myself it is probable that there is some mistake," Mrs. Rankin returned. There was a slight relaxing of her features, she drew a tiny breath of relief, and put her handkerchief to her lips for a moment, as Sir Anthony turned to speak to Mrs. Dawson.

Lady Palmer crossed over and took the chair next Mrs. Rankin, her soft black gown falling in graceful folds round her slim figure. "I want your girl to dine with me one day this week," she began in her sweet caressing tone. "I have a young cousin in town, and though of course I can't do any real entertaining just now I thought I might give the two a little dinner, and perhaps some music afterwards. Your girl sings, doesn't she?"

"In an amateurish way; still, it is useful in the parish sometimes," Mrs. Rankin replied.

Lady Palmer's eyes watched her from beneath their lids. What was it the woman was afraid of, she asked herself. What brought that look of being on the defensive on her face directly Judith's name was mentioned? Why did she turn pale and shiver when Sir Anthony was speaking to her?

She leaned forward a little in her chair. "I am going to try and make Miss Rankin as fond of me as she is of my cousin, Lady Carew."

Mrs. Rankin's face stiffened instantly. "It is exceedingly kind of you."

"Now which day can she come?" said Lady Palmer. "Let me see—Thursday or Friday will suit me best. Which would she prefer, do you think?"

Mrs. Rankin shook her head. "I am afraid neither day is possible. On Thursday we are all dining out, and on Friday she is having a friend from the country to spend the day with her."

Lady Palmer's eyes narrowed. "Next week then. Of course I am not going out now, so I am comparatively free. Which day shall we say?"

"Oh, next week?" Mrs. Rankin was sitting bolt upright now, her hands in their black kid gloves were folded in her lap. "Next week," she went on, "Sophie will be away from home, I am sorry to say, Lady Palmer. She is going down to stay with some cousins in the Isle of Wight."

"I am so sorry," Lady Palmer said gently, as Mrs. Dawson rose, and Mrs. Rankin, with an air of relief, followed her example. "Well, I must hope to be more fortunate another time." She gave Mrs. Rankin one of her flashing smiles, as she spoke.

The smile was still lingering round her lips when, Sir Anthony having escorted the visitors to their carriage, she lay back in her chair and awaited his return. "So Sophie knows," she murmured beneath her breath. "Sophie knows at least enough to put me on the track. Ah, well! I think I shall manage to have an interview with Sophie before very long, and then Lady Carew may look out."

CHAPTER XIX

"So—so I am disappointed!" Peggy ended with a little shiver in her voice.

Stephen Crasster, walking by her side down the Dower House drive, set his teeth together for an instant before he turned and looked down at her, his features relaxing.

"Why are you disappointed, Peggy?"

"I have told you," Peggy answered, her eyes downcast, her face looking mutinous. "I wanted you and Lorrimer to be friends—real friends!"

There was a smile in Stephen's kind eyes as he glanced at the long upcurled lashes, at the pretty, wilful mouth.

"Won't you bring Lord Chesterham to lunch with me at Talgarth to-morrow?"

Peggy clapped her hands childishly, her small face aglow, her vexation for the time being forgotten.

"I should love to. I have been wanting to see what you have been doing at Talgarth so much. I thought it was so funny you didn't ask me."

"Did you?" Stephen questioned quietly. "Well, you must come to-morrow, Peggy, you and Chesterham. I wanted Talgarth to be in apple-pie order before you saw it. Certainly to-morrow you will have to make allowances."

"That will be ever so much more fun," Peggy returned rapturously. "I don't think I like places in apple-pie order. Oh!"—a rich blush mantling her cheeks, as a motor turned in at the lodge gates. "Why I believe this is—"

"So do I," returned Stephen with a whimsical half smile.

But she was looking at the motor; her eyes were smiling at the man in the driver's seat. She hardly heard Stephen's hurried apology for a leave-taking, hardly noticed that he had left her, striding off to the side gate which was nearest to Carew village. Chesterham pulled up the car and jumped out.

"Will you come for a spin, sweetheart? What do you think of the car? Isn't she a beauty, goes like a bird—sixty miles an hour, when the police are not about."

Peggy laughed. "I should love a ride, Lorrimer; will you take me over to Talgarth to lunch to-morrow?"

"Talgarth!" His face clouded over. "That is that fellow Crasster's place, isn't it? Why do you want to go there?"

"Because it is Stephen's place," Peggy said, with an uplifting of her brows. "Don't you realize that he is a great friend of mine, Lorrimer?"

"Friend!" Chesterham laughed out, though his eyes were glittering evilly. "I don't think friendship was exactly the gift Mr. Stephen Crasster wanted from you, Peggy."

"What do you mean?" She looked up at him with big, startled eyes, in which there lay a kind of wakening consciousness. "Stephen was my friend always."

"You were blind, child," Chesterham said with a touch of roughness that Peggy had never heard in his tone before. "The man is in love with you, it is easy to see that. And you belong to me, I cannot allow this walking and talking with him."

He drew her arm through his and led her across the grass to the shrubbery, leaving the car to the chauffeur.

"You can't allow me to talk to Stephen!" Peggy's fugitive colour was coming and going. Lorrimer was looking unlike himself to-day, she thought; he was flushed, his eyes were shining. "Don't you know that Stephen has been my friend all my life, Lorrimer? As for what you say it is nonsense— nonsense," vehemently as if trying to convince herself. "He is my friend."

"Ah, well, I am going to be your friend in the future!" Chesterham said masterfully, gazing down at her. They were out of sight of every one now, screened from the house by the belt of rhododendrons that bordered the shrubbery. He clipped his arm round her and caught her to him with a sudden warmth that half alarmed the girl. "You are mine, and I cannot spare one little bit of you, one iota of your time or thought to Crasster!" he declared vehemently, punctuating his words with hot, passionate kisses.

Half frightened, wholly indignant at his roughness, Peggy managed to free herself at last.

"How dare you?" she demanded, her face scarlet, tears of anger and humiliation standing in her eyes. "How dare you?"

"How dare I?" Chesterham laughed aloud. His bronzed face had distinctly deepened in hue, his blue eyes were gleaming oddly. "Do you think I am made of milk and water, like your friend Stephen Crasster? No! No! I am flesh and blood, Peggy, and you are most adorably pretty." He moved towards her as though to take her in his arms again.

Swift as lightning Peggy eluded him, ran past him down the path. She had never seen Chesterham quite like this before. His words about Stephen Crasster had startled and shocked her; his kisses, his passion, had filled her with a sense of humiliation. In a double sense he was tearing the veil from her eyes.

When Chesterham, giving up his undignified pursuit, stepped quietly into the drive, she was scudding across the little stretch of lawn that lay between the shrubbery and the house. He shrugged his shoulders and his face was black with anger as he followed slowly.

Meanwhile, Crasster, absorbed in meditations that were none of the pleasantest, was making his way down the road to Carew village. At the top of the street near the Carew Arms, he nearly collided with no less a person than Mr. Lennox.

"The very person I was wishing to see," he exclaimed as he stopped. "I was thinking of calling in at the Carew Arms. If you have nothing better to do this evening come in and have a taste of bachelor fare with me at Talgarth. I met with a curious case the other day that I should like to talk over with you."

Mr. Lennox paused. "You are very kind, sir. But;" with a certain hesitancy in his manner, "I am afraid that this evening it is impossible. I have an engagement—and, as a matter of fact, I am expecting some important news."

Crasster looked disappointed. "I am sorry, I am getting tired of lonely evenings, I am going back to town next week."

"I am sorry to hear that, sir." The detective took rapid counsel with himself. "I was wishing to ask your advice about something, sir. If you have nothing to do this morning, maybe you would step into my rooms at the Carew Arms."

Crasster hesitated a moment, then he turned to Lennox. "I don't mind if I do. Although," he said, "it doesn't look as if I should be much help to you, Mr. Lennox."

"Oh, I think you will, sir," the other returned confidently as he led the way to his private room at the Carew Arms."

The detective's room was a very pleasant one overlooking the garden, and with a capital view of the arbour outside. Two high-backed wooden arm-chairs stood in the window, and Lennox drew one forward.

Please to take a seat, sir. I know you have been wondering what brought me down here, sir.

Crasster laughed. "Well, I must acknowledge to a little natural curiosity. A prolonged residence at the Carew Arms seemed hardly in keeping with what one expects of the best-known of modern detectives. One wouldn't expect to find any very interesting criminals in Carew village."

"Perhaps not," the detective said slowly. "And yet my stay here has distinctly forwarded me in my investigation into one of the most mysterious of modern tragedies."

"Really?" Stephen looked up a trifle incredulous. "I must confess at times, inspector, that I have been inclined to attribute it to Célestine's bright eyes."

Mr. Lennox waved his hand as if to brush the very suggestion aside. "Pish! Célestine," he said lightly. "Célestine has her uses, sir, but," looking Crasster full in the face with his keen frosty blue eyes, "I came here in connection with the Abbey Court murder, sir. You must have guessed that, knowing what you do."

"Impossible!" Stephen stared at him. "You don't mean that you placed any reliance— what in the world could Carew have to do with the Abbey Court murder?"

"Not much at first sight," the detective returned amicably. "As a matter of fact it wasn't so much what I expected to discover at Carew village, but that it was a sort of centre. Still I may say that my stay has not been unproductive. I am glad I came to the Carew Arms."

"You don't say so!" Stephen sat back in his chair and looked at him.

It was essentially a peaceful and pleasant scene they looked upon through the open window, one that seemed far removed from that horrible, sordid crime in the Abbey Court flats. Yet, as he looked at the inspector's face, a terrible prevision of evil took possession of Stephen, a certainty that the shadow of some frightful calamity overhung the quiet village.

"What do you mean?" he said at last curtly.

The inspector did not answer for a moment, his eyes strayed to a wooden box that stood on the sideboard at the end of the room. At last, he said slowly:

"You may remember that nothing was ever discovered with regard to the identity of the man who called himself C. Warden—I mean no hint as to his past, no knowledge of his friends or where he came from."

"I remember," said Stephen slowly. "That was one of the most baffling features of the case. Not a single paper of his was to be found. It looked as if he had deliberately destroyed everything that could give any clue to his identity."

"Yes! either he had or his murderer had," Mr. Lennox finished significantly. "Well, sir, I don't say I have found out who it was, or where he came from; but it was because I thought the answer to those two questions might be found in this neighbourhood that I came down to the Carew Arms."

"The last place in the world where I would have thought you would be likely to obtain any help," Stephen said energetically; yet the inspector saw plainly enough that a shade passed over his face as he heard the words. "Why, man alive, haven't you discovered that in a country place like this everybody knows everybody else and everybody else's business? There is no room for mysteries or unknown personages down at Carew."

The inspector nodded. "I know what you mean, sir. But now let me tell you. I believe Lord Chesterham is a great friend of yours, isn't he, Mr. Crasster?"

The suddenness of the question, of the extraordinary change of topic, almost took Crasster's breath away.

"I know him of course. Yes, he is a friend," he answered, loyal to Peggy's trust in him: "But what possible connexion do you imagine he could have had with the—"

The inspector laughed a little. "Oh, I don't go so far as to imagine that he had any connexion with the tragedy, sir. But my stay here is indirectly connected with him all the same. You may not have noticed the paragraphs that appeared in the papers when he succeeded to the title?"

"I don't think I did," Stephen said uncertainly. He was watching the inspector's face. What in the world had all this to do with the Abbey Court murder? He could not make it out.

"I am sure I did not," he added more positively.

"I always look through the papers pretty carefully myself," said the inspector, "and note anything special that strikes me. It often comes in useful. Well, sir, I had two reasons for coming to Carew. The first one—well, that I may tell you later; the other I found in those paragraphs relating to the succession to the Chesterham peerage. Several of them spoke of a blue star which was supposed to be the peculiar birth-mark of the Chesterham family, and which, of course, distinguishes the present peer. Perhaps you didn't notice it, sir?"

"Certainly I didn't!" Stephen answered, a gleam of sudden comprehension lighting up his eyes. "I don't even remember hearing of his succession at the time. But you don't mean that—"

"Just that." The inspector nodded. "I made inquiries and the Chesterham Star is a blue mark, on the arm, just above the wrist, identical in every respect with the mark you will remember seeing on the arm of the man who died in the Abbey Court flats."

"I remember," Stephen said slowly. "But it is inconceivable that—"

"It is almost certain to my mind that he was a member of the Chesterham family—either with the bar sinister or otherwise," the inspector went on, "though I haven't traced him yet. But, when I have, half the mystery surrounding the Abbey Court murder will be cleared up, sir."

"But how—" Stephen began.

He was interrupted by a familiar ting-ting, from the other end of the room.

"The telephone," said the inspector. "If you will excuse me one moment, sir, I am expecting an important message!"

CHAPTER XX

Crasster waited while the inspector went over to the writing-table that stood at the other end of the room, and took down the receiver.

"As I expected—exactly. The man is certain—there can be no mistake. I must see him before we do any more—tell him to be at my office at Scotland Yard at six o'clock to-morrow." He rang off and restored the receiver to its hook.

As he came back to Stephen at the window his face was very grave. Stephen, glancing up, caught the questioning look and wondered.

"I am lost in amazement at finding a telephone at the Carew Arms, inspector," he said lightly. "Who would have thought of anything so modern in this old-fashioned house?"

Lennox laughed. "It is a bit out of the ordinary, isn't it, sir? Mrs. Curtis explained to me when I came about the rooms, that, as Sir Anthony was having the telephone put in at Heron's

Carew, it was not a matter of much difficulty to get it here, and I gratified her greatly when I told her that it was my crowning attraction to the Carew Arms. But for its being here I should probably have gone to private rooms somewhere in the neighbourhood. As a rule I prefer them; folks get to know less of your business."

"I don't fancy anyone gets to know much of your business here," Crasster said, laughing in spite of himself. "I think the length of your stay is put down entirely to Célestine's account. But about what you were telling me, inspector: The mark on that poor fellow's arm; I can't believe it is identical with the Chesterham blue star."

"Can't you, sir?" The detective went back to his table, and, opening a case, came back with a paper in his hand. "There is a painting I had done on the spot, an exact copy of the mark on C. Warden's arm."

Stephen took the paper in his hand and looked at it closely. "Yes! Well, it certainly is like the description I have heard of the Chesterham star."

Lennox handed him another sheet. "This is a likeness of the Chesterham star, done from memory, by the nurse who attended the late Lord Chesterham in his fatal illness."

Crasster studied the two in silence for a minute, then he handed them back.

"Certainly they do look identical. But it seems to me inconceivable that C. Warden should be a member of the Chesterham family. Possibly it is only a coincidence."

"Hardly probable," the inspector said dryly. "I have seen Lord Chesterham, sir, and I have been round the hall and looked at the old family portraits, and I have come to the conclusion that the murdered man bore a certain resemblance to the Chesterham family. Not a striking one by any means, but still sufficient to be noticeable. Oh, I think there's no doubt the clue to C. Warden's identity is to be found in this neighbourhood, Mr. Crasster."

Stephen handed him back the two drawings.

"Well, have it your own way, inspector. Only granted that C. Warden was a left-handed connexion of the Chesterhams, I doubt whether you will find anything about him here."

"Well, I may or I may not," the inspector remarked oracularly. "In any case my stay here hasn't been entirely unproductive. I told you I had another reason for coming down, sir."

"Connected with the Abbey Court murder?" Crasster questioned, shading his eyes with his hand.

The inspector nodded. "You will remember the porter told us who he thought the lady he had taken up in the lift resembled."

"I remember," Crasster said shortly. "Absolutely absurd, as I said at the time." His hand went to his chin and pulled it forward restlessly.

The inspector watched him closely, his keen little eyes marking every movement. He did not speak for some minutes; it was evident he was weighing some course of action. At last he looked up.

"Yet, but for that supposed recognition, we should have taken you into our counsel long before this, Mr. Crasster. You must have thought it strange you did not hear from me."

"I fancied that you did not think much of my talents as a detective," Stephen answered. "But what do you mean about this porter's recognition? You cannot surely imagine—"

The inspector got up and closed the open window before he spoke. "I have had the man down here, sir, there is no doubt about it."

"No doubt about it," Crasster echoed as he sat back and stared at him. "What in the world do you mean?"

The inspector leaned forward and spoke almost in a whisper, glancing round as if afraid that even the walls themselves should overhear his secret. "When Davis, the porter, told us that the lady he had taken up the lift into C. Warden's rooms was very like a fashionable beauty whom he had seen once or twice in the park, like you I was inclined to pooh-pooh the whole business. Then later on, when the affair seemed to have grown more inexplicable than ever, my mind went back to it, and I questioned Davis again. As a result I had him down here; he has seen Lady Carew twice, and has no doubt at all as to her identity. He says that he is prepared to swear to it anywhere."

Crasster drew a long breath with a sharp inaudible exclamation. Then he waited, his keen, clean-shaven face distinctly paler, his eyes watching the inspector's face closely, his hands clasping the arms of his chair.

Though at the bottom of his heart he had never cared for Lady Carew, though he had always been conscious of a certain latent antagonism towards her, the inspector's words came to him as a terrible shock. Anthony Carew was his dearest friend. To believe this horrible, this inconceivable thing, was to know that an abyss of horror and humiliation was opening before him. Peggy—ah! Crasster's heart failed him, he closed his eyes for a minute, as he thought of Peggy—how would she bear it, the shame and the terror and the sorrow? For that Peggy loved her sister-in-law very dearly, he knew well.

"It is impossible," he exclaimed at last, springing to his feet, and beginning to pace up and down the room. "Impossible, I tell you. Oh, Davis may be wrong, he may be lying; that Lady Carew should have had anything to do with that tragedy at Abbey Court is impossible, an absolute, physical impossibility."

The inspector did not move. His small blue eyes had a gleam of sympathy as he looked across.

"The fan—you may remember a fan was found in the room, Mr. Crasster."

"Well?" Stephen questioned hoarsely.

"It has been identified as Lady Carew's by her maid."

"My God!" Stephen sat down heavily.

The inspector went over to the sideboard and came back with a tiny glass of liqueur in his hand.

"Drink this, sir. It will pull you together. There is more for you to hear this morning and I want your help."

Crasster tossed off the absinth; it had the more effect upon him as he was habitually abstemious.

"You want my help," he repeated. "But I—good Lord, Lennox, I cannot help you! Don't you know that the Carews are my dearest friends?"

"You haven't heard all yet, sir," the inspector said slowly. "And we shall need wise heads and clear brains before we see the end of the Abbey Court murder, it strikes me."

Stephen leaned forward, his head on his hands, his elbows on the table.

"Is it possible there is more to hear?" he said with a groan. "Well, let me know the worst, Lennox."

The inspector coughed. "You don't need to be told, sir, that we have had one or two little bits of evidence that were not allowed to leak out at the inquest. They would not have enlightened the jury, and, through publicity being given to them, the murderer might have escaped."

Stephen nodded. "I know what you mean. Go on, inspector."

"Well, sir"—the detective hesitated, and seemed at a loss to choose his words—"the policeman on point duty at the end of Leinster Avenue that night saw a man loitering about for some time outside the Abbey Court flats—a man who was apparently waiting and watching for some one. Finally, he went inside and stayed some little time, then he came back again, and stood about a while. Of course, on the face of it, there is nothing to connect him with the murder in that. But, wait a minute, sir," as Stephen uttered a quick exclamation of surprise. "The pistol that was found in the room. You saw it, no doubt."

"Of course I did. The doctor's evidence proved that Warden was shot with it."

"Exactly," the inspector drew in his lips. "Well, the finding of the owner of that pistol has been no end of bother. In fact, I don't mind telling you, sir, that I look upon its accomplishment as a pretty considerable feather in my cap."

"You have discovered that?" Stephen exclaimed quickly. "Why then—"

The inspector looked at him. "You heard my summons on the telephone just now? Well, that was to tell me that the affair was finished. We have had some trouble first of all in finding the maker, secondly in tracing the shop at which it was bought, and lastly in identifying the purchaser, but to-day all three have been successfully accomplished. The revolver was one of a pair in a case which was supplied to Sir Anthony Carew in June of last year."

"To Sir Anthony Carew." Stephen's right hand clenched itself.

"To Sir Anthony Carew," the inspector repeated. "It was what I expected to hear, sir. I had the constable I was telling you of down here last week, and he identified Sir Anthony Carew as the man who stood about in the Leinster Avenue for so long, and, as I said before, entered the Abbey Court flats and stayed some little time."

If Crasster's face had been pale before it was absolutely ghastly now. Judith Carew had been up to Warden's room, Anthony had been loitering about outside, the dead man had been shot with Anthony's pistol. What did it mean? What could it mean, he asked himself? Not yet could he grasp the full significance of those damning facts.

"What are you going to do?" he asked with stiffening lips.

The inspector drew in his lips and, taking off his pince-nez, apparently studied it carefully for a minute.

"That is where I want your help, sir."

A hoarse sound broke from Stephen. "Man alive! How can I help you? Haven't I just told you that the Carews are my dearest friends?"

"That is why I asked you to help me," the inspector repeated. "Don't you see, sir, if it were merely a question of arresting Sir Anthony and Lady Carew, I should do that on my own responsibility? When I ask you to help me—"

Crasster lifted his head, a gleam of hope dawning in his eyes.

"You mean—"

The inspector scratched his head. "I don't exactly know what I do mean, sir, and that is the plain truth of it. I never believed in instinct before, and the facts seem plain enough on the face of them, but I can't bring myself to believe that either Sir Anthony or Lady Carew is guilty of the Abbey Court murder. I may tell you that those in authority above me don't share this view, and any day may bring orders for the arrest of one or both. I am holding back as long as I can, however, for I have the strongest feeling that some even darker mystery is behind the flat tragedy. Now, it came to me yesterday that I would ask your advice. You have helped me to solve many a knotty problem in the past; it seemed to me now that, if you were fighting to save your friends, you would be doubly keen."

Stephen's head dropped again on his hands. Despite his lifelong friendship for Sir Anthony Carew, his thought now would fly to Peggy, with her innocent pride in her engagement, in her handsome lover.

"If I could see a loophole," he groaned.

The detective stepped back, drew up a chair so closely that it touched the arm of Crasster's, and sat down.

"Suppose I tell you a suspicion—not that—a vague thought that I have had sometimes, I wonder whether you will think me mad, sir?" He bent his head down to Crasster's and murmured a few words in his ear.

Their effect upon Stephen was magical. He sprang backwards and looked at the inspector.

"Impossible! How could there be any connexion between the two?"

The inspector shrugged his shoulders. "I don't pretend to explain it, sir, yet. But that is the direction my suspicion takes."

"But it is madness—absolute madness!" Stephen reiterated, his face still oddly white.

The inspector spread out his hands. "Then, Sir Anthony Carew—"

Stephen dropped back in his chair. "Heaven help me, inspector, I don't know what to think."

CHAPTER XXI

"It is no use, I shall go up to town and have it out!" Lady Carew was standing in her dressing-room, her dark brows drawn together in an expression of pain, her handkerchief held to her face.

"O—h! But that would be a pity, when Miladi has such beautiful regular teeth." Célestine held up her hands. "If miladi would try a little more of the mixture perhaps it would relieve her now."

But Lady Carew shook her head. "I am tired of all those messes, Célestine; I can't stand any more of them. Look me out a train. I shall get up and see a dentist. You will find a Bradshaw in the library."

"But Miladi has courage," Célestine remarked as she left the room. "I would rather apply remedies all the day than go to see the dentist—me. He give you too much pain."

Left alone, Judith dropped the handkerchief from her face and began to walk restlessly up and down the room. "What else can I do?" she breathed. "And yet—and yet, if she should guess."

As if taking a sudden resolution, she went out of the room and up the stairs to the nursery. Paul was just awake; he stretched out his arms to his mother, and as Judith took him, and he nestled his fair head down into the hollow of her neck, for a moment the pain at her heart was lulled.

"It is for your sake, my little boy," she whispered, as she pressed her lips to the soft gold down on the top of his head. "For your sake, and your father's. For myself, what would it matter?"

"Ah, miladi, is it that the pain is better?" Célestine stood in the doorway, her sharp black eyes regarding Lady Carew curiously. "There's a train up to town from Carew village at 11.30, miladi."

"Eleven-thirty!" Judith repeated. "That will do very well. Tell them to bring the pony carriage round, Célestine. I will drive down."

"Yes, miladi." Célestine waited while Judith went to the inner nursery and gave Paul back to his nurse. "Shall we be coming home to-night, miladi, or do we spend the night in town?"

"Oh, I shall come back to-night," Judith said quickly. "But I shall not take you, Célestine. I shall have a taxi straight from the station to the dentist's and manage quite well alone."

At the station, as Lady Carew got out of the carriage, a man on a bicycle came swiftly up and dismounted at the steps. When she took her ticket to London, he was just behind her. When Judith got out at St. Pancras the same man was close behind her again and took the next taxi to hers.

But once in London Lady Carew's toothache apparently disappeared. The taxi rolled rapidly westward, and passing down Park Lane and by Hyde Park Corner, made its way to Chelsea.

As it drew nearer it became increasingly obvious that Judith was exceedingly nervous. The taxi passed through the better streets, and finally came to a stop before a quaint old-fashioned house standing a little back from the road. Judith paid her cab and dismissed it, then went up the steps, and rang the bell with fingers that trembled visibly.

"Is Mrs. Rankin at home?" she asked when a smiling, white-capped maid had answered the door.

"Yes, ma'am," the girl showed her into a pretty, unpretentious drawing-room.

Judith did not sit down. She turned and waited, standing with her face towards the open door, her hand clutching at the small inlaid table at her right.

At last there was the sound of a door opening. Judith's eyelids flickered slightly, her hand tightened its grasp.

Mrs. Rankin was coming slowly across the hall, obvious lagging unwillingness in every step. As she entered the room she looked at Judith with cold condemning eyes. "So you have come at last, Lady Carew?"

"Yes, I have come," Judith assented quickly.

Mrs. Rankin had not offered her hand; she had not attempted any sort of greeting, but as she spoke she turned and carefully closed the door.

Judith did not appear to resent her manner, or to expect any other kind of welcome. "I had to come," she said, her breath catching her in the throat with a hoarse sob. "You saw Anthony the other day. Sophie was down in our neighbourhood, I had to come to ask you. You will not tell Anthony—if he questions you—you—"

Mrs. Rankin cast one swift look at her visitor's agitated face, then quickly glanced away again. "You may rely on me, as you have always relied on me for the past two years, Judith.

Has not your very silence proved your trust? Or had you forgotten?"

"Ah, no!" Judith caught her breath with a sob. "I had not forgotten—how could I ever forget? But I was afraid. I—I knew you would say I was doing wrong."

"You might have trusted me, Judith. It was not my place to judge another. I might have tried to persuade you to be brave— to be true to yourself."

"Ah, yes," Judith cried with a great sob that threatened to choke her. "I know you would. And I only wanted to be happy, to forget—if I could."

The pity in the other woman's eyes grew and strengthened.

"Happiness does not come that way, Judith."

"I know that, I know that!" cried Lady Carew recklessly. "Nothing comes but misery—utter hopeless misery." She thrust back her golden hair from her brow; she held out her hands. "Do I look like a happy woman?" she demanded. "I tell you that I am wretched, wretched."

Looking at her tragic face, beautiful even in its pallor, Mrs. Rankin could not doubt the truth of her words. The elder woman's face softened involuntarily, she moved a step or two nearer, then she stopped before she reached her visitor.

"What does he—Sir Anthony—know of the past? What have you told him?"

Judith laughed drearily. "What should he know? Nothing, except that I was Sophie's governess. He has heard of peaceful days in the old convent at Bruges before, that is all. He does not guess, how should he, at the blackness of the shame and the misery that lie between."

Mrs. Rankin drew a deep breath. "Ah, Judith, if you had only trusted him—if you had only told him. Surely, surely he would have forgiven, he would at least have taken care that you were safe."

"That I was safe!" A sudden change swept over Judith's face, the passion, the pain died out, leaving it white and rigid. "What do you mean?" she said hoarsely, speaking slowly with a little pause between each word. "What do you know?"

Mrs. Rankin's face was white, too, now. She leaned across the little table, her voice sinking to a whisper.

"I know nothing. But one night last spring we had a visitor." She paused and drew a handkerchief across her trembling lips.

"Yes!" said Judith, in a harsh, loud tone. "Yes! you had a visitor?" Her eyes watched Mrs. Rankin's in a very anguish of dread. "You had a visitor, you say. Who was it?"

Again Mrs. Rankin glanced round, her voice dropped until it became almost inaudible.

"He—he called himself Charles Warden."

There was a long silence. Judith's eyes wandered round the room, it was all so familiar, so homelike.

Mrs. Rankin's voice sounded a very great way off when she began to speak again. Judith could hardly bring herself to attend to it. What was she saying?

"He called himself Charles Warden, he wanted to know where you were to be found. When we professed entire ignorance of your whereabouts, he told us that he had come into a large fortune, and that he meant to share it with you And he begged me if I should hear of you, if I could recall any clue that would help him in his search for you, to let him know at once at the—"

At last Judith brought her eyes back to the face of the woman standing opposite. "Yes! Where were you to let him know?"

"At Abbey Court, at—at No. 42," Mrs. Rankin whispered.

"Ah!" Judith slipped sideways from her hold on the table on to the chair behind.

Mrs. Rankin did not move; she went on speaking with stiff, pale lips.

"That was on Tuesday, and when I saw the papers on Thursday evening I—I was frightened. Judith, tell me, you do not know who was in the flat that night, who fired the fatal shot?"

"I wish to Heaven I did."

The words and accent alike had the force of complete truthfulness. Mrs. Rankin's face altered; the reserve, the hardness broke up, melted. She came round the table, she took both the ice-cold hands in hers.

"Forgive me, Judith, if I doubted," she whispered. "I was frightened—terribly frightened! I know the awful temptation it might have been. Forgive me, child!"

Judith's hands lay listlessly in hers. "There is nothing to forgive!" she said dully. "You only judge as the world will judge when it hears the story of that night. And something tells me the time is drawing very near now."

The grey shadow was stealing over Mrs. Rankin's face again, now her clasp of the cold hands loosened.

"What do you mean, Judith; you were not there, child? You do not know who the woman in the flat was?"

Judith drew herself slowly from the encircling arms, she freed her hands.

"I was the woman the papers spoke of. Yes, you were quite right when you thought so," she said slowly. "I was at the flat in Abbey Court that night, but I did not kill Cyril Stanmore. I do not know who did."

"Judith!" Mrs. Rankin's cry was full of horror—horror that changed to pity as she looked at the white worn face, at the passionate pathetic eyes.

"Yes, I am the woman the papers speak about, the woman the police are looking for," Judith went on in low, monotonous tones. "What do you think it feels like, Mrs. Rankin, to know you are being hunted, tracked down, that every day your doom is growing closer, a little more certain? I wonder what it feels like to be hanged, if it hurts one much?" in a curiously impersonal tone.

"Hush! hush! I can't stand it, Judith!" Mrs. Rankin cried, in tones of passionate pain. "You did not hurt Cyril Stanmore; haven't you just told me so? You could prove your innocence."

"I couldn't," Judith contradicted dully. "I was there in the dark, when somebody shot him, but I didn't see—I didn't know."

Something in the slow colourless voice seemed to strike a passionate chord of pity in the elder woman's heart. She laid her arms round Judith again. "Tell me all about it, Judith!"

And Judith feeling the help of the womanly sympathy that had never failed her in her need before, in a few faltering sentences told her the story of that terrible night.

Mrs. Rankin's arms never relaxed their hold. When the last words of the bald recital of terrible facts was said, a little fluttering sigh escaped her. Judith, looking up, saw the kindly face was as white as death, the eyes looking down at her held a great dread, an infinite pity.

"My child! my child!" Mrs. Rankin said brokenly. "What a terrible tangle you have involved yourself in. What can we do to help you, Judith?"

Judith stirred restlessly. "There isn't anything to be done but to wait—for the end—till the blow falls," she said drearily. "But you won't help it on, you won't tell them what you know?"

"Never, never, Judith!" Mrs. Rankin lowered her voice. "I suppose it isn't possible—it couldn't be that Lady Palmer suspects? She has taken to coming here. Mrs. Dawson, her sister, lives in the parish, and Lady Palmer seems positively to haunt me. She often asks me about you, and sometimes I have fancied that she is trying to find out."

"I dare say." Judith caught her breath with a bitter laugh. "Probably she is in league with the police. I know she hates me; I have felt it all along. She would do me any harm she could.

She loved Anthony, you know, years ago, and he—he loved her. If I were out of the way they would be happy together."

"I don't think so," Mrs. Rankin said gently. "Your husband loves you, Judith. I have only seen him once, but I am sure of that, and he is an honourable, upright man. There is only one thing for you to do now."

Judith's slight form grew rigid. "And that?"

"Go to Sir Anthony," Mrs. Rankin said in a firm, decided voice, though her eyes looked frightened, "tell him everything from the very beginning as you have told me. He would believe you, and he would help you as no one else can. Promise me you will do this. You will go to him, Judith."

"Never!" Judith set her teeth. "Rather than do that, rather than Anthony should know, I would kill myself!" she declared passionately.

CHAPTER XXII

"I thought I was never going to see you again, Peggy."

"Did you?" The girl was walking with a slow listless step through the Home Wood.

Peggy had altered curiously of late, her spirits had become capricious and variable, she was noticeably thinner and paler. She flushed hotly now as she heard Stephen Crasster's voice behind her. Since the day when Chesterham had so rudely torn the veil from her eyes, she had avoided her old friend as much as possible. To-day, for the first time, she found herself alone with him.

"And it seems to me that our lunch at Talgarth is never coming off," Stephen went on lightly. "You are always engaged."

"Yes." Peggy's voice sounded muffled as she turned her face away. "Yes, it is very unfortunate. I was very much disappointed. It is so kind of you to ask me."

"Kind to myself," Crasster smiled. "You might take pity on my loneliness, Peggy; more particularly as my time for giving invitations to Talgarth is getting short."

"What do you mean?" Peggy turned a startled face upon him.

Stephen did not answer for a moment.

"The Annesley Wards have always had a fancy for Talgarth," he said slowly at last. "I am going to let it to them, with the option of buying it at the end of the year."

"You are going to let Talgarth?" Peggy repeated in tones of consternation. "Oh, Stephen, we thought you had come to settle down among us."

"So did I at first," Stephen assented. "But I am beginning to fancy I am a bit of a rolling stone, Peggy. And, in any case, if I went on with my profession I shouldn't have much time for Talgarth. It is no use keeping on a big house like that for one man."

"It isn't so very big," Peggy said wistfully. "And why do you say 'if I went on with my profession,' Stephen?"

"Why, because—" Crasster hesitated a moment and bit his lip. "The fact is that since I have come into money, as the country folk say, I suppose I am getting lazy. I feel I should like to see rather more of the world. There is an expedition starting for Central Africa in a couple of months' time, and I have a chance of going with it, if I like."

"But you wouldn't, Stephen." Peggy exclaimed in startled tones.

"I think I must, Peggy."

The girl winked back her rising tears. "I don't see why."

Stephen glanced at her half-averted cheek, at the long upcurled lashes, at the mouth that trembled as she spoke. It took all his manhood's strength of will to restrain the words that would have torn the last vestige of doubt from Peggy's mind, to keep up the light jesting tone that had become habitual to him of late when he was speaking to Peggy.

"I think everything is changing," the girl went on, her voice quivering. "And I—I like things to stop always the same."

Stephen's smile held more of sadness than of mirth. "Change is the law of this world, little Peggy. Haven't you learnt that, child?"

There was silence for a minute, broken by a hoarse sob in Peggy's throat.

"I ought to have," she flashed out suddenly. "Anthony has changed, so has Judith. I should not know either of them now, and you have altered, and—and Lorrimer." She dropped her voice as she spoke her lover's name.

"Surely he has not changed!" Stephen was half laughing as he spoke, but his eyes showed a keen anxiety. "Or, if so, it is only for the better!" he concluded jestingly.

Peggy did not look round, she shivered a little.

"Oh, he is only like everybody else. I suppose you will tell me I must get used to it."

"I, at least, shall never change in one way," Stephen said gravely. "I shall always be your friend, Peggy."

"Oh, you say so now," the girl answered pettishly, still keeping her face turned away. "But a friend isn't much good to one, if he is at the other end of the world."

"I would come from the other end of the world to serve you," Stephen declared hoarsely. "You know that. Don't make it too hard for me."

"I should like to make things so hard for you that you couldn't go at all," Peggy retorted with some of her old spirit. "Tell the Annesley Wards they can't have Talgarth; keep it for yourself!"

"I can't, Peggy. Don't ask me."

Peggy took one swift glance at his face, then looked away, her own cheeks paling. But she did not speak, and they walked on in silence, past the Heron's moat, with its giant bulrushes, and its glory of golden kingcups, to the Dower House.

The Dowager Lady Carew was sitting out on the lawn. At sight of the two figures beside her, Peggy's face altered curiously, her footsteps faltered, she glanced behind as though she would willingly have turned back. But it was too late; already she had been seen, and Chesterham was coming to meet them.

"I didn't expect you to-day," Peggy said as he greeted them. "I thought you were in London."

"Did you? That isn't a very warm greeting, Peggy. I found my business could wait awhile," Chesterham said carelessly, as he took possession of her, and he and Crasster exchanged a curt nod. "Your brother and I have been having a business talk, and now Lady Carew has asked me to stay to lunch."

They all walked back together to the weeping willow, where the Dowager Lady Carew had established herself, her stepson beside her. He looked up as they approached.

"What is this I hear about your letting Talgarth, Crasster?"

"I don't know what you may have heard," Stephen laughed. "But I am going to let it to the Annesley Wards."

Sir Anthony looked at him. "I thought you had come here to be near your friends. We looked upon you as a permanent neighbour."

"You are very kind, all of you," Stephen responded, speaking with apparent carelessness. "But I find that I am lost without my work, and it is better to wear out than rust out, Anthony. However, it is possible there may be a hitch yet; the Wards may draw back."

"I hope they will," Sir Anthony said heartily. "We can't afford to spare you, Stephen, things have gone crookedly enough of late, goodness knows, without that. His eyes went across to his future brother-in-law, who was standing by Peggy's side a few paces away.

Sir Anthony frowned as he noticed the girl's freshness and innocence, the man's coarseness, his marks of evil living.

"Chesterham," he called out suddenly, "I hope it isn't true you have given the Westerburys notice to leave the Home Farm, and that you are letting it to Hiram Lee."

"Oh, yes." Chesterham affected to laugh, though there was a gleam in his eye that betokened anything but amusement. "I may put Hiram Lee in to manage it. I think I shall until I see how things turn out. Hiram has come into some money from a distant relative lately; he has turned over a new leaf."

"He has need," Sir Anthony said significantly. "They are a bad lot, those Lees, Chesterham. I am sorry to hear they are favourites of yours."

Chesterham darted a swift look at him, frowning the while. "I don't know that they can be called exactly favourites of mine," he said shortly, "but I don't forget old friends. And I used to spend a good deal of my time here when I was a child, Sir Anthony, a fact that has probably escaped your memory."

"No, I remember you well enough," Sir Anthony contradicted. "But I don't know where the Lees came in."

"You wouldn't," Chesterham said gently, "but I had rather a bad time of it at Chesterham in those days. I was only a bit of a boy, you know," he continued in his slow drawling tones, "and my grandmother was dead, so my grandfather turned me more or less over to the servants' care. My happiest days were spent at the Lees' cottage, playing with old Betty's grandson, Ronald. Hiram, he was a stripling then, was very good to both of us, to me and the boy Ronald. Even if the Lees have managed to fall into disrepute with the good folk of the neighbourhood, I can't quite forget them. You wouldn't wish me to, would you, Peggy?" raising his voice as his fiancée sprang from her seat on the table and came towards them.

"Wouldn't wish you to forget the Lees?" Peggy repeated doubtfully. "N—o, I suppose not. Not if they were really good to you, Lorrimer. But I don't like them. That old Betty Lee always frightens me, I shouldn't care to see much of her myself. She looks a dreadful old woman, I think. But don't let us talk of her or any more of the Lees; I want some tennis, Stephen, and I will take you and Lorrimer, Anthony."

"It is much too hot to play," Sir Anthony grumbled.

But as usual Peggy had her way. She had the first service. As Stephen stood opposite to Chesterham, and the latter raised his arm to take the ball, Stephen for the first time caught sight of the Chesterham star just above the wrist. It was, as Lennox had said, almost identical with the mark which Crasster himself had seen in the very same place on the arm of the man who died in the flat.

CHAPTER XXIII

"Now you understand what you have to do, Germain." Mr. Lennox's tone was firm and decisive.

Opposite to him there stood Superintendent Germain, of the local constabulary; the third member of the little group was Mr. Lennox's *quondam* friend, Mr. Barker.

Superintendent Germain evidently found himself in a quandary. "I think I understand, sir; but I can't say I like the job, and if his lordship should take it amiss—"

"We will bear you guiltless," Lennox finished. "But, if you carry out my instructions properly, there is no likelihood of your being blamed by anybody."

"Well, I will do my best, sir," the superintendent said unwillingly. "Though I can't see what is meant by it."

Lennox laughed. "I will tell you all about it in a day or two, superintendent. Now, you understand, Sir Anthony being away from home, you have come to Lord Chesterham as the nearest magistrate to apply for a warrant for the arrest of Peter Wilkins, on a charge of obtaining money by false pretences.

Mr. Barker and myself have accompanied you to make our affidavits before him. The rest I will manage. Now, is that plain sailing?"

"Plain enough," the superintendent grumbled. "I will do my best, sir."

"And no man could do more," Mr. Lennox finished cheerfully. "Now, superintendent, here is our dogcart, jump in."

When at last they came in sight of Chesterham Hall, Lennox roused himself and glanced about from side to side with evident interest.

"Pretty place," he said approvingly. "I don't wonder Lord Chesterham prefers it to his castle in the Highlands. That will be the Home Farm we see over there, I suppose, Mr. Germain?"

The superintendent nodded. "His Lordship will soon find he has made a mistake in getting rid of decent tenants like the Westerburys and putting in those good-for-nothing Lees, I fancy."

"Ay! It is a funny notion of his, that," Lennox observed thoughtfully.

"When his lordship was here, a bit of a boy in his grandfather's lifetime, he used to run in and out playing with the old woman's grandson, Ronald, and it seems he has a good memory."

"Ronald! Mr. Lennox repeated thoughtfully. "That isn't the man that is going into the Home Farm, is it?"

The superintendent shook his head. "No, no! That is Ronald's uncle, Hiram Lee. Old Mrs. Lee had one daughter; she was in service at the Hall, and she had one boy. The old Lord Chesterham was a very bad lot; it is said he knew something about young Ronald's parentage. Be that as it may, young Ronald grew up a fine upstanding boy. I remember him well. When I was a lad we were at school together, but he ran away from home, Ronald did; he was mad on being a sailor, and the end of that was he was drowned on his first voyage. So there is only Hiram and the old lady left.

"I see." Mr. Lennox was looking up at the Hall as they approached. It was a fine red brick mansion of the Queen Anne period; below it the grounds slanted down to the lake.

Lord Chesterham was at home, they were told, and, explaining their errand, the three men were shown into a small room on the ground floor, evidently used for the transaction of business.

Chesterham came to them without delay. "Well, superintendent, what can I do for you?" he inquired.

The superintendent explained. A warrant for the arrest of one Peter Wilkins was needed, and as Sir Anthony Carew was out they thought it best to come on to Chesterham Hall. Chesterham laughed.

"Well, they have put me on the bench, I know, but I am not very expert at my new duties yet. You will have to tell me what to do, superintendent; I have the forms here."

He unlocked a drawer and drew them out. The superintendent leaned over and showed him how to fill up the vacant spaces, the other two men watching interestedly.

Mr. Lennox put his hand in his pocket and drew out a fountain pen.

"I brought this for the affidavits. I never can write except with my own pen," he observed to Barker confidentially.

As he spoke he tried to take off the top, but apparently it stuck. He tried again, using force, and suddenly the whole thing split in his hand. The ink flew out, spattered his face, flowed out in a murky stream on the table, on the warrant, to which Lord Chesterham was just affixing his signature, on to his hands. He looked up with an expression of annoyance.

"I beg ten thousand pardons. I cannot say how sorry I am. If your lordship will allow me." Lennox caught up a sheet of blotting-paper.

Lord Chesterham took it from him but it was too late to stay the mischief. Superintendent Germain turned for a new form; Chesterham crumpled the warrant up and threw it aside. He rubbed his fingers on the blotting-paper and then, rolling it into a ball, tossed it into the waste-paper basket.

"I am sorry, my lord," Mr. Lennox went on apologizing profusely.

Lord Chesterham did not look particularly gracious. "I suppose you couldn't help it," he said shortly. "We shall have to have another form, superintendent."

"I am afraid so, sir."

While the superintendent and Lord Chesterham bent over the new form Mr. Lennox quietly walked round the table, and secured two balls of paper from the wastepaper-basket. He slipped them into his pocket with a satisfied smile, as he came back to affix his signature to the affidavit.

The rest of the business was soon over and they took their leave, Mr. Lennox's quick eye moving round the hall as they were shown through.

"Very well done, Mr. Germain; very well done indeed," he said genially as they drove off. "Couldn't have been better."

"I am glad you are satisfied, sir," the superintendent replied quietly.

Mr. Lennox's first proceeding on reaching his room at the Carew Arms was to take out the papers he had extracted from Lord Chesterham's waste-paper-basket and spread them on the table. Then, with a look of grim satisfaction, he laid them in a drawer.

He locked it and was turning away when his eye was caught by a vision sailing up the garden path. Célestine, to wit, attired

in all the glory of her holiday attire. With an exclamation of
surprise the inspector went round to the door.

Seeing him, Célestine bridled coyly. "See you, Mr. Lennox
this is not convenable!" she exclaimed as he went to meet her.
"But I could not that you should hear my story from anyone
else."

"Your story!" the inspector repeated. "But what is it,
mademoiselle? Come in, come in! You know I stand your
friend whatever happens."

Célestine looked down and did her best to blush. "But that
is what I hoped, monsieur. But I will not come in. If monsieur
has but the time to spare, there is the arbour where we talked
the other day. If we sat there but for five minutes it is not
possible that anybody could object. Is it not so, monsieur?"

"The most censorious minded couldn't see any harm," the
inspector agreed cheerfully as he caught up his hat. "I hope you
are not in trouble, mademoiselle."

Célestine clasped her hands as she sank on the rustic seat.
"The worst of trouble, monsieur, I have been insulted. That Sir
Anthony."

A curious expression compounded of mingled annoyance
and amusement had crossed the inspector's face as she began.
It changed to one of interest now.

"Sir Anthony!" he repeated. "But surely he has not insulted
you, mademoiselle."

"But—yes," Célestine confirmed, nodding her head. "Figure
to yourself, monsieur, I am trying to find some old things of
miladi's that are mislaid. I think perhaps they are in the
morning-room, and I go and search in the drawers there, and
while I am looking Sir Anthony comes in. He says that I am
poking, prying. Then when I denied it he says that I am
dishonest, because I have with me one little brooch of brilliants
of miladi's, which she has lost for a long time, and which I have
just found. He call me thief. He says he will send for the police,

have my boxes searched. I lift up my head. 'You can send for your police, Sir Anthony,' I say to him, 'and you can search my boxes, I leave them with you. But I myself, I go out of your house at once. I will not stay in it for one minute to be insulted, me.'"

"I admire your spirit, I am sure, mademoiselle," the inspector responded, lowering himself to the chair beside her.

Notwithstanding his commendatory words, however, his countenance was both perturbed and perplexed as he glanced across at the maid.

"And now—" he prompted.

Célestine was too much absorbed in her own story to note the obvious embarrassment in his face. "Now," she said, "I stay with Mrs. Varnham. She have a farm on Milord Chesterham's property, and I—I take my revenge. You understand?"

Lennox looked at her. "No," he said bluntly, "I don't know what you mean, mademoiselle. How can you revenge yourself?"

Célestine looked wise. "That is my business, monsieur. I shall have my revenge, and there are two or three people who will help me to get it, look you; I know one leetle secret of miladi's, just one," holding up her finger. "But it is enough to give me my revenge. There are those who would give me good English gold to know that secret—Miladi Palmer, she would pay me well, for she do not love miladi. And there is somebody else too, but I do not go to them, I wait now—I wait until Sir Anthony send for the police, until he have my boxes searched, and then—then I go up to Heron's Carew once more, and I say 'Ah! you think it one very fine thing, Sir Anthony, to set the police upon poor Célestine, do you not. How if I have a secret—I—that will put the police on to miladi, your wife?' How would Sir Anthony look then?"

Undoubtedly Mr. Lennox was keenly interested now. "He would look pretty much of a fool, I should think, mademoiselle.

But how would it be possible for you to put the police on miladi's track. I can't see?"

"Ah! But I see," and Célestine nodded wisely. "And I do not speak without what you call the book. I have a proof of every word that I shall say to him."

"Have you really?" Mr. Lennox leaned forward to look into her face. "And is it something that puts miladi in the power of the police. You must be very sure of your ground before you speak, you know, mademoiselle."

Célestine laughed. "Oh, but I am sure, and it is something that the police are but now looking for—something that they will give a great price to know."

There was no mistaking Mr. Lennox's interest now; his breath quickened. "I tell you what, mademoiselle, it seems to me that this is a case that needs careful handling. It won't do for you to go to Heron's Carew, yourself."

"But I tell you that that will be my revenge," Célestine reiterated.

"Suppose Sir Anthony gets the first look in," Lennox suggested. "Suppose he has the police at Heron's Carew, and before you have time to speak he gives you in custody, on some trumped-up charge of course. He might, you know, mademoiselle, and you wouldn't enjoy that, to think nothing of what I and your other friends would feel if we saw you marched down the village street by the police like a common thief. No revenge you could take would make up to us for that, mademoiselle."

Célestine hesitated, her change of countenance showed that the prospect was an alarming one.

"But what can I do then?" she debated. "I don't see—"

Lennox leaned across the little wooden table that divided them. "You could let a friend go, mademoiselle," he suggested. "A friend might manage it for you. If you look upon me as a friend, and I am proud to hope you do, if you would put the matter into my hands, why, you know it would be an honour and a pleasure to come to serve you."

Célestine considered the matter a minute, then she looked up at him through her eyelashes. "If Monsieur would be so good, I see now that it would be safer. But indeed I do not like to trouble you."

"Trouble taken for you is a pleasure to me, mademoiselle," the inspector declared gallantly. "I will walk up to Heron's Carew without delay if you will give me the track to go upon."

Célestine looked all around and lowered her voice. "I will tell you all from the beginning. You remember perhaps that I say that on the night of Lady Denborough's dinner party miladi have a migraine, that she stay at home and go out later."

Lennox nodded. "I remember thinking that she must have gone out to meet a lover myself."

Célestine shook her head. "It was no lover as I told you before, monsieur. The next day I find that one of the wardrobes door is locked. I wonder and I wonder why it is, and at last I find a key that fit the lock, and I get it open. Inside, pushed down in what you call the well, I find the white tea-gown Miladi was wearing the evening before. It is all dusty now, and bedraggled, and there is ink on the skirt and the bodice and the sleeves are all stained with blood. Yes, indeed, monsieur," as Lennox, in spite of his self-control, uttered an exclamation of astonishment. "Well I say nothing—me. But I take out the gown, and I put it away in one of my places, and when Miladi come to look for it, it has gone and she never guess who has it."

"Still I don't see," Mr. Lennox debated. "Her nose might have bled."

"Pah!" Célestine said contemptuously. "You have not heard all, monsieur. That night a man was killed in Leinster Avenue, and all London was trying to find a woman who visited him, a tall woman with golden hair, and only I, Célestine, knew that it was miladi for whom they were looking. Miladi went up to see that man in the flat that night that he died. Now, monsieur, shall I not have my revenge?"

"Perhaps," Lennox said slowly, "but it won't be the easy affair you think, mademoiselle. It can't be dealt with by the local police. And it isn't a matter that I can walk up to Heron's Carew and lay before Sir Anthony; that would be to spoil everything—to give the whole show away. I have got a friend at Scotland Yard; if you will allow me we will take his advice upon it, and see what he thinks we ought to do."

"As you like," Célestine's eyes narrowed into slits. "We will ask your friend what you like, only I will have my revenge," she said decidedly. "You understand, monsieur, I must not be deprived of my revenge."

CHAPTER XXIV

"Peggy is in the garden; you will find her there." The Dowager Lady Carew looked vaguely at the window. It was evident that she did not want to be disturbed.

With a word of apology Chesterham stepped out on to the terrace. He knew where he would be most likely to find Peggy. At an early stage of his engagement he had been made free of her favourite haunts. At the very end of the shrubbery a drooping copper beech made a shelter on the hottest day. Peggy had a table there and a couple of lounge chairs. As he parted the branches, she looked up with a quick exclamation. Her face looked white and wan, her eyes were heavy and there were purple shadows beneath.

"Peggy, sweetheart, what is the matter? What have you been doing to yourself?" Chesterham dropped the leafy screen and came forward eagerly.

But Peggy drew back, she put aside his outstretched hands. "Not to-day. Please don't," she said, with a little air of dignity that sat oddly on her small childish face.

Chesterham paused, the smile died out of his eyes. "Why, Peggy, what is it?"

Peggy laid her hand on her breast as if to hush its throbbing; she raised her eyes and looked straight at the man before her.

"An hour ago," she said steadily, "I was in Lount Wood."

"In Lount Wood?" the man's eyes fell guiltily. "Peggy, what do you mean?"

"I think you know," the girl said quietly, "I saw you—you were not alone."

"You would not blame me for a few minutes' idle talk Peggy, I overtook the girl and these Frenchwomen always try to entangle you—"

Peggy gave him one contemptuous glance. "I was there when you came," she said icily, "I was sketching the Three Beeches, I saw you meet her."

"You saw us meet!" For a moment the man had the grace to look disconcerted, then he made a desperate effort to recover his usual manner, to brazen it out. "It was only a little idle flirtation, Peggy. I was a fool and worse, I acknowledge it, but a thing like that does not affect my feeling for you. That—"

Peggy's slight contemptuous glance did not alter.

"Does it not?" she questioned icily. "I had hoped the contrary, for I must confess the knowledge that you could make appointments with my sister-in-law's dismissed maid, that you could walk with her, kiss her—Ah, you did not know I saw that—has altered my feeling towards you entirely."

She drew the glittering circlet from the third finger of her left hand, and held it out to him.

"Will you take this, please?"

He let her put the ring in his hand. "You loved me once, Peggy," he said imploringly. "You will again; you will let me give you back the ring."

"Never!" the girl exclaimed with sudden fire. "I was flattered by your attentions when we first met, Lord Chesterham. I liked you, but I never loved in the true sense of the word. I know that now, never at all."

"And who has made you so wise now?" he sneered. "But I need not ask, it is your good friend, Stephen Crasster, of course."

For a moment Peggy went very white; her great brown eyes blazed back their scorn at him, then the colour flowed slowly back to her cheeks, she held her small head very high.

"Stephen has never said a word of love to me," she said slowly. "Not a word. But it may be that from his chivalry I have learned the difference between love and what passes as love with such men as you."

"Have you really?" Chesterham laughed recklessly. His eyes were glittering, his face was red and puffy, the restraint that had marked his relations with Peggy was disappearing. "Ah, well, I am not going to lose you, my pretty Peggy; if you do not come to me for love, you shall for fear."

"Fear!" Peggy echoed disdainfully. The courage of her ancestors sounded in the thrill of her sweet young voice, she drew up her long, slim throat. "Do you imagine that I am afraid of you—of anything that you can do?"

"Not for yourself," Chesterham said slowly. As his bloodshot eyes wandered over the tall svelte figure, the charming *riante* face, the sullen anger in them changed to an unwilling admiration. "But for those you love."

"Those I love," Peggy said blankly. "What do you mean?" shrinking a little as if some cold wind touched her.

"Those you love," Chesterham repeated deliberately. "You would do a great deal to save them from danger, it may be from death itself, wouldn't you, Peggy? You would even for their sakes keep your promise to me," with a laugh that drove the colour from Peggy's cheeks once more.

"Will you explain yourself?" she said. "You are talking in riddles. If there is anything in your words beyond a mere empty threat you must be more definite, please."

"It is no mere empty threat," he said slowly. "A word from me would bring disgrace and ruin upon Heron's Carew. Such disgrace and ruin as you have never dreamed of. It is for you, Peggy, to say whether that word shall be spoken."

Something in his tone carried the conviction home to Peggy that he was not speaking without foundation, and for the moment her brave young spirit quailed.

"I have said that you must be more explicit," she found herself saying in a dull, level voice that did not sound in the least like her own. "Disgrace and ruin are strange words to use in connexion with Heron's Carew."

Chesterham pulled his long moustache; his eyes watched her in a savage underhand fashion. "A word from me would send your sister-in-law to prison—it might even be to the scaffold itself—would bring such a terrible disaster upon Heron's Carew as you have never dreamed of."

Peggy gathered up her courage in both hands. She looked him in the face fully, contemptuously.

"It is a lie!" she said very deliberately. "Will you kindly allow me to pass? I have nothing more to say to you."

"But I have something to say to you," Chesterham said grimly. He bent forward and caught her slender wrists in a grip of iron. "You can go to your sister-in-law; you can tell her what I say; I will give you a week to think it over, and then, unless you keep your promise to me, I shall speak and the blow will fall."

Peggy did not speak, she only looked up at him with big, wide-opened eyes in which there lay something of the anguish of a wild trapped thing; then made her way gropingly across the lawn to the house.

A mist seemed to rise up before her and all the pleasant familiar surroundings. The scene she had witnessed in the Lount Wood earlier in the day had shocked her, had completed the tearing of the veil from her eyes that Chesterham's own words with regard to Stephen Crasster had begun, but it had not prepared her for the crass cowardliness, the depth of moral turpitude this interview with the man she once thought she loved had revealed.

From her window she saw Chesterham walk across the lawn to his car, and then, with a curt word to his chauffeur, drive out of the gate.

She had hardly had time to realize the meaning of his threats against Judith; that he should have any power to carry them into effect was impossible, she told herself. Yet Judith had altered so strangely, so terribly of late. The girl remembered her own misgivings, her fear that something was wrong between Judith and Anthony, her certainty that ill-health alone would not account for everything. Her doubt became a certainty that Chesterham's words held a key to the mystery. Not that Peggy believed that Judith's silence veiled any guilty secret. She trusted her sister-in-law too well to think that; but she did fancy that Judith's past might hold some mystery, innocent enough in itself, Out of which Chesterham was trying to make capital. One thing grew clearer out of the chaos in which Peggy's mind was enveloped—the only person who could help her now was Judith.

At this hour Judith was pretty sure to be found at home and alone. She would go to her. Peggy caught up her hat, and without giving herself time to change her mind set off through the Home Wood to Heron's Carew. Judith was not on the lawn; Peggy found her in the morning-room, lying back on the couch among her cushions, looking white and wan.

She started up with a cry of alarm as she saw her young sister-in-law's face.

"What is wrong, Peggy?"

"Nothing much, I hope; but that is what I have come to you to find out," the girl answered vaguely, as she put her arms round Judith and made her lie back. "It may be that everything is right instead of wrong," she went on, while Judith waited, watching her with a nameless fear, her breath coming and going in soft gasps. "I have broken off my engagement with Lord Chesterham."

"You have broken off your engagement to Lord Chesterham!" Judith echoed; then, to Peggy's consternation, she burst into tears. "Oh, it is because I am so glad, Peggy," she sobbed. "So glad; he is a bad man; I don't like him, I am afraid of him."

"Yes," said Peggy softly, taking Judith's hands in hers, and chafing them against her warm young cheek.

"Why didn't you tell me so before, Judith?"

"Oh, it wouldn't have been any use," Judith said beneath her breath. "You wouldn't listen to Anthony or to Stephen."

"No," Peggy said, still keeping the cold hands against her cheek. "But I think I should have listened to you, Judith, if you had told me everything."

"Told you everything?" Judith tore her hands away, she raised herself on one elbow and stared at the girl. "What do you mean?"

Peggy pressed her soft red lips to the pale cheek. "If you had told me all you knew of Chesterham. Do you know that when I told him just now that all was over between us, that I could not marry him, he said that I must, for your sake. That if I did not he would bring some terrible trouble upon you—upon Heron's Carew?"

Judith sat as if she had been turned to stone; her face was marble white, while all her tortured soul seemed to look out of her straining, burning eyes.

"What trouble?" she said hoarsely. "Did he tell you?"

Peggy hesitated a minute, but it seemed to her that perfect frankness was the only thing that could save them now. "He spoke of trouble that would end in open disgrace, in prison—even on the scaffold itself."

"Ah!" Judith drew a long breath.

From beneath her long lashes Peggy's brown eyes watched her very lovingly. "He says he will keep silence only if I marry him. Judith, what am I to do? What are we to do?"

Judith did not answer. She sat motionless, only her eyes altered. Very gradually the light of a great decision dawned in them. At last she moved; very slowly she raised herself to her feet; she held out her hand to Peggy.

"Come!" she whispered. "Come, Peggy."

"Where?" Peggy looked at her with a new-born awe, in which some fear mingled. "What are you going to do, Judith?"

"What I ought to have done long ago," Judith said slowly with her stiff lips. "I am going to take you to Anthony, to tell him everything—so that you must not be sacrificed."

Filled with fear, she hardly knew of what, Peggy tried to hold her back.

"Wait, Judith, wait. Let us think."

But Judith would not pause. Her cold hand gripped the girl's insistently. "Come!"

As they passed into the hall they heard a sob on the staircase. Some one came swiftly towards them. "Oh, my lady—my lady, Master Paul!"

Peggy felt the poor mother's form stiffen. "What is it?" Judith cried wildly. "Speak, woman, speak! What is wrong with him?"

"My lady, we are afraid it is convulsions," the woman faltered. "If your ladyship would come at once."

CHAPTER XXV

Talgarth was a pleasant old-fashioned house. Tradition had it that it had been built out of the stones from the walls of the convent that had stood close by, and that had been pillaged and destroyed by the orders of the eighth Henry. For the past twenty years Squire Hunter, from whom Stephen Crasster bought Talgarth, had not had money to keep the old place up, and it had acquired a forlorn, neglected look. Stephen Crasster had projected wide-spreading improvements, but the tidings of Peggy's engagement had taken the heart out of him.

Inspector Furnival found Stephen in the library when, in response to repeated invitations, he walked over to Talgarth one summer evening.

Crasster sprang up in surprise as "Mr. Lennox" was announced.

"Why, inspector, this is a welcome surprise," he said, shaking hands cordially. "I have been looking over the notes of a case and trying to make up my mind about it. You are just in the nick of time to give me some help with it."

"Well, I don't know that I shall be of much assistance, sir. It seems to me that my brain is pretty well addled." The inspector laughed as he took the chair that Crasster indicated opposite to his own. "As a matter of fact I have come up hoping that you would let me talk over one or two little matters with you—things that are puzzling me a bit."

"Are they in connection with the Abbey Court case?" Crasster's face had grown suddenly grave. His hand, as he resumed his seat, beat a restless tattoo on the arm of his chair. "Well, inspector, what is it? Anything fresh?"

"Well, it is and it isn't, sir," the inspector replied enigmatically. He drew out his notebook, and, extracting an envelope, handed it to Stephen. "This came by this morning's post."

Stephen looked at it curiously. It was addressed to Mr. Lennox at the Carew Arms, in odd-looking handwriting—one that sloped backwards and was evidently disguised.

"Well?" he said at last inquiringly. "What sort of a communication is this, inspector? One would say at first sight that your correspondent did not wish to be identified."

The inspector smiled. "Precisely the case, I fancy, sir. However, will you read the enclosure?"

Crasster made an involuntary movement of distaste as he drew out the thin oblong sheet of paper, and saw the crooked misshapen writing inside:

"If Inspector Furnival wishes to inquire into Lady Carew's antecedents he will be able to get all the information he requires from Canon Rankin of St. Barnabas' Vicarage, Chelsea. The Canon might also be questioned with regard to a mysterious visitor who came in one day this spring. These hints may be more useful to Inspector Furnival than anything he will obtain from the maid, Célestine, and they are offered for his consideration by a well-wisher."

Stephen read the rancorous words over twice, then he flicked the paper on the table contemptuously.

"From Célestine herself?" he hazarded.

The inspector smiled as he shook his head. "No, Célestine hasn't discovered my real business yet. That paper was bought in Chesterham village, sir. I made it my business as soon as this epistle arrived to go round all the little shops in the neighbourhood and discover, if possible, where it was purchased. I ran it to earth at an old dame's in Chesterham village. I laid in a stock of it myself, and the old lady was quite pleased, and said she would have to order extra supplies, as it was quite wonderful how the gentry were taking to it."

Stephen raised his eyebrows. "Gentry?" he questioned gently.

The inspector laughed. "She said that a lady who was staying at General Wilton's a week or two ago came in one afternoon and bought a whole box."

"You surely don't mean—" said Stephen.

Inspector Furnival nodded. "Lady Palmer, sir. There can't be any question about that. I have compared the writing too, with a specimen of hers that I managed to get, and I don't feel any doubt at all that it is hers. My mind might not have gone straight to her, though, but for Célestine," he added candidly. "She told me one day how Lady Palmer was always asking her questions about Lady Carew, and now she is a widow, and none too well off, and Sir Anthony has come into the title and estates, nothing would suit Lady Palmer better than to get rid of Lady Carew. Do you take me, sir?"

Crasster did not answer for a minute. He sat looking at the paper; at last he raised his eyes.

"How could Lady Palmer have become possessed of the information that this note presupposes?"

The inspector shrugged his shoulders. "It is impossible to say, sir, otherwise than that probably Célestine on her dismissal from Heron's Carew did not hold her tongue. However, that is neither here nor there. I brought this note to you to show you that our time is short. Something will have to be done soon."

Stephen got up and threw open the window as though the atmosphere stifled him.

"The woman must be a perfect fiend!"

The inspector smiled as one tolerant of the idiosyncrasies of the weaker sex.

"Ah, well, sir, when jealousy gets hold of a woman! There is something else I have got to show you, Mr. Crasster." He drew a small package done up in brown paper from his pocket and began to open it. When at last the inspector laid the opened paper upon the table, he turned. "There sir."

Stephen leaned forward eagerly; then as he saw the object lying in the midst of such careful unfolding, he looked amazed. "Why, what is this, inspector? Surely nothing but an ordinary latch-key."

The inspector gazed at it almost affectionately; then he turned and glanced sharply at the other man's interested face.

"It is Mr. C. Warden's latch-key, sir, found in his pocket after death."

"Oh!" Stephen looked puzzled. "I remember; it was among the contents of his pocket. But I don't see what you are doing with it now, inspector. Where does it come in?"

Inspector Furnival smiled quietly, not ill-pleased.

"Well, I think it will ultimately form an important link in our chain of evidence, sir. If you will examine it a little more closely I think you will come to the same conclusion."

Crasster picked up a magnifying glass, and laying the key on the table bent over it a minute or two without speaking. At last he looked up.

"I see particles of wax adhering to the wards."

Inspector Furnival nodded as he looked at him. "The inference being that some one had an impression in wax taken of the key, or lock, or both?"

"Of—of—course." Stephen sprang to his feet in his excitement. "Then this clears Lady Carew. It proves—"

"Nothing," the inspector said curtly.

Crasster standing up now on the hearthrug, with his back to the fire-place, glanced at the other man's expressionless face.

"It proves nothing except that another person, probably not Warden himself, had taken means to procure a key to the flat," the inspector went on after a pause. "It would count for nothing in comparison with the weight of evidence against Lady Carew. And yet it does give us a loophole—"

"We must work it up," Stephen exclaimed eagerly. "It gives me real hope, Furnival. My heart has been as heavy as lead these last few days, though I knew there wasn't—there couldn't be—anything in your theories. With this we shall clear both Sir Anthony and Lady Carew yet."

"We may implicate Sir Anthony, it seems to me, sir," the inspector said slowly. "For anything we know yet, sir.

"Implicate Sir Anthony!" Crasster stared at him.

"I said, for anything we know yet," the detective corrected. "It may be that Sir Anthony found out where her ladyship was going, and provided himself beforehand with the means of getting into the flat, and ascertaining what went on during her interview with Warden. Mind, I don't say this is my view of the case, but it is one which has found some belief at headquarters. My chief is not inclined to believe in the possibility of any third person being mixed up in the affair."

Looking at the detective's impassive face, listening to his carefully modulated voice, Crasster felt his heart sink. He had been telling himself, ever since he saw the detective on the preceding Monday, that there must be some way out of this horrible impasse in which the Carews were involved. To-day, however, it seemed to Crasster that Furnival spoke as if the matter were one entirely out of his control, as if he had to some extent lost interest in it.

"What are you going to do now?" Crasster questioned.

The inspector looked up as if startled from a daydream. "Well, I have a plan, sir. Not much of one, but still it may answer. I should have put it into execution to-day but for this illness of the child's."

"Child's, what child's?" Stephen questioned. "What child is ill?"

Furnival looked surprised. "I thought you would have heard, sir. Sir Anthony Carew's little boy. They telegraphed to London for a specialist an hour ago."

"What?" Stephen looked at him in consternation. "It must be terribly sudden. I saw him last night, he was all right then."

"Children are like that," the inspector observed philosophically.

Stephen hardly heard the conclusion of the sentence. He looked at his watch.

"You will forgive me, inspector, I must go over and see how the boy is."

The inspector stood up and buttoned his coat. "I must be getting back too, sir. There may be some news waiting for me. If you will be so good as to give me a lift, I shall be greatly obliged."

"Delighted, I'm sure," said Crasster cordially. "Though I wish you would stay, inspector."

"Not to-day thank you, sir."

It was a drive of nine miles from Talgarth to Heron's Carew, but Stephen's powerful car made short work of the distance. The night was dark and threatening. The air was sultry and heavy with the weight that presages the coming of the storm, To Stephen it seemed prophetic; the very elements were in sympathy with his mood, with the tragedy that overhung Heron's Carew. He put the inspector down at the Carew Arms and drove on to Heron's Carew. As he passed the Dower House he caught sight of a white figure leaning against the gate. With a quick exclamation he stopped the car and sprang out. "Peggy, what are you doing here?"

"Waiting for Dr. Bennett." The girl let him take her cold hand in his; she looked at him with dull, uncomprehending eyes. "Paul is ill, you know, they say he is dying. They— Judith—sent me to tell Mother, because she always loved him, and the shock has made her quite ill, so ill that I can't leave her and go back to Heron's Carew. So I came down here to watch for Dr. Bennett to ask him—"

"You poor child," Stephen said tenderly. "Let me take you back to the house, Peggy. I will go up to Heron's Carew and bring you back word how he is."

She let him draw her arm through his and lead her up the drive. She shivered, her fingers clung more closely to Stephen's arm.

"I—I am frightened, Stephen," she whispered.

He looked down at her with a smile. "Of what, Peggy?"

She gave a little hoarse sob. "Of—of everything."

"Of everything. Nonsense!" Stephen spoke in a tone of calm authority. "Paul's illness has upset you, of course."

Presently, there rose the low rumbling of distant thunder.

"There!" Peggy caught her breath. "It is coming. I can feel it. And—and—" She drew Stephen onward quickly. She looked up at him with big, fear-laden eyes; her lips trembled; the hand lying on his arm shook as if with ague. "I have helped to bring trouble. What shall I do, Stephen? What shall I do?"

Inside the hall Crasster stopped determinedly. "You are overwrought, tired out, Peggy. And there is thunder in the air. It upsets many people. Promise me you will put these fears aside, and to-morrow, when Paul is better—"

Peggy had dropped his arm now. She stood apart, her white face lifted to the sky. To his last sentence she apparently paid no heed at all.

"There are other things in the air to-night as well as thunder," she said breathlessly. "There is trouble and treachery and—and worse. It is terrible not to know, to wait here and imagine the horrors the darkness hides. Oh, Stephen, when shall we—"

A forked, zigzag tongue of blue flame seemed to shoot right between them, almost simultaneously the thunder broke overhead, and pealed and reverberated around.

With a despairing cry Peggy turned and rushed into the house.

CHAPTER XXVI

Dawn was breaking slowly, as the first rays of the rising sun filtered through the unclosed windows of the nursery. Judith, with her child in her arms looked up wildly into the doctor's face. But the doctor's expression was inscrutable, his watch was in his hand, his gaze fixed on the tiny waxen face.

Sir Anthony stood opposite; daylight made him look haggard. There were wearied circles round his eyes. Suddenly the doctor stooped, looked more closely at the child in Judith's arms, then with an imperative gesture he pointed to the white cot. "Lay him there," he whispered. "Nay, my dear Lady Carew, you must! It is most important that he should have all the air he can possibly get."

Judith obeyed. Then she waited, standing back, waited for the doctor's word that should bid her look for the fluttering of the wings of the Angel Azrael.

On the other side of the cot the doctor stood, his eyes bent on his little patient. Sir Anthony crossed over to his wife, he took her ice-cold hands in his.

"Judith," he said softly. "My poor darling."

For the time being the dark abyss of sin and horror that lay between them was forgotten; they were not the estranged husband and wife now; they were simply Paul's father and mother, watching together by their sick child's bed.

Judith let her hands rest in her husband's; she rested herself against him as if she were too much exhausted to stand alone. "Anthony, will he live—will my little baby Paul live?" she questioned beneath her breath. Sir Anthony put one strong arm round her and held her up. "Pray we may keep him, Judith, our dear little Paul," he whispered, his whole frame quivering, strong man though he was.

As in a vision all that the future might hold rose before her, the torturing shame, the horrible fear and disgrace. A long shiver shook her from head to foot.

"Perhaps it is best that he should go," she said dully. "Perhaps it is best, Anthony."

She felt his form stiffen, then very gently he put her from him; he moved away and stood by the mantelpiece, waiting.

Dr. Bennett was standing at the foot of the cot, his eyes fixed intently upon his little patient. He bent forward now, then beckoned to the nurse who was standing behind. She handed him the cup from which she had been trying to get Paul to take some nourishment, and with a spoon he managed to get a few drops between the parted lips. Then he set the cup down on the table and glanced round.

Sir Anthony stepped quickly to his side. Surely the last moment had come, he thought, but the doctor looked beyond him at the mother's face.

"It is good news, Lady Carew," he said softly. "The one chance that I had hardly dared to hope for has come to pass. Nature is righting herself, the stupor has passed into natural sleep, and little Paul is saved. Please God he will do well now!"

"Please God!" Judith echoed the words mechanically, staring at Dr. Bennett as though her benumbed brain failed to grasp the meaning of his words, then her whole face quivered, she burst into tears. "He is going to live, our little Paul," she gasped. Sir Anthony drew her to an easy chair and made her sit down.

Dr. Bennett eyed her benevolently. "The best thing for her," he said in answer to Sir Anthony's look of anxious inquiry. "She is worn out by anxiety and watching. Now, if you could get her to her room—I shall be here for some hours yet, and I want the patient kept as quiet as possible."

But for some time Judith resisted both his and her husband's entreaties to rest, to leave Paul to his nurse and the doctor. At last, however, the night's vigil, coming on the top of her previous weakness, made of her compliance a thing outside her own will, and Sir Anthony half carried her from the room. She clung to him as he laid her fully dressed on the bed, and drew the quilt around her. "Anthony," she whispered, "don't leave me. Stay with me here, where I can see you." For the moment, Sir Anthony hesitated; then he laid his hand on hers as he sat down beside her.

"Try to sleep, Judith," he urged. "Nothing will do you so much good as that. And when Paul wakes we will call you."

Judith closed her eyes obediently, but her brain had been too thoroughly overtaxed to rest at once; one thought obsessed it now; there was something she must tell Anthony, something she had promised to tell Anthony, but she could not remember what it was.

She turned feebly to her husband. "Anthony, there is something you ought to know, something I ought to tell you—"

Sir Anthony's face was very sombre. His mind was revolving that sentence that had fallen from her lips in the room above. Perhaps it is best that he should go. Would it have been best, he was asking himself, that the little life should have flickered out? It might be that in the future baby Paul himself might wish that to-day had been the end of all, that he had died before he grew up to share in the horrible shame that might fall any day now on the Carews of Heron Carew.

Judith's weak voice went on insistently. "You don't listen, and I—I want you to help me. I can't remember what it is I have to tell you."

Sir Anthony glanced at her. She was looking very ill, he noted it dispassionately.

"Help me, Anthony. What am I to tell you?"

"Nothing," he spoke sternly. "Nothing, there is nothing you can tell me, Judith. You are to be still and go to sleep."

But the great eyes that looked purple now in the shadow only gazed at him more anxiously. "But I must tell you, I promised Peggy—"

"Promised Peggy!" Sir Anthony echoed, startled in spite of himself. "What did you promise Peggy?"

Judith drew her brows together. "I—I don't know," she said faintly. "Peggy said I must be brave; we were coming together to tell you—something. Then they came, and said that Paul was ill, and I think a black cloud burst in my brain; everything is dark and mixed up together. I can't remember what I wanted to say to you. I—I wish I could." The tears sprang into her eyes, ran down her cheeks; she began to sob pitifully.

Anthony felt that this was no time for further questioning. He soothed her agitation as well as he could, and Judith yielded herself to his influence and presently fell into a restful slumber.

Sir Anthony waited until the soft regular breathing told him that she was really asleep, then he went into his dressing-room and closed the door. He felt a certain prevision that the day that he had been dreading for so long, the day that he had always known in his heart was inevitable, was close at hand.

It was wearing towards seven when Lady Carew woke at last with her mind fully conscious of her surroundings. She got out of bed then, and walking slowly, helping herself by the balustrade like one recovering from a serious illness, she made her way to the nursery, and satisfied herself that Paul was going on well.

The nurse cried out when she saw her mistress's face, but Judith only smiled wanly, and told her that she was going to speak to Sir Anthony, and that she would come up again presently.

The irony of her words made her smile as she went back to her room. What would have happened before she saw her child again? What pity, what help could she hope for, from Paul's father, when he had heard her story?

She took the nourishment her maid brought her, and forced herself to swallow it. She would need all her strength, she knew, for the coming interview, if she could hope in any way to make Anthony understand.

As she went downstairs she heard voices in the hall— Anthony's and Crasster's. "I'll just show you what I mean, Crasster," Anthony was saying. "But I won't come any farther to-day. Truth to tell, I have had such a fright about the boy, I don't care to be out of hearing of him." There was an inaudible reply from Stephen. Judith drew back out of sight on the bend of the stair. They crossed to the front door.

The door slammed behind them. Judith waited a minute or two to make sure the coast was clear, then she came down slowly and, after a moment's hesitation, opened the study door. Anthony had said he was going to do some work there; well, he would find her waiting.

The study was a large room, furnished in a severely masculine style, with big leather covered easy chairs and solid looking tables, a low divan ran across one end of the room, since Sir Anthony preferred it to the regular smoking room.

A big screen of stamped leather stood near the window, Judith took the chair it shaded, the partial gloom was very grateful to her tired eyes. Anthony was longer in coming back than she imagined he would be. At last, her eyelids drooped, her thoughts trailed into unconsciousness, and she was asleep once more.

How long she had been there she never knew. She was awakened by the sound of voices on the other side of the screen, strange voices, but they were speaking of things that concerned her. She caught words that drove the blood back from her heart. "The Abbey Court murder." She realized that the speakers believed themselves to be alone, that they were speaking of her and Anthony. She leaned forward and listened, her white face aglow with a strange eagerness.

CHAPTER XXVII

"Sir Anthony will see you in a few minutes, if you will please to take a seat." The butler ushered Mr. Lennox and his companion into the study.

Mr. Lennox glanced about him keenly as he took the chair the man indicated; then his face assumed a satisfied expression.

"I think it is the only thing to be done. We can't afford to pick and choose in our profession, Barker."

"No, sir," the man acquiesced.

Mr. Lennox straightened himself suddenly. "I should say the Abbey Court murder has been as puzzling an affair as we ever had in hand, take it from first to last."

Mr. Barker looked at his superior in a little surprise. "And we are not out of the wood yet, sir."

"We are pretty well through with it," the other contradicted. "There will not be much left to the imagination when I have finished with Sir Anthony Carew, I fancy. You understand what you have to do, Barker?"

"I think so, sir."

"Be careful! A word or two too much or too little might do untold mischief. On the other hand, if you manage successfully there will be a promotion for you over this business. Ah, here is Sir Anthony," as they caught an echo of his voice in the hall.

Both men stood up as Sir Anthony came into the room. He was looking manifestly tired and ill.

"Sorry to keep you waiting," he said as he bowed. "But my time is rather full up to-day. I understand that your business is important, Mr.—er—Lennox," glancing at the card in his hand.

"It is, sir," that functionary answered. "Had it been possible to delay it longer I would have done so, knowing that you had a good deal of anxiety to-day. But I am acting on instructions from headquarters. And I think I had better begin by telling you, Sir Anthony, that, though I have called myself Lennox down here for reasons that you will understand, I am really Detective-Inspector Furnival, of Scotland Yard."

"Indeed!" There was a slight stiffening of Sir Anthony's muscles that did not escape the detective's keen eyes. "I should be glad if you could make your business as short as possible," he went on politely, "since my time is, of necessity, much occupied."

"I quite understand, Sir Anthony. If you will allow me." He spoke a few words in an undertone to Mr. Barker. "My friend will wait for us in the hall, sir, if you have no objection." He opened the door and showed the man out. Then as he closed it, his manner changed; he came back to Sir Anthony. "I am down here to investigate the Abbey Court murder, and I want your help, sir."

"My help!" Sir Anthony echoed, his countenance changing, in spite of his best effort to maintain his composure. "I am at a loss to understand you. In what way can I help you?"

"I will tell you, sir," the inspector looked round. "But as it is likely to be a long story, might I suggest a seat—"

"Take one!" Sir Anthony said curtly. He went ever to the fire-place as the inspector availed himself of his permission, and took up a position on the hearthrug, with one elbow on the high wooden mantelshelf. His dark face was absolutely impassive now, as he looked at the inspector and waited for him to begin.

The detective cleared his throat. "It would help me greatly, sir, it would help everybody who is interested in the case, very materially, if you would tell us the facts as you know them."

"The facts as I know them! I am unable to guess your meaning, you must be more explicit, please! What facts do you imagine I am likely to know?" Sir Anthony's tone was cold, his countenance was absolutely unmoved, the inspector was obliged to admire his self-command.

"The testimony of anybody who was on the spot near the time of the murder, if not at the actual moment, is bound to be useful," the detective said quietly.

Sir Anthony eyed him more carefully. "Your words imply that you imagine I was on the spot."

"We know you were," the detective said decisively. "Sir Anthony, won't you deal openly with me? I will not conceal from you that matters may become serious for you. Any moment I may have definite orders from Scotland Yard to effect your arrest. I am here, because, in spite of circumstantial evidence, I cannot believe in your guilt. I am hoping that you may tell me something that may put me on the track of the real criminal. I know you can help me, Sir Anthony. Will you?"

Sir Anthony did not answer for a minute. He drew a box of cigars that stood at the other end of the mantelpiece towards him, and selecting one carefully, cut off the tip and lighted it, then he held the box to the detective.

"Help yourself, inspector; they are first-rate Havanas. Well," watching his smoke curling upwards, "how much do you know?"

Inspector Furnival hesitated. The situation required careful handling.

"We know the identity of the lady who visited the flat on the night of the murder," he began tentatively at last. "We know that while she was inside you were watching from the shelter of a doorway opposite; we know that after she had come out you entered the block of flats, and that it must have been very near the time the fatal shot was fired. The pistol found in the room has been identified as your property."

Sir Anthony's start was not lost on the keen-witted detective, but there came no other answer. Inspector Furnival sat back in his chair and waited.

"Well, sir?" the detective said at last.

Sir Anthony took his cigar from his mouth. "Well?" he echoed with a slight weary smile. "There does not seem much more to be said, does there, inspector?"

The interest in the detective's eyes grew keener, he leaned forward and watched Sir Anthony's face closely.

"You mean, sir—"

Sir Anthony shrugged his shoulders. "There does not seem to me to be much to say, inspector! You have got your facts all very pat—well, there is nothing for you to do but to act upon them, I should imagine."

Something in his tone, some faint contemptuous menace made the detective momentarily wince.

"I have told you my reading of the facts, sir, won't you help me?"

"How can I?" Sir Anthony parried. "You couldn't expect it, you know, inspector. But I thought there was a certain formality, a little warning that was always given by the police to a suspect, before they questioned him. I fancied he was always told that what he said would be taken down in writing and might be used in evidence against him. You are not so generous as your confrères, inspector!"

The inspector stood up and buttoned his coat. "If you take it that way, sir, there is no more to be said. I came to ask your help. If you refuse to give it me—"

"You will have to fall back upon Scotland Yard's plan," Sir Anthony finished, a resolute touch of lightness in his tone, though his deep-set eyes were sombre. "Understand, inspector, you will find me here when you want me. I shall not run away, I assure you."

"No, I think you are too wise for that, sir," the detective's tone was grim: "I knew you could help me; I thought you would. I may have taken an unprofessional course, but I think the circumstances justified it. I hope you may not regret your refusal to be frank with me later on." He moved a step backwards, a little nearer the leather screen as he spoke.

"I hope I shall not," Sir Anthony responded imperturbably. "The law does not force a man to incriminate himself, you know, inspector."

"I know, and I tell you that I believe you could not only free yourself from every shadow of suspicion, if you chose, but could also help us materially to discover the real criminal." Inspector Furnival's tone was clear and distinct; he looked straight into the strong impassive face of the man in front of him. "But that won't avail us much when instructions come down from Scotland Yard, to apply for a warrant for the arrest of Sir Anthony Carew for the murder in Abbey Court."

Sir Anthony bent his head in acquiescence. "I know you mean well, inspector. Many thanks for your good intentions. I am sure—"

"Stop!" the voice rang out imperiously, the leather screen was pushed aside and fell to the floor. Sir Anthony's face went white beneath its tan. A curious satisfied gleam shone for a moment in the detective's eyes, as a tall, slim figure, in a light dressing-gown rose, and steadied itself tremblingly against the high back of a chair. "Stop!" the clear voice commanded again.

"Judith!" Sir Anthony exclaimed hoarsely. He went forward quickly. "What is it, dear? Why are you here? Come, let me take you back to your room—to Paul."

"No!" Judith put his hands aside decidedly, she held tightly to the high chair in front of her, her eyes glanced, not at the face of the man she loved, but past him at the lynx-eyed detective. "You will not apply for a warrant for the arrest of Sir Anthony Carew for the Abbey Court murder," she said in a high unnatural voice. "Because he is innocent. I killed the man who was known as C. Warden, in the Abbey Court flat."

Sir Anthony caught her rigid figure roughly in his arms. "You are mad, Judith! You do not know what you are saying! Your night of watching, your grief, have turned your brain."

His face was grey; the expression was changed now into one of terrible overwhelming fear. He tried to draw his wife to the door, but she resisted him, she freed herself resolutely, and turned again to the detective.

"I—I killed the man," she cried feverishly. "Are you taking it down? Don't you understand?"

"Not quite, Lady Carew," replied the plain-spoken detective. "Why should you kill this man?"

Judith put her hand to her throat, she would not look at her husband's agonized face.

"He—I had known him in the past"—her breath caught in cruel gasps between each word—"I thought he was dead, but he met me and threatened me. He ordered me to come to his flat that night. Then when I got there he insulted me—he—" She paused, her hands clenching.

"Judith, Judith! for pity's sake," Sir Anthony put himself between her and the detective. "For Paul's sake, for my sake, for the sake of all that is past, be silent."

But even Anthony himself had receded into the background of her mind. Judith looked at him with dull, non-seeing eyes.

"I had taken one of my husband's revolvers, to protect myself with, and—I shot him—Warden—with it." She finished with a hoarse sob. "That is all. Now—now, you can arrest me—not Sir Anthony."

The detective bowed. "I have no warrant to arrest anyone at present," he said stolidly. His eyes were downcast, but there was a gleam of triumph between their heavy lids. "When I hear definitely from Scotland Yard—"

"Ah! Yes, I see," Judith said unsteadily. She swayed with a little sobbing moan.

Sir Anthony sprang forward and caught her as she fell. He placed her on the couch. Then, he turned and faced the detective—merciful unconsciousness had come to his aid; the situation was in his hands now.

"Of course you know that Lady Carew was raving," he said hoarsely. "The night of watching we have had with the child, the anxiety has been too much for her. She has imagined—"

Inspector Furnival let his eyes stray to the unconscious form on the couch. "I told you that the identity of Warden's visitor was known to us, sir."

Sir Anthony drew himself up. "You told me the inferences you had drawn from the circumstances as you knew them. You were right; I followed Lady Carew; I waited till she came out, then I went into the flat. I quarrelled with Warden, I threatened to horse-whip him, he closed with me and in our struggle the pistol went off. You know the rest, and now, you must do your worst inspector. You will understand that I am anxious that Lady Carew's name should be kept out of the affair as much as possible."

The detective permitted himself to smile. "Not much chance of keeping her ladyship's name out of it as matters stand, sir. We should have been more likely to do so if you had been as I asked you to be, open with me from the first."

"Umph!" Sir Anthony straightened his broad shoulders. He cast one glance behind him at the couch, then he turned again to the inspector. "I shall plead guilty, you understand. So—well—you will not have much difficulty."

The inspector met his gaze fully.

"No! I suppose not, sir. Under the circumstances I must leave my man Barker in the house. Later on when I have heard from Scotland Yard, I will—"

"You will make the arrest," Sir Anthony finished. "I understand. You will find me ready, inspector!"

CHAPTER XXVIII

"Six, seven!" It was the clock striking from the little church on the hill. Judith opened her eyes and looked about her vaguely, the oppression on her brain prevented her from thinking coherently, from realizing what had happened. For a time she lay motionless; then something roused the dormant memory, the hazel eyes grew dark and troubled, the curved lips twitched. Slowly Judith raised herself in bed, and gazed round the room fearfully. Every detail of that terrible scene in the study up to the moment she fainted was coming back to her, was being mentally reproduced with the fidelity and the accuracy of a photograph. She hardly knew what she expected to see as she glanced from the closed door leading to Sir Anthony's apartments, to the open one of her own dressing-room, but she asked herself pitifully, was it usual to leave people alone who had confessed to having committed a murder?

What had been passing downstairs while she was unconscious? She was oppressed by a vague, horrible fear—the terror that had made her take upon herself the responsibility for Cyril Stanmore's death hung over her and paralysed her. The detective had been about to arrest Anthony—what if he had disbelieved her, what if already Anthony was in prison?

She pulled herself to the side of the bed and slipped out. Her limbs felt strangely weak and heavy, almost as if they did not belong to her; holding by the furniture she made her way slowly to the other end of the room. The dressing-room was empty.

She did not forget the impulse that had bidden her to take the crime in the Abbey Court flat on her own shoulders. Anthony had been driven mad by jealousy and anger; her responsibility was as great as though her hand had fired the fatal shot. It was her guilty silence that had led to the whole catastrophe. It was right that the punishment should fall upon her!

She went up to her dressing-table mechanically and smoothed her hair. Her eyes wandered over its luxurious plenishings, and rested on the photograph of Anthony in its big silver frame. But though she looked at the old familiar surroundings she felt a curious sense of detachment. She had done with all those things, life was over for her. Only one thing remained now—death. As she thought of death a strange fascination stole over her. It was the only way out of the tangle in which she had become involved. Perhaps, when she was dead, in time Anthony would grow to think more kindly of her—perhaps even if she died now, they would hush things up, Paul would never hear his mother's story. She caught at this last thought feverishly. Yes! That was the only thing she could do now for the sake of the two she loved. She must die—now, to-night—before the keen-eyed detective came to take her away to be pilloried in a criminal court.

But how was she to die? She looked round the room despairingly. Assuredly there was no means of taking her life here. There might be pistols in Anthony's room, but the communication door was locked. Then, like an inspiration, there recurred to her wandering mind a memory of the cool waters of Heron's Moat. That would scarcely be death surely, to sink softly in the clear limpid ripples.

She went across to her wardrobe and drew out a dark loose cloak that would cover her all over, and a garden hat. Then she hesitated. There was a door in her dressing-room that was never used, concealed from view by a hanging cabinet; the key of it was in her possession.

If the detective was having the other door watched, he would never think of this; and from it she could make her way to the back part of the house.

She unlocked the door, then paused again. Dazed and weary though she was, it seemed to her that she must leave some word of farewell for her husband. She went back to her writing-table, and took a pencil and a sheet of paper and wrote quickly:

"I do not ask for forgiveness, Anthony, for it seems to me that forgiveness is well-nigh impossible, but, if ever in the years to come you give a thought to the unhappy woman who was once your wife, try and think of her as kindly as you can for the sake of the first golden days of our love. Tell our boy as little as may be of me, only that his mother loved him very dearly, and that she is dead. I go now to make the only expiation possible for my sin; for it has been my sin all along. When you married me I let you think I was an innocent girl. I did not tell you that five years previously I had been married to Cyril Stanmore, the man who, as C. Warden, died in the Abbey Court flat. My life with him was a veritable hell; he was a libertine, a gambler, and I was his decoy, that was all. The climax came. I refused to obey some particularly degrading command of his, and he told me that our marriage was no marriage, that I was no wife of his! That night I left him! In my hour of direst need I met Canon Rankin. He and his wife were kindness itself to me and I stayed with them until I came to Heron's Carew as Peggy's governess. I had seen Cyril Stanmore's death in the papers. I never doubted that he was dead until he spoke to me outside St. Peter's, on the day of Geraldine Summerhouse's wedding. The rest you know. Life has been one long torture to me since then, and the prospect of rest is very sweet. I dare not ask for pardon from you whom I have so deeply wronged, my dearly loved husband, but I pray you to think in the future as kindly as you can of your poor lost Judith."

Tears from her eyes fell and blotted the paper; more than once she pressed it to her lips. At least Anthony would see it, his hands would touch it, when she would be lying still beneath the water of the Heron's Moat. Then with another lingering look round the room, at the inanimate things that had been so familiar and so dear, she opened the little door behind the hanging cabinet, and went out into the passage.

She listened a minute, there was no sound of any living presence to be heard. She went down slowly by the servants' staircase, meeting no one by the way. As she reached the side entrance at the bottom, she paused, and looked towards the green baize door that gave access to the front part of the house. If only, herself unseen, she could look upon Anthony's face once more, if she could hear his dear voice. Then, with a gesture of despair she passed out and drew the door to behind her. Outside it was growing dusk, the grass in the park was heavy with dew as she crossed to the Home Wood.

It was very strange to her to think that she was treading that familiar path for the last time. She opened the little wicket that led into the private path into the Home Wood, and walked on more quickly now, looking neither to the right nor left. She took no heed of a rustle among the undergrowth as she passed; she did not hear stealthy steps creeping behind her at a distance. She saw only Anthony's face that seemed to smile on her, Paul's baby hands that were beckoning her on. So—only so—could she atone! The Heron's Moat looked a thing of mystery when at last she came to it; the twilight was closing in, the water was dark and turbid, not smiling and limpid as when the sun shone on it.

She left the path and walked round the edge of the pool more slowly. Where should she throw herself in? Then she remembered that from the opposite side, in the daylight through an opening among the trees it was possible to catch a glimpse of Heron's Carew. Perhaps even tonight, if they had lighted up... At any rate she would go to her last long sleep with her feet turned towards the home she loved. She put up one last prayer for her dear ones as she hesitated on the brink. "Help them to forget; oh, help them to forget."

For herself—for pardon for the act, she was about to do, she did not pray, it seemed to her so natural, so inevitable a thing— God, in His heaven would understand! He would know she could do nothing else. A life for a life, that had been His ordinance of old.

She sprang forward, the dark waters closed over her head; she sank, rose struggling helplessly, since she was young, and, when the earnest purpose of her was dimmed, the strong firm limbs struggled against their fate. All the past was rising before her too: her life at the convent, that terrible year when she had been Stanmore's wife, dear memories of her and Anthony's love. Mingling with the noise and the roaring of the water in her ears there was another sound, a great shouting.

But it was growing dimmer, she ceased to struggle, she was sinking again, deeper and deeper, right into eternity.

CHAPTER XXIX

"A gentleman to see you, sir."

"A gentleman to see me. Didn't I tell you I was engaged?" Mr. Lennox, *alias* Inspector Furnival, looked up angrily.

But his words came too late. The little rosy-cheeked maidservant was already standing back to allow the tall man behind her to pass in.

"Not too much engaged to spare me a few minutes, I hope," a familiar voice said pleasantly.

With a quick exclamation Furnival started to his feet. "Mr. Lawrence, sir! I had no idea—"

"No idea I was in the neighbourhood," the new-comer finished for him with a smile. "Well, I was not until ten minutes ago, when I arrived at the station. I have come down from the chief, Furnival. He is getting impatient."

"So I gathered, sir." The inspector frowned as he looked at the papers on the table before him, and pulled his red beard thoughtfully.

His visitor smiled a little as he watched him. Mr. Frank Lawrence was a well-known figure in the Criminal Investigation Department. Though his only official recognized position was that of junior secretary to the chief, he was rapidly becoming a power to be reckoned with by virtue of his quick brain, of his almost uncanny power of seeing the right path to be pursued through the many intricate problems presented to the department. In person he was rather above the middle height, of slim build, with slightly rounded shoulders, and a keen, dark face with a high Roman nose, on which a pair of gold-rimmed eye-glasses were perched.

"Yes; the chief is anxious to hurry things up a bit," he went on easily. "Going to ask me to sit down, inspector? Thanks!" sinking down lazily into the chair which Furnival with a word of apology drew forward.

"Have you seen this paragraph in one of the evening papers, inspector? I met with it on my way down. It may interest you. This is the sort of thing that makes the chief mad." He handed the paper to Furnival, who read it slowly:

THE ABBEY COURT MURDER

"The extra inactivity, not to say stupidity, which the police are exhibiting with regard to this case is exciting universal comment. It is an open secret that the lady who visited the flat on the night of the murder was very shortly afterwards identified, and yet no steps whatever in the matter appear to have been taken by the authorities. A feeling is gaining ground that this is not entirely owing to official incapacity, but that strong social influence has been brought to bear in order to have the matter hushed up. True or not, this impression is greatly to be regretted inasmuch as it introduces a new and disagreeable element into our public life. Hitherto, English justice has been deemed to be beyond and above corruption; it is to be hoped that speedy action in the Abbey Court case may show that the tradition remains with us that retribution, though slow, is sure."

Furnival threw the paper down contemptuously. "Who would notice a rag like that?"

"No one, perhaps; if it were an isolated case!" Frank Lawrence said in his lazy drawling tones. "But the whole press has been full of such innuendoes lately. You must have seen them, inspector?"

Furnival nodded. "Oh, yes; I have seen them, as many as I have time for. So the chief thinks I have been negligent?"

"Scarcely; or I should not have been sent down," Frank Lawrence corrected softly. "But he does not understand why the warrant has not been applied for and the arrest made before now."

"I didn't want to make a fool of myself!" The inspector's face was very grim. "But the warrant is applied for now. You are just in time to be in at the finish, Mr. Lawrence. You will be able to tell the chief it isn't quite such plain sailing as he fancies."

Mr. Lawrence raised his eyebrows. "How do you mean?"

The inspector glanced at the clock. "It is a long story sir. And I am due at Heron's Carew in half an hour. I went up there earlier this afternoon. And perhaps I need hardly tell you my men are on guard there now."

Mr. Lawrence looked momentarily astonished.

"Really! Then you may as well say the end is at hand. I shall stay here until the arrest."

Inspector Furnival smiled meaningly. "I expect the arrest to take place to-night or to-morrow morning at the latest."

"I am glad to hear it," Mr. Lawrence said hastily. "It was time it was made, Furnival, quite time. Between ourselves, I have never known the chief so impatient. And now I suppose we shall have what the papers call a *cause célèbre*."

The inspector's smile deepened a little. "I suppose we shall," he assented.

The younger man did not speak again for a minute or two. "It will be a nine days' wonder, the trial," he said at last. "And no knowing how it will end after all, in spite of our evidence. For she will fight to the bitter end of course, and the Carew influence and the Carew money will go far—"

The inspector pulled his sandy beard and watched the dark clear face.

"Lady Carew will make no fight, sir; she confessed to me this afternoon."

"What!" Young Lawrence stared at him, for once thoroughly taken aback. "Lady Carew confessed to you that she had committed the Abbey Court murder! Impossible!"

"Quite possible and quite true!" the inspector affirmed. He looked across at the grandfather clock in the corner. Very soon Sir Anthony would be expecting him up at Heron's Carew. "As a matter of fact," he added, his mouth twisting in a curious smile, "Lady Carew's is not the only confession of guilt I have had today in the matter of the Abbey Court murder!"

Mr. Lawrence took off his pince-nez and stared at him. "I can't understand you to-night, Furnival. Can't you be a little more explicit? It is impossible that you can mean that two people can have told you that they committed the murder in Abbey Court?"

The inspector nodded. "That is just what I do mean. Lady Carew says that Warden forced her by some power he had over her to come to his flat, that she took her husband's revolver for her protection, and that, stung by Warden's insults, she shot him with it."

Lawrence's interest manifestly quickened. "Much as the chief has always surmised. But you said—"

"On the other hand," the inspector went on very deliberately, "Sir Anthony Carew states that he discovered his wife was going to Warden's flat, that he followed, and watched her, and that when Lady Carew had gone he went in, quarrelled with the fellow and in his rage—I dare say you have heard of the Carew temper, sir—he shot him. Sounds a likely story, doesn't it, Mr. Lawrence? And it is by no means incompatible with our evidence."

"But—but—" objected Lawrence, wiping his brow. "They can't both be telling the truth."

Again that curious smile came into the inspector's eyes.

"So much is self-evident, sir. The only question to my mind now is—is either of them?"

Young Lawrence's astonishment deepened.

"You mean—"

The inspector leaned forward confidentially.

"Lady Carew fancied that I was about to arrest Sir Anthony when she came forward with her confession. Sir Anthony, on his part, was beside himself with fear at the peril in which his wife was placed, when he took the responsibility of the crime on his own shoulders. Therefore the situation stands thus: Lady Carew says that she is guilty; Sir Anthony says he is— each, as far as I can judge, believing the other to be. Now do you see the position of affairs? Each is trying to save the other."

"But—" Mr. Lawrence rubbed his hand through his hair. "I don't understand, Furnival. Which of them is guilty?"

The inspector looked at him. "Neither of them," he said curtly. "If each of them thinks the other is, doesn't that prove to you that both of them are innocent? Oh, it hasn't been as easy a task as you folks at Scotland Yard expected, to get to the bottom of the Abbey Court murder." He got up, looked at his watch, and compared it with the grandfather's clock. "I am afraid I must be starting, sir. I promised to be at Heron's Carew, by eight, and I don't want to keep Sir Anthony waiting."

Mr. Lawrence rose too. "I will walk up with you. If this is your opinion, inspector, how is it that you told me just now that you were about to apply for a warrant for the arrest of the Abbey Court murderer?"

"That I had applied," the detective corrected, as he opened the door leading into the garden, and they went down the path.

"But whose arrest have you applied for?" Lawrence questioned, as they unlatched the garden gate, and let themselves out into the village street.

"Whose?" The inspector glanced on either side of him, behind and before. "Ah, that is my little secret for the present, sir. You will soon know all."

They walked on briskly. The church clock chimed eight, the inspector quickened his step. "I was afraid we were late. We will take the short cut through the Home Wood if you don't mind, Mr. Lawrence."

As they passed the Dower House they heard voices, and caught a momentary sight of Peggy and Crasster pacing up and down the drive together. The inspector's face brightened as he looked after them.

It was fairly light in the street, but in the Home Wood it seemed almost dark. The two men walked along quickly, their feet making little sound on the pine-needle covered path.

As they came near the Heron's Moat they became aware of footsteps coming from the opposite direction. A man was running, sprinting as if for dear life, towards them; at the same moment Inspector Furnival caught sight of a tall figure in a dark gown on the other side of the pool. He started forward with a quick exclamation of dismay.

Simultaneously, there was a splash, a loud cry rang out. The tall figure had disappeared beneath the waters of the pool. Inspector Furnival ran for all he was worth, the man who had been racing down the path towards them ran too. But some one was before them, some one who sprang into the pool, and, as they reached the spot, reappeared, holding an inanimate burden, endeavouring to keep her head above water.

With a sharp cry the man who had been running, tossing off his coat as he ran, threw himself into the water, and swam to the other's help. Inspector Furnival and Mr. Lawrence, racing their hardest, arrived on the scene in time to assist at the landing.

The two men who had been in the water, and whom Furnival now recognized as Sir Anthony Carew and his own subordinate, Barker, laid their inanimate burden on the bank. Judith's face was white, her eyes were closed, her golden hair lay dank on the grass. Sir Anthony bent over her in agony.

"She—she can't be dead!"

"No, no!" the inspector said soothingly. "She was not under the water a minute. I have had some experience of first aid. If you would let me come nearer." He stooped over her. "She has fainted from the shock, that is all," he said quietly. "There is a keeper's cottage close at hand, Sir Anthony, we had better take her there, and the man can fetch Dr. Bennett."

Sir Anthony assented dumbly. His heart had given a great suffocating twist of relief at hearing that Judith lived. And yet assuredly, Anthony Carew said to himself, as he gathered her unconscious form in his arms and, refusing all other help, strode off with her to the cottage, it would have been well for Judith if by any means she could have escaped the calamity that was coming upon them.

As they neared the gamekeeper's he felt the fluttering of her breath, her eyelids wavered, then opened, the lovely eyes looked up into his.

"Anthony!" she said.

Spite of all his dread of the future, his horror of the past, his heart leapt with thankfulness to hear the beloved voice again. He bent his head lower.

"Judith, my darling."

A faint colour flickered for a moment in the white cheeks. "Am—am I dead?" she questioned. "Is this heaven, Anthony? Do you forgive me for—"

Anthony pressed his lips to the fair hair. "Everything, my darling."

"It is my fault—all of it. If I had not dropped the paper that told you where I was going; if I had not taken your pistol," the weak voice went on, unheeding the look of astonishment that spread over her husband's face as she proceeded, "you would not have been tempted; you could not have used it against him!"

A strange sound burst from Anthony Carew as he laid her on the couch in the keeper's front room.

"Judith! Does this mean that you think I was guilty?"

"I—I never blamed you," she returned incoherently. "Oh, Anthony!"

There was a strange glad light in Sir Anthony Carew's face as the gamekeeper's wife, with her willing helpers, took possession of Judith. "She thought I was guilty," he repeated to himself. "Then surely she, she was—she must be innocent."

CHAPTER XXX

It was one of those chilly mornings that come sometimes in early autumn. The white mist from the park seemed to rise like a pall right up to the window of the morning-room at Heron's Carew; a bright fire burned in the grate, making the weather outside look more damp and cheerless by contrast. Lady Carew was leaning back in her favourite low reclining chair near the fire-place; Sir Anthony was standing on the hearthrug. The front door bell rang, their eyes met in a smile of perfect confidence. Then Judith began to shiver.

"Oh, Anthony, I am frightened! Do you think they really know who shot Cyril? I don't see how they can! Suppose—suppose they are only trying to make us incriminate ourselves?"

Sir Anthony's face was a little overclouded. "I can't tell, dear. But I feel inclined to trust Inspector Furnival, and he tells me that if we speak out we have nothing to fear. Anyhow, the truth must be the best policy, and, at any rate, we both know that the worst dread of all that has haunted each of us these past terrible months has been only a delusion; don't we, Judith?"

"Yes, yes!" she whispered, looking up at him with dewy eyes. "Oh, Anthony! How could I have been so foolish?"

He caught his breath. "You couldn't help it. How I—" He broke off as three men were ushered into the room: Stephen Crasster, Inspector Furnival, and Mr. Lawrence.

Sir Anthony greeted them all courteously, and invited them to be seated.

"Lady Carew and I have decided to take your advice," he began, addressing Furnival. "We will tell you our story—our stories, rather—without any reservation. And, if you can find any loophole to help us; I am sure we need not assure you of our boundless gratitude. I think we are all here now—except Mrs. Rankin. Ah, here she is!" He opened the door.

Mrs. Rankin's comely face was pale and anxious. She went over and took the seat Sir Anthony drew up for her, near Lady Carew, and clasped Judith's hand in hers. Crasster stood by Sir Anthony on the hearthrug. Furnival and Lawrence occupied seats nearer the door, placed so that they had a good view of the faces of the other three.

"If Lady Carew will begin—" Furnival said, glancing at Sir Anthony.

The firelight gleamed on Judith's delicate face, shone on the masses of pale gold hair, gave for a moment a fictitious colour to the transparent skin. She drew herself up among her cushions, bracing herself for the ordeal that awaited her. Her fingers caught convulsively at Mrs. Rankin's hand, her eyes sought Anthony's. It was to him she was telling the tale, it was to him that she must vindicate herself! Her voice was very low and trembling when she began, it gathered strength as she went on.

"I was very young when I married Cyril Stanmore, entirely in ignorance of his real character, and so friendless that I had no one to warn me that he was only a professional gambler. Our quarrels arose from the fact that when I did discover how his money was obtained I refused to help him to be a party to his schemes.

"Everything culminated on the night he told me I had never been his wife at all, that our marriage had been illegal. That night I left him for ever. Chance had made me acquainted with Canon Rankin. I knew his kindly character. I told him my miserable story, and appealed to him for help. He took me to his own home, placed me in Mrs. Rankin's care, and promised to find me work.

"Finally he suggested that I should act as his daughter's governess until I had had time to live down the past, to obtain a satisfactory reference for the future. How kind both he and Mrs. Rankin were to me in that terrible time no words of mine could ever tell! Finally, when there was no more work for me with them, they procured me an engagement at Heron's Carew. When I was going to marry Sir Anthony Carew, I did not tell them, because I knew that they would want me to tell him the secret of the past, and I couldn't—I couldn't put my happiness away from me with my own hands. I had heard, as I believed, of Cyril Stanmore's death before I left Canon Rankin's, therefore, his sudden appearance on the steps of St. Peter's, was a double shock to me. When he ordered me to come to his flat I was too bewildered to know what I ought to do—too overwhelmed to do anything but obey. When I got there—I had taken my husband's pistol to protect myself with—he, Stanmore, mocked at me, took it from me, and threw it down. Then I rubbed against the switch, and put out the electric light. In the darkness a shot was fired, I heard a fall and a groan. It was a long time before I could find the switch, but I could hear some one in the room, some one breathing heavily—"

She paused and drank feverishly some water that Mrs. Rankin handed to her. Then with a shuddering glance round the circle of expectant faces, she went on.

"When I did find the light," she whispered, "there was no one there but Cyril Stanmore and myself. When I saw that he was dead I was too terrified to do anything, or give the alarm. No one would believe me, I thought; everybody would think I had shot him. I hurried away."

Her voice sank into silence.

Inspector Furnival had been busy making notes in his pocket-book; he looked up now.

"You were not alone when you left the block of flats, Lady Carew; a man came down the stairs with you?" he paused suggestively.

Judith looked at him with wide-open, amazed eyes. "You know that too. But he—I met him on the stairs outside the flat; he had known me in the old time—and he turned with me and walked with me to the entrance."

A spasm of fear that momentarily contorted her face, that caught her throat, making her voice husky and dry, did not escape the sharp-witted inspector's notice.

"Will you tell us his name, Lady Carew. Can you say why, when the police were searching high and low to discover the identity of the visitor to the flat, he did not come forward to say he had met you?"

There was a long pause. Judith's eyes turned about from side to side. The inspector waited, holding his pencil pointed over his notebook. Mrs. Rankin's mouth quivered painfully as she chafed the cold hand she held. At last Lady Carew spoke.

"I suppose he was sorry for me!" she said faintly. "He had been a great friend of Stanmore's in the old time. I—I used to think then that he made Stanmore worse, that he was his evil genius, but perhaps—when he knew what had happened that night—he was sorry for me!"

"His name?" the inspector questioned, writing rapidly.

Judith hesitated again; she put up her handkerchief to her lips, she glanced across at Anthony. He was not looking at her.

"I—I knew him as Jermyn Leigh," she stammered at last.

"And you parted from him at the entrance to the flats, you say?" the inspector went on quickly. "You must pardon my putting these questions, Lady Carew; if this tangle is ever to be straightened out, we must have the truth and the whole truth now. Have you ever seen this man—Jermyn Leigh—since he left you that night?"

"Y—es!" the word fell across the listening silence.

Sir Anthony stood perfectly motionless. Crasster gave a quick inaudible exclamation as he leaned forward.

The inspector waited. "Where?" he questioned at last. "In London, or since you came down to Heron's Carew?"

"Since we came down to Heron's Carew!" She seemed to repeat his words mechanically. "Yes, yes, he is here, though I never thought—I never dreamt of such a thing till I saw him—" Her voice failed her; she caught her breath.

"Ah, yes," the inspector assented. "The name by which he is known here, please."

Judith looked at him; for a minute her lips seemed to move inaudibly.

"He is Lord Chesterham."

"Chesterham!" The exclamation burst from Crasster.

Sir Anthony did not stir; Mrs. Rankin, as if moved by some sudden impulse of pity, leaned forward and kissed Judith's pale cheek.

A little satisfied smile played round the inspector's mouth as he made another entry in his book.

"He would recognize you when he met you down here of course?"

"Oh yes, yes; he knew me!" Judith said faintly. "He promised to keep silence if—if I would not try to stop his marriage," she went on feverishly. "But now—now I can't any longer."

"Thank you, I think that is all for the present." The inspector wore a curiously triumphant expression as he looked up. "Sir Anthony, will you gives us your help? Please tell us what you know of the night's doings."

Sir Anthony glanced up.

"It is so; little I know, as I told you, inspector. I picked up a paper that Lady Carew dropped, having on it Warden's address, and the hour at which she was to be at the flat. Sometimes now, it seems to me, looking back, that the very suspicion that my wife had made an appointment with another man drove me mad. I went to the flats at the time named; I waited in a doorway opposite, and I saw my wife go in, and come out again after some time. Then I went in. A man was standing in the vestibule; it struck me that he was watching Lady Carew, he was smiling to himself as he looked after her, but I had only a very cursory glimpse of him. I went up to the flat, but, of course, I could not get in. Of the tragedy itself I know nothing."

"Did you recognize Chesterham as the man who was standing in the vestibule watching Lady Carew?" Crasster asked eagerly. It was the first time he had spoken.

Sir Anthony shook his head.

"I cannot say that I did, though I have sometimes felt that his face was vaguely familiar. But as I say, it was only a glimpse I had of him that night. Can we help you any further, inspector?"

"A little, I think, sir." Inspector Furnival drew a paper from his pocket and studied it in silence for a minute or two. "If Lady Carew will kindly answer a few questions? The dress you wore that night has been placed in the hands of the police by your late maid, Célestine, Lady Carew. There are splashes of blood on the bodice that must have come from the murdered man and the skirt is stained with ink. How do you account for this?"

"I—I tried to raise him—Stanmore—in my arms," Judith faltered. Her voice wavered and broke. The very effort of speaking of it brought back the whole terrible scene before her eyes. "And—and—when he threw the pistol on the table he upset the inkstand; I tried to get it back; that is how the ink must have got on my dress."

"Ah! The ink was on the table with the pistol," the inspector commented with a far-away look in his eyes. "One more question, Lady Carew. There was a blue star on Stanmore's wrist." Judith bent her head in assent. "Were you aware that there was a similar mark on the wrist of the man whom you knew as Jermyn Leigh?"

Judith's face grew strangely white, her eyes glanced obliquely round as though oppressed by some horrible fear.

"I—I never saw one—I did not think he had one." A hoarse sob rose in her throat.

The inspector went on apparently scrawling hieroglyphics in his pocket-book. Lawrence and Crasster knew that his look, his very silence, betokened that he was satisfied.

Nobody spoke for a minute or two, as if by common consent. Every one avoided looking at the agonized face of the woman in the big chair. Lawrence glanced at Crasster, some faint foreshadowing of what was coming upon him, unreal, fantastical, as must appear the happenings it involved. Inspector Furnival glanced at Mrs. Rankin. "You have nothing more to tell us, I think?"

"No," she answered with a little catch in her breath. "Only that on Tuesday before the murder Stanmore called on us and asked us if we could tell him where Lady Carew was to be found. We declined to give him any information of course, and he went away asking us if we should hear of her later, to let him know at the Abbey Court flats, where he told us he was staying under the name of Charles Warden."

The inspector tapped his notebook thoughtfully. "Did he tell you why he was anxious to find Lady Carew?"

Mrs. Rankin shook her head.

"No further than that he said he had come back to England to claim some great inheritance that had fallen to him, and we gathered that he wished her to share it with him."

"Um! Um!" The inspectors did not speak for a minute or two, then he looked up suddenly. "Did he give you any notion of the sort of inheritance to which he had succeeded?"

"No—no," Mrs. Rankin said slowly, "further than that he spoke as if it meant rank as well as wealth. But I think he was too much excited to talk coherently, and we, of course, were only too anxious to get rid of him.

"Naturally!" the inspector assented. "Well, I don't think we need trouble you any further to-day."

Mrs. Rankin sat back in her chair with an audible sigh of relief.

Sir Anthony looked at the detective. "Can you help us, Furnival, or are we too hopelessly in the mire?"

"I think I shall be able to do something, Sir Anthony." The inspector glanced over what he had written, then he closed the book and fastened it. "But before we go any further I should suggest Lady Carew goes to her room. I am sure Mrs. Rankin will agree with me that it is the best thing for her."

"They—they do believe me, Anthony?" she said piteously, as her husband came forward and drew her arm through his.

The inspector took the answer upon himself.

"Well, I do, for one, Lady Carew," he said heartily. "And later on Sir Anthony will tell you the name of the Abbey Court murderer."

"Thank you!" Judith murmured brokenly. She felt strangely bewildered, scarcely able even to think. All she could realize was that there was hope at last, hope that the awful black cloud that had brooded over Heron's Carew for so long was going to be dissipated.

Her husband half-supported, half-carried her to her room, and then, whispering soothing words, he left her to Mrs. Rankin's care, and went back to the morning-room. The three men had their heads close together when he entered. He fancied that Crasster looked strangely disturbed.

"Excuse me, Sir Anthony," murmured the inspector. He went across to the window, and, throwing it open, put his head out with a curious whistling sound, like a bird's cry. It was answered from the bushes on the other side of the terrace. He stepped back and closed the window.

"It is all right," he observed enigmatically. "You are going to have a visitor, Sir Anthony. I hear a car in the drive."

"A visitor!" Sir Anthony stepped to the bell.

"Allow him to be admitted, please, Sir Anthony," said the inspector. "I fancy it is one whose evidence may be very germane to the case."

Sir Anthony started.

"Germane to the case! I don't see—"

"One moment, Sir Anthony!"

The inspector held up his hand.

The bell pealed loudly, they heard the old butler open the door, a murmured colloquy, then Sir Anthony's face altered.

"Chesterham! Ah, of course his testimony—"

"Will supply the missing link!" the inspector finished.

"Exactly." Sir Anthony opened the door. "Ah, Chesterham, we were just speaking of you. Come in."

Chesterham was distinctly paler than usual, his face looked anxious and worried.

"I only heard half an hour ago of the accident that happened to Lady Carew last night," he began, advancing to meet Sir Anthony. "I trust its gravity has been exaggerated. How is she? I—" He broke off as he saw the men behind Sir Anthony.

Inspector Furnival stepped forward. Sir Anthony with a puzzled expression moved aside.

"You do not disturb us, Lord Chesterham!" the inspector remarked suavely. "As Sir Anthony said, we were just speaking of you. You can supply exactly the evidence we want!"

"Evidence! I don't understand you!" Chesterham's face darkened as he spoke, and he drew back. "I came here to speak to Sir Anthony Carew," he added with an assumption of hauteur that brought a slight smile to the inspector's lips.

At the same time there was a knock at the front door. Furnival signed to the butler to open it. A couple of men in dark clothes entered and stood on the mat. As soon as they were fairly inside, the inspector advanced towards the astonished Chesterham.

"Ronald Lee, *alias* Jermyn Leigh, *alias* Viscount Chesterham, I arrest you for the wilful murder of Cyril Stanmore, Lord Chesterham, at the Abbey Court flats on the night of April— 19—. And it is my duty to warn you that anything you say in answer to the charge will be taken down in writing and may be used against you."

He drew his hand from his pocket, something of steel dangling from it suggestively.

For an instant, it seemed to the lookers-on that Chesterham visibly cowered and shrank, the next he had to some extent pulled himself together.

"You must be mad!" he said loudly. "Stark, staring mad! When you hear that the visitor to Stanmore's flat on the night of the murder was—"

"We have been aware of that lady's identity from the first." The inspector's tone was ominously quiet. "Your game has been a bold one, Mr. Lee, but I think it is played out now. I shall have to trouble you to come with me to the police station at Caversham. One of my men will get a conveyance from the Carew Arms, or if you would prefer to use your—I should say Lord Chesterham's—motor, perhaps it would be better!"

Chesterham's eyes wandered slowly round from the pale shocked faces of Sir Anthony Carew and Stephen Crasster, to the inspector's keen alert countenance and to his solid-looking assistants behind. Then he drew something from his pocket, something that gleamed in the light. The next instant there was a shot, a sharp exclamation from the inspector, and the men gathered round the prostrate figure on the floor. Furnival was the first to look up.

"The fool I was not to think of this! But he has missed his aim—it is nothing but a flesh wound in the thick part of the leg; I can manage to dress it for the present, and we will call in at Dr. Bennett's as we go through the village."

CHAPTER XXXI

"Committed for trial, is he? Well, they couldn't do much else!"

It was the verdict of Mrs. Curtis, at the Carew Arms, as she watched the crowd pouring down the village street.

Carew village had never known such excitement within the memory of man. Lord Chesterham, in some extraordinary way, had turned out not to be Lord Chesterham at all, but Ronald Lee, whom many of the villagers remembered as a child, and, as if this news was not thrilling enough, he had been brought before the magistrates that morning charged with having murdered somebody—the true Lord Chesterham, some people said it was—up in London.

He had attempted to commit suicide too, and had been carried into court that morning with his leg swathed in bandages. Small wonder was there that there had not been standing room in the magistrates' court—that the whole population of the neighbourhood seemed to have turned out, eager to learn all that there was to be learned of this astonishing story.

Inspector Furnival came down the street with Stephen Crasster.

"I congratulate you, inspector," Crasster was saying, as they neared the Carew Arms. "You have done a difficult piece of work marvellously well. I wonder what it was that first gave you the clue that enabled you to straighten out the tangle?"

The inspector pondered a minute, his hand on the garden gate.

"I think it was the blue star of the Chesterhams! But I must premise that I never believed Lady Carew guilty. Though very soon it was a matter of certainty with me that she was Warden's mysterious visitor, I felt a premonition all along that Warden's murderer must be searched for elsewhere. The blue star made me feel sure that there was some connection between Warden and the Chesterhams too."

"It seems a very slight thing to have led to so momentous a conclusion," Crasster said thoughtfully. "I can't make out how you guessed the man to be an impostor, either. I say inspector, I think I will come in with you for a minute or two"—as he became suddenly aware that their colloquy was exciting an unusual amount of interest from the passers-by—"we shall have a crowd round us in no time if we stand here."

"By all means, sir." The inspector stood back. "It is not often the folks down here get anything like this to talk about," he added as he shut the gate.

They did not enter the house, but walked up and down the garden paths.

"You want to know what made me think him an impostor, sir?" the inspector went on. "Well, when the idea first occurred to me I had nothing to go on but guesswork. His friendship for the Lees was the first definite thing I had to put me on the track. I had the pleasure of 'assisting' at one of his interviews with old Betty, as our French neighbours say, and that was enough to show me that she, at any rate, suspected a mystery. Then I could find no trace of anyone who might have been Warden among the Chesterham collaterals. Although his likeness to them, as well as the blue star, proved that he must have been related. The only illegitimate descendant of whom I could find any definite trace was young Ronald Lee, and he had no blue star. Later I found that young Lee had a passion for tattooing, and also from his gipsy relatives he had learned many tricks of colouring. I became sure that one of them, either Warden or the man called Lord Chesterham, had simulated the star, and, on the whole, it didn't seem to me it was so likely to be the dead man. The impersonation supplied the motive for the murder, you see."

"As one can't doubt after to-day's evidence," Crasster assented. "The murder must have been premeditated, inspector.

"Distinctly," the inspector agreed. "He had discovered that Lady Carew was to be there, and laid his plans accordingly, so the suspicion should turn upon her. There can be no doubt that he was waiting in the outer room to accomplish his purpose; the accidental turning out of the light gave him his opportunity, and he instantly availed himself of it. He must then have gone out of the flat and watched. He met Lady Carew on the stairs designedly, to frighten her, to show her that she was in his power; and when he had left her he went back to the flat, having previously provided himself with a key—you remember the wax on the lock—and took all the papers that proved Stanmore to be the heir to the peerage of Chesterham. He trusted to his knowledge of the family history, and his undoubted likeness to the Chesterhams, to enable him to carry out the rest. It was a diabolical scheme, and might have succeeded, but that he gave himself away over the pistol. Undoubtedly he left it in the flat to implicate Sir Anthony or Lady Carew. He had forgotten that when he picked it up there was ink on the table-cloth, that some of it got on his hands, and that therefore his finger-prints were left on the revolver. That was what turned my suspicion into a certainty. When I applied to him for a warrant later I managed to upset some ink, and obtain some impressions of his thumb and fingers. They corresponded with those on the revolver, and thus practically clinched the matter."

"Well, it has been a pretty smart thing," concluded Crasster. "And it will be a feather in your cap for years to come, inspector. There are not many men who could have cleared up the mystery as you have. Bless my life"—with a sudden change of tone, as they suddenly turned a corner—"who is this?"

A woman stood before them on the path, a small scarlet fury of a woman, her little *piquante* face distorted with rage, her black eyes blazing. The inspector cast one glance at her, and then, distinguished police officer though he was, looked as though he was about to run away.

But Célestine placed herself directly in front of him.

"Good day to you, Meestare Lennox—or Inspector Furnival," she said, subduing her shaking voice to accents of ironic politeness. "So it is a—well what you call—police officer you are, after all!"

Crasster with difficulty repressed a smile; the inspector's face threatened to become a copper colour.

"That is it, mademoiselle," he responded, with a gallant attempt to appear at his ease.

Célestine doubled up her little black-gloved fist.

"And the things you collect," she went on with a catch in her breath, "they are poor silly women's secrets—and their hearts. Ah! ah! is it not so, Monsieur Lennox?"

But the inspector was pulling himself together now.

"Their secrets perhaps," he said with a little hard laugh. "We poor police officers haven't much time to think of other things, mademoiselle."

Hearing the new note in his voice, Célestine stared at him in astonishment for a minute: then to his consternation she burst into tears.

"Oh it is hard—hard!" she sobbed. "You are a very cruel man, Mr. Lennox. You have broke my heart just to amuse yourself to find out my little secrets. And now what am I to do? No lady will take me for her maid again. Oh, yes, you have ruined me and broke my heart!"

The inspector wiped his brow. "Mademoiselle—"

Crasster glanced at him. "Let me speak to her, inspector. Oh, I don't think your heart is broken, mademoiselle!" he said in a bantering tone. "Unless it is at the fate that has overtaken your friend, Lord Chesterham. That must have been a delightful walk you took with him in the Lount Wood the other day."

Célestine flashed a wrathful glance at him from beneath the shadow of her lace-trimmed handkerchief.

"I do not know what you mean, monsieur!" she said.

"Don't you?" Crasster questioned, still smiling. "I think you will remember presently, mademoiselle. I was taking a short cut through the wood, and it happened that I was behind you and the prisoner who was brought before the magistrate to-day. I saw—"

"Ah!—you are a devil! I hate you!" Célestine burst forth, her whole frame shaking with fury, her eyes blazing.

"Do you? I am sorry for that!" Crasster said coldly, "but you will forgive me by and by, mademoiselle, when you realize that your friend the inspector is guiltless in the matter of breaking hearts. And as for another situation, why I am sure Lady Palmer will be pleased to do all she can to help you to get one. It will be the least she can do, since you tried so hard to help her when you were at Heron's Carew."

"Ah, ah!" with a moan like some wounded animal, Célestine stared at him for a moment, then she turned her back on them, and flew down the path, a small tornado of wrath.

"Phew!" The inspector took off his cap and rubbed his forehead. "That was an awkward quarter of an hour, sir. If it hadn't been for you—"

"Well, I have no scruples, in dealing with Célestine," Crasster laughed. "She was perfectly willing to sell her mistress to anyone. She was carrying on an underhand flirtation with that scoundrel Lee, or Chesterham, and doubtless giving him information, which he could use for his own purposes; and certainly at one time she was in Lady Palmer's pay, and that lady is, as we know, anything but a friend of Lady Carew. Oh, I don't think you have anything to reproach yourself with, inspector."

Sir Anthony Carew led his wife, at the close of the proceedings at the police court, from the seat she had occupied between the Dowager Lady Carew and Mrs. Rankin, to their own carriage. As he took his place beside her, he saw that she was very pale, that every line in her attitude spoke of utter exhaustion. Though every impulse was bidding him to take her in his arms, tell her that he would hold her thus against all the world, the whiteness and the weariness of her seemed to forbid it.

She did not open her eyes, or move unless it were to shrink further from him into her corner, as he looked at her, and for very pity her husband forebore to speak. That day's ordeal had been terrible to her he knew, though the kindness of the magistrates and the counsel had minimized it as far as might be. Though the nature of the tie that had bound her to Stanmore had not yet become common property, he knew that it must be inevitably disclosed at the trial, and the knowledge was gall and wormwood to him.

Yet his thought now was not of his sullied pride, of the disgrace she had brought upon his name, but of her, his wife, the woman he loved, lying there before him, humbled to the very dust, her fair beauty dimmed, the very life of her seemingly quenched. His touch was very tender as the carriage stopped before the door of Heron's Carew, and he helped her up the steps and across the wide low hall into the drawing-room. A great roomy Chesterfield stood before the fire, and he placed her in it, propped her up with pillows. Then, seeing her wanness, her utter exhaustion, he went himself and brought wine and delicate sandwiches, and coaxed her to eat and drink, not resting until he had seen a fair amount swallowed and a faint tinge of colour coming back to the white cheeks and lips.

As she gave him back the glass, and lay lack in her cushions, he bent over her.

"Judith!"

The big eyes, looking almost black in the shadow, glanced up at him for one moment, then veiled themselves in their long lashes, her breath quickened. "Is it really true that you—that I am—"

He knelt down beside her, and took the weak hand, on which her wedding ring shone, in his. "It is certain, Judith. I put Shapcote on, and there can be no doubt that Cyril Stanmore"—he gulped over the name—"married an actress, one Phyllis Champion, when he was a young fellow, not one and twenty, and she was living a year ago. Therefore there can be no doubt. You are my wife—you have always been my wife!"

"Your wife!" Judith stirred restlessly and turned her face towards the sofa cushions. "Anthony, what can I say? I am not worthy—it is only for Paul's sake—and yet how can I be glad when I remember that but for this you would be free—you could begin again."

"Begin again!" Anthony had captured both the small cold hands now, he chafed them, laying them against his heart. "How should I begin again, child? What do you mean?"

Judith's head was very low now; her golden hair dropped on the cushions.

"I thought perhaps you were sorry you had married me before—" she said painfully. "When Sybil Palmer—" in answer to his questioning exclamation.

There was a moment's silence; then Judith found her arms drawn round her husband's neck. "Sybil Palmer!" he repeated, with a contemptuous laugh. "I never knew you had heard that story, Judith. Yes, I thought myself very fond of Sybil in the old days, but I know now that it was never real love at all, never for a day. And now—now, surely my wife knows that the world holds only one woman for me."

A soft ray of light was stealing over Judith's white face now, and yet it seemed too good to be true. Her arms slackened their hold.

"You will never be able to forgive me for deceiving you."

Sir Anthony drew her slight form to his breast. He laid his face against the gleaming hair. "There is no need for forgiveness between us sweetheart," he said tenderly. "But," as he felt her quick movement, "if there were—if you had done anything that in any way wronged me, don't you know that a man forgives anything—everything to—"

Judith was resting now against his broad chest, her cheek pressed against the rough cloth of his coat, her hair lying across his shoulder in glittering disorder, her soft white arms twined round his throat. She trembled as she lay there, as she heard the quiver in his strong voice.

"Yes, he forgives everything to whom, Anthony?" she questioned softly.

He stooped nearer, drew her closely to him in his strong arms, laid his lips tenderly, passionately on hers. "To the woman he loves," he whispered. "Didn't you know that Judith, my darling, my wife."

THE END

33595232R00121

Made in the USA
Middletown, DE
19 July 2016